THE REAL WORLD

THE REAL WORLD

ROY HEWETSON

In memory of my good friend Kathy Murphy

CHAPTER 1
RETURN TO THE REAL WORLD

One of Trenchard's many vices led to his downfall. Not that his actions justified such an extreme response. After all it was only a game of cards, even if the stakes were high. He was gently goading his big fat opponent, constantly pronouncing on this and that, making sure the man couldn't concentrate upon what was probably a better hand. Suddenly the fellow jumped to his feet, nostrils bulging, face the colour of beetroot, mounds of blubber that encased his frame trembling in rage.

The table was flung sideways, scattering money, cards, drinks and glasses about the room. All except one bottle. Somehow that appeared in the big man's fist, clasped around its neck. Trenchard watched the green coloured sparkle of its rounded shape rise above his head, hover, and then descend. A single blow. That was that. Trenchard was gone, releasing an imprisoned spirit back to the invisible confines of an alternative world.

It was a relief to the liberated soul to circle the ceiling, observing guests, some tending to the human body, breathing into the mouth, thumping the chest. Others looked on, expressing surprise, indignation, irritation at the unseemly disturbance during what was supposed to be a dignified, upper-class reception in aid of charity. No use. He was definitely gone. No longer did the spark of life that activated his frame inhabit Trenchard's being.

Watching their continued efforts, content that the human was beyond their attention, the spirit was fascinated to hear of the support for the large attacker. All the surviving guests, or at least those sufficiently roused to take an interest, conspired to cover up the deadly deed. By the time ambulance men and police arrived, the general agreement was that the aggressor was no more than the innocent victim of an unprovoked attack. What had left the deceased dead had become his inebriated stumble and the blow when his head hit the corner of the table. A lie. A cover up. A deceit.

Slowly the spirit adjusted to his freedom. He was once again returning to his world. Despite the unfortunate choice of his last trip, detachment from the human form had its moment of nostalgia. No one believed the story of Trenchard's demise. He could see that from the expressions on the faces of the inquisitors, but the big man was more important than the dead one, and the age of bodily fluid testing, chemical clothes analysis, inch by inch inspection of the scene and psychological breaking down of witnesses had yet to dawn. Out of a sense of loyalty, the spirit had tried to intervene, shouting at them from the ceiling, until he remembered his limitations. His kind had no vocal chords so all his exertion achieved was an occasional rustle of the curtains.

He watched his recently inhabited human being placed on the stretcher and transported out of the room. Apart from a religious dignitary, intent upon securing the funeral service for his establishment, and one or two actors or politicians seeking a mention in the obituaries, the guests had shown no sympathy for the departed. The phrase 'good riddance' could occasionally be heard before they, too, had gone.

The spirit had to concede that it was a shock to have been ejected so suddenly from what now was another of his experience trips into humanity. At least he was no longer burdened by the strictures of declining human behaviour, yet the route had had its moments of drama not to mention a sizeable helping of emotion. As ever he was equipped with complete recall. He told himself it had been a complex journey, especially the debt, the stress, the conflict, but, overall, his store of earthly knowledge had increased considerably.

Amidst these deliberations he realised he was beginning to sink from the ceiling. Despite efforts to the contrary, managing to again disturb the curtains on the way down, he landed in the third wooden panel along from an ancestral painting that dominated the room. He sighed, consoling himself that he had become part of a stately home. It could have been much worse. His return to the Real World could have had him in the bedpost of one of the many women with whom Trenchard had dabbled, relieving them of their boredom and some of their riches, whilst their more permanent partners were elsewhere. There had been lucky escapes. He might have been released into the structure of a ship, similar to one of an earlier journey across the high seas. That had been his fate last time, tied to the rigging of a three-master for decades. Only when the boat had been re-discovered for modern use as a training vessel had he been dumped on the quayside amongst the rest of the rubbish and taken his chances.

No. If he had to re-enter his pure electronic existence, a stately home would do, even if there were signs of deterioration and decline from what had obviously once been a vibrant household. He settled and began to feel for currents around him. At first there was nothing, then he detected a wave of thought.

"Who's there?" he enquired in silent spiritual projection. No answer. "Come on. I know you're around," he persisted. "At least we can compare notes." Still nothing. "All right. Have it your own way. Be like that." He'd never been one to impose himself where he wasn't wanted, not in the Real World.

Several measures elapsed. Day had turned to night and back a number of times before he tried again, not that such variations were of value to him any more. Then she relented.

"I'm not sure I should be speaking to you," she began.

"Go on, spoil yourself." He was able to latch onto her impulses and look into her last human trip. She wasn't as innocent as all that.

"You weren't in a very nice person," she said.

"Luck of the draw," he replied. "Your last journey wasn't purer than pure either."

3

"That was many measures ago."

"So why are you still here? There must have been opportunities for another trip."

"This time I want it to be right. I've had enough of subservience."

In the silence that followed she didn't cancel her impulses and he had a good look at her history, knowing she was doing the same with his. She'd been in a chamber maid called Mavis when the stately home was still at its most active. The servants with which she had come into contact suggested the estate was large and the owners very wealthy; probably employing upwards of 50 or more to keep them in the type of comfort which, at the time, was denied to lesser mortals. Then he latched onto her undoing. Mavis had been unfrocked, literally, by the Master's son. What he couldn't understand was why, following her human's death in childbirth, she had landed three storeys down in this room. He asked her.

"I didn't," she replied. "Not at first. I just kept floating around up in the attic."

"You must have attached to something. You couldn't have kept floating."

"There was this old abandoned rocking horse. That's where I landed at first. Mavis had been virtually imprisoned there in that room during her pregnancy, nothing but a store before. The Mistress was hard. She only provided minimal comforts and had no emotion at all for the promise of a grandchild. The staff, the few who knew, weren't any better."

"I can see," he said, able to telepathically share her recollections.

"Well, after a while, when my human departed their world and the room had become a store again, I discovered I could move the horse."

"Nothing new there. I can move things too. Those curtains for example." He sent them a blast just to prove his point.

"I know all that," she said, impatient at his ignorance. "But I was in the horse. I was in its wood. It was me moving, not just pushing some other object about."

"I see. Yes, that is different. But it still doesn't explain how you got down here."

"Well, if you just let me finish, I'll tell you."

He remained quiet, waiting for her to continue.

"I was having a gentle rock one day when I tried a treble burst of energy. You know, try to meet the horse in its mid rock and stop it."

"A bit daft," he told her. "Using so much of your energy could have drained you for a human century. Is that why you're still about now? Surely you realised what it would do to your store."

"I didn't care. I just did it out of boredom."

"And it's taken you all this time to recover," he concluded for her.

"No it hasn't. D'you want to hear this or not?"

"Yes, yes. Please go on. I'm sorry I interrupted. I really want to know how you landed down here." There was silence. He knew she was still there by the current and he also knew that if he said more he might put her off completely. He kept quiet and waited until his patience gave out. "Please go on," he pleaded, not able to contain himself any longer.

"I will if you shut up and listen."

"I promise."

"Right, then. Well, you were correct to begin with. It was a silly thing to do and I was stuck. It lasted I don't know how long. No one entered. The dust settled and being in the attic there wasn't even any light, not that that mattered. And the roof reflected any chance of helpful energy in another direction. Then, one day, some children came in. They had a light - not the usual oil lamps and candles, but a torch. I didn't know what it was at the time because batteries hadn't long been in common use. The children wanted to look at what was on some shelves in the corner, so they put the torch on the saddle of the rocking horse and propped it up so it shone where they wanted. I thought I should test my current to see if there was a chance of latching on to humanity again, so I tried to move it – the torch, that is."

"But you would only have discharged more energy," he said. "And none of us need vision. Night and day are the same to us. It would have made more sense to enter one of the kids."

"Will you stop interrupting. I knew that, but I was fed up. I wanted some action. Well, it didn't move. But I suddenly felt something. A surge and then the torch went out. I didn't understand at the time, but I do now. I'd drained the battery and all that lovely energy had come into me. It was such a bolt it shot me out of the horse and I actually materialised for a moment or two. The kids screamed and fled. And I discovered I could follow them. My visual image didn't last long but my power was restored. I was mobile, without relying on a human. I had enough energy to propel myself along the corridor."

"How did you know you had an image?"

"Because I followed the kids downstairs and heard them shrieking they'd seen a ghost."

"So that's how you landed up here."

"Not quite. I drifted about a bit and found myself in the kitchen. You appreciate I was using quite a lot of energy and suddenly I was slipping back to the old state, being drawn to the kitchen table. You can understand I didn't want to get stuck in that, with all the pounding and spilling and things humans did with it. Electricity was all over the place. I didn't know what it was then, but I do now. One piece of equipment was the electric stove with the hot plates in use. It was tucked in a corner, not capable of replacing the ovens but it was throbbing away to itself. I managed to get over and got a fix straight away, the same way I'd drained the torch. That's when I realised, for us electricity is energy... power. I was a bit clumsy. Took too much too quickly. That fused the circuit and they had to replace the stove but my image had faded before anyone noticed. Since then I've perfected the technique and can plug into the supply for a controlled top-up without causing any damage to the apparatus. And, if I wish, I can do it without materialising. It's good fun."

There was a long silence whilst he tried to grasp the implications of what she was saying. She seemed to be enjoying herself and to be free. In their state there was no emotion, no pain, no stress and no desires except the drive to discover a suitable body with which to blend and take on human form again. At least that was how he'd seen things; how it was and had always been. But, now, here she was contradicting the lot, and expressing feelings. She'd been bored, wanted to do things quite separate from re-entry into the human chain. And she had done them… was still doing them for all he knew.

"I'm finding all this very hard to believe," he admitted.

"They all do."

"You mean you've told others."

"Of course. This place is packed with them. I've communicated with every departed soul here since I've made my discovery." She was well away now, and he couldn't have stopped her even if he'd wanted to. It was an incredible story. Not only had she perfected a method of increasing her force-field to exist free of all inanimate resting places, but she had trained others to do the same. All those who had wanted treatment had received it. Some had refused, sticking to the traditional line and waiting for a suitable candidate to get them back into humanity, but the rest, apparently, were dotted about the mansion thoroughly enjoying themselves.

It sounded attractive. He'd had a skinful of earthly life over the centuries and, each time he came back to Reality, his recollections seemed more tedious than the time before. He decided he wanted to stay in his Real State, especially if he, too, could achieve the freedom he was hearing about. He wondered if his new companion would teach him. He didn't know her, not even her current name. He'd never bothered with names before. Spirits didn't communicate that much and didn't need them, at least not until now.

"Call me Antedote," she said, reading his musings.

"That's a daft name."

"No it's not. I like it, so you're stuck with it."

She also latched onto his intentions. Responding to his request she proceeded to introduce him to the art of electrifusion, dragging him from the woodwork with a bolt from her ample supply. It was sufficient to have him following her for the next human week, first out into the hall, where he met others of their persuasion, and then on into rooms, all with their occupants. Spirits made their presence known to each other by movement of their force-field, except when they forgot and overdid it. Then they took on an almost human form, still invisible to the others, but if there were any humans about on these rare occasions their ghostly appearance caused chaos and was to be discouraged. If the spiritual residents began to run short of power, they latched on to their nearest companion and were able to share.

"And what if there's no companion available?" Hedstrong asked. He'd been named Hedstrong by Antedote.

"You come to me," she told him.

"But why can't you teach us how to plug into the mains?"

"Because I don't want to. I'm quite happy with it as it is, thank you."

"That's not fair."

"Tough, because that's how it is. You can always go back to humanity if you don't like it."

He didn't like it, but he didn't not like it so much that he wanted to slot back into the alternative, which meant he was obliged to accept the situation. So what if she wanted to keep control? She was a woman and, apparently, they generally did keep control in this world as well as in the other.

CHAPTER 2

FREEDOM TO ROAM

"Thank God they've all gone," he said to no one in particular. Indeed there was no one within earshot. What remained of the staff were somewhere else in the house or outside enjoying the last of the daylight. The family had departed and those ghastly gamblers had gone too, including one feet first. He'd been assured there'd be no repercussions in his direction concerning the death. He still had influence.

Suddenly he was aware of a young girl standing in the hall watching him.

"And where did you come from?" he asked.

"The garden," she replied.

"And what were you doing in my garden?"

"Just looking, seeing what I could find."

"And what did you find?"

"Nothing really," she said. "I just like looking at the plants and the trees and picturing how it all was and how it all will be."

His Lordship was intrigued. Further questions revealed that the girl's name was Phyllis and she lived in the village. Apparently she frequently visited the estate to escape what she called the 'throbbing of her home'.

"We live in an old house and it has an evil past. I can feel it," she explained.

"Has it, indeed?" his Lordship commented. "And are there any evil pasts up here?"

"Not really," she told him. "Not in the gardens, but I don't know about your house. It's the first time I've been in it. Are you going to sell that painting?"

"What makes you ask?"

"You've been studying it a long time. And things I've heard in the village," she added.

"What things?"

With little need for persuasion she told him of talk of the decline of the estate and speculation as to what would happen to it. He pressed her for more information, discovering that she'd picked up much of the gossip just by keeping quiet and unnoticed during discussions. She'd then explored the kitchen garden, the greenhouses, looked in at ground floor windows that remained unshuttered, all, she claimed, just to verify what she'd heard. When asked, she confirmed that she'd kept most of it to herself. She didn't believe it was fair what was being said.

"Are you going to sell everything and move?" she asked. "Now your mother's dead."

"No, I doubt if I shall do that," his Lordship told her, for some reason not disturbed by such a blunt question so soon after the funeral. It would certainly be different, he knew that, but this was his home.

"I'm glad. They would all be upset if you did and all this went." She opened her arms in a gesture to envelop the room. "Although I doubt if they have any idea what keeping it means."

"And who might 'they' be?" his Lordship asked.

"You can't see them, can you?" In a matter-of-fact manner Phyllis went on to describe the various spirits inhabiting the library into which they had progressed. With a surprising degree of accuracy she included Antedote, who happened to be drifting through at the time. Phyllis described how she would have looked if she'd materialised, defining the dress of an early parlour maid. His Lordship put everything down to the young girl's imagination, suggesting that it was probably time she returned to the village in case her parents wondered where she was. He did, however, agree that she be allowed to visit the grounds when she wished and perhaps also, on occasion, come to talk to him in the house.

Meanwhile, in the Real World, for the first time Hedstrong was able to move about in his spiritual state. He was in his element, although it took time to adjust to the new freedom, time being the most important contrast. Whilst in human form, he'd been governed by the sun and the moon, creating days, nights, hours and minutes. Real World 'measures' were different. They were devoid of the same regularity, each coming to an end when a spirit sensed the next ought to start. That way one period could envelop night and day, extending even up to a human year or more, or it could be as short as the tick of a clock.

He'd not felt this a problem in the past, because he'd always been static without the opportunity to mix with other like-electrified beings. Now, spending more time with Antedote, things were different. They felt comfortable in each other's company and were pleased at their frequent chance encounters. Inevitably, Hedstrong reached the point where he wanted to arrange to meet Antedote at a set time. Measures didn't allow them to do that.

"This is stupid," Antedote declared. "Why shouldn't we meet when the desire is there? I enjoy having you around, generally speaking, and I want to know when I can see you."

"What d'you mean, 'generally speaking'?"

"Don't get uppity. I was just saying."

"What were you saying?" Her comment annoyed Hedstrong, particularly the casual implication that he should be 'around' for her.

"I was just saying that there are times, like now, when you get uppity. Then it would be better if we had our own space."

"We've got our own space. I can go back to my wood panel whenever I like and you can go back to…" He realised he wasn't sure where Antedote had established her resting place or, indeed, if she still had one. It certainly wasn't the rocking horse where she'd started these current measures and there was no certainty she was to be found in the panel where he had first discovered her. "Where exactly are you based?" he asked.

"Never you mind. Do you want to talk about time or not?"

He did, so he let the other subject drop, realising that he was developing a feeling. It was a strange sensation for him, in the Real World. He was experiencing an emotion.

"It's a pity we can't just communicate forward like we can back," he said.

"What d'you mean?"

"Well, I can see your past, your human past, just by twitching onto your wavelength and, unless you block me, I can see what you've thought, a fraction of a measure after you've thought it. If we could bring that up to the present so we could actually communicate even without jointly having to twitch on each other's wavelength, that would do the trick."

"We can't. Both of us have to be willing to communicate. Otherwise it would be an invasion of privacy. We might merge into one."

"I'm getting confused," he admitted.

"Then stick to what we should be discussing, if you really want a date with me."

He did. Yes, he really did. He wanted a date with her. He wanted what was, in reality, identical to a human emotion. Was this a unique development in the Real World? Evolving because of their new-found freedom of movement? Or was it just something he hadn't discovered before? He quickly blocked off these thoughts, because they would have been regarded by Antedote as straying from the point and might end up with her ignoring him. He didn't want that - another sign of his feeling. So he settled for consideration of how they could devise a system where both could pick a moment in the future which they would both recognise - a time and place where they could meet

There was no use in trying to rely upon night and day. To spirits there was little contrast between the two. Although, due to the energy variation, they could recognise the difference, vision to them was the same, light or dark. The debate moved to whether they could use the position of the sun or the moon, but this was too unreliable because, although they could project through solid objects, their power would be tested to the limit if they both tried to penetrate too much atmosphere, especially with the increasing number of radio beams humans seemed to messing about with. Then it came to him.

"I don't know what we're fussing about," he said. "There's enough clocks about in this house. Why don't we use human time?" He felt proud of himself at the suggestion and rattled a cup on the kitchen table past which they happened to be drifting. Antedote was not impressed, either by the rattle of the cup, which she considered showing off, or the suggestion.

"How would you know which clock to rely on?" she asked. "There are numerous ones crowding this place and they're all displaying different time."

He pointed to the one on the main kitchen wall. "We'll go by this one. It's operated by a battery. It keeps decent human time so it should be good enough."

"And when we looked at it, how would we know we were in the same measure, on the same human day?" she asked scornfully.

"Ah," he said. "That would be difficult."

The problem was becoming quite a power drain, so much so that Hedstrong felt a pull back to his static state. He mentioned the fact to Antedote and requested a charge to save him descending into the table. She obliged and he felt new energy surging through his being. He also began to recognise another emotion.

"I love it when you do that to me," he admitted, adding, impulsively, "in fact I always like you with me. I don't really need to work out time, because the urge for your presence is always there. I want to be with you all the time."

"That's all right, then. Problem solved."

13

"How d'you mean?"

"You want me all the time, so that will be a constant wave."

"Yes," he agreed, his feeling for her surging almost to the point of materialisation.

"So I can dock into that whenever I want to share," she concluded.

It wasn't quite what he'd meant, but he was reluctant to say so at that moment, especially just after she'd given him such a good feeling of energy.

***

The arrangement worked well for several measures. Hedstrong's wave of devotion remained constant and Antedote latched onto it whenever she felt in the mood. To be fair, although 'fairness' wasn't top of Antedote's list of attributes, it had to be said that she quite regularly felt the mood, but there were periods when her growing obligations to the other spirits became such a drain that she needed time on her own to recover. Those occasions apart, she liked his presence around her.

Seeking to keep pace with the charging demands of her fellow spirits, she was still refining her technique of tapping into electrical sources. She was well beyond her first accidental discovery, and had become much more organised and skilful. She'd identified the mains power at the point where it entered the big house: the other side of the electric meter. Generally there was a constant, unvaried current which she could siphon off without adding cost to the household bill. Earlier attempts on the in-house side of the meter had shocked her at the speed at which the dials started to spin around. She'd added so much to the human electric account and stressed the mechanism to such an extent that the equipment had collapsed. Aware of the declining human activity in the mansion she'd feared it would be another blow to their efforts to keep the big house going.

She'd been wrong. The opposite had occurred, the failure of the meter allowing residents a whole human quarter year whilst they enjoyed a free supply. Humans being humans, they took full advantage of the period before it was discovered by officialdom. Even then they had a further brief spell before replacement instrumentation arrived, during which they rushed to complete the maximum amount of maintenance or repair requiring use of power equipment. It had been a surprise to her how agile they became in improving their standard of living when it could be done for nothing.

The last thing she wanted was to cause excessive demands that would pressure the household monetary resources even further. So, following the installation of the new equipment, except for emergency boosts, she kept to the outward side of the meter, taking her main charge before it passed through to be recorded as consumption. She still managed to dim the lights for a moment and could mess up the timing on alarm clocks and the like, but she knew the ancient wiring would be blamed – not her.

That deteriorating wiring had also caused her to master some adjustments – mansion voltage being considerably weaker than the flow on the supply side of the meter. When first taking a charge from the stronger current, like her initial attempt in the kitchen, there'd been one or two micro-measures when she'd materialised. A gardener had been passing underneath the point where the mains supply connected and suddenly he'd seen her in the wall. Fortunately, she'd disappeared before he could believe his eyes.

What if she materialised too close to a human, she wondered? She had an uncomfortable feeling, echoing from a distant vague recollection of her planetary arrival, that she would enter the mind of the being whether she liked it or not. Especially if he or she was already occupied by one of her compatriots, such a sudden unplanned absorption could land them in a lunatic asylum: not an adventure she was inclined to favour. All these concerns weighed down upon her during her secret visits to the meter ard. She'd also seen the outside of the house when receiving ... boost and it looked so inviting but she knew she couldn't escape the confines of the stately residence unless entering the human chain again. At least she believed that was the case but, so much had happened to her, she wasn't sure. Maybe one day she should try, or get Hedstrong to go first. There was still so much to learn and such a responsibility that she felt her burden was growing by the measure. She confided in Hedstrong when she next twitched him and he was sympathetic.

As usual, during their communication, he didn't put a block on his thoughts, happy to present an open book to his companion, so she read his full reaction to the confidence. He was going to ask her to teach him how to recharge, so he could help. Her initial impulse was to reject the idea. Whatever relief a sharing would bring it would reduce her control, not especially over him, she felt she could probably maintain that for the most part, but over the rest of the mansion's spiritual community.

If she gave in, there would be two beings from which the others could seek a top-up. At present, they had to turn to her and she was able to dictate the terms. If they didn't accept they were soon back to static, with entry into the human chain their only option. One or two took that course, telling her in no uncertain terms what she could do with her power, but the majority conformed, granting her an army which, she realised, she could use in whatever manner she chose to influence their environment. Perhaps, she thought, the burden of power was worth it.

***

At about this time, spirits caring to notice could observe the Lord of the Manor wandering about the house sighing at the increased signs of dereliction. Damp was coming into the servants' quarters and he suspected the cause was a leak in one of the roofs. That wasn't an immediate problem, because he was down to a skeleton staff with much of the stately home empty, almost abandoned. More serious were the signs of damp in some of the main rooms and the damage it could cause to items of value. There was no alternative. He'd have to sell something.

The world around him wasn't doing much better. With his now distant army experience in North Africa, he could have told the Russians they'd never succeed in bringing Afghanistan to heel. And, to think, here in the UK there was a woman Prime Minister. Despite her determination and community work, he doubted if his mother would have approved, especially someone without the background expected of Conservative leaders. If not before, the 1980s confirmed to him that there would be no return to the days his parents had known. Not even the Royal Wedding of Prince Charles, the successor to the throne, would change things.

The Lord had never known his father, who'd died very early in his life, but he knew that the, then, King and Queen attended his parents' wedding. Things were different now, but he was damned if he was going to give up his house and estate. His mind made up, he called in an expert to advise. He requested the presence of Jenner Makethorpe without delay. The expert arrived to encounter a major stumbling block. His Lordship had great difficulty coming to any decision on ideas put forward. Undeterred, Makethorpe produced a regular flow of suggestions, including a massive reduction of books in the library. They'd only been returned three or four decades ago, following resumption of the room, plus much of the house, as a normal residence after Second World Wartime hospital and children's accommodation.

The shelves would go, as well as books, Makethorpe's suggestion being a revamp to make it available for conference and other commercial letting. The man went even further, opting for a comprehensive reorganisation of the whole house into luxury apartments. He enjoyed messing about at someone else's expense, especially in a dwelling the size of the mansion. He flooded the place with workmen, unlocking doors and casting aside dust sheets in rooms that had lain idle for some time. Their tests and examinations led to more plans which his Lordship simply left lying around. He was unable to countenance anything which would destroy the reclusive nature of what, despite all beginning to crumble around him, was his comfortable solitary home.

***

Antedote happened to notice the latest plans whilst they lay scattered over the snooker table. She had a good look and became convinced the owner was about to do all manner of evil to their spiritual resting places. Jenner Makethorpe's prowling through the corridors added to her concern, as did his importing of even more experts.

She established the library as a centre of activity and, taking the sudden influx of humans to be a serious threat, she called a conference to discuss matters. With spiritual opinion united behind her, she mobilised her supporters into an electrified army aimed at stopping the work. When one workman arrived, he mysteriously lost control of his equipment, sustaining an injury which called for hospital treatment. An expert was next when a step ladder he had been climbing shook him off. Others followed, adding to a regular flow of ambulances between mansion and hospital.

Local gossip ran riot. One human day, correspondence (including quotes from auctioneers chosen to market library books and other ornaments) had, with skilful manipulation of the relevant force-field by Antedote, fallen out of a file at the feet of a visiting council official. He'd surreptitiously read letters advocating the stripping of what was part of an historic building. Undetected, he pinched enough of the paperwork to pass details to a parishioner who, with a petition signed by hundreds, persuaded an emergency meeting of his Parish Council to request a Grade 1 Preservation Order.

Contrary to their usual policy when a lesser authority dared approach them uninvited, especially when backed by a local residents' petition - the District Council made the Listed Building Order. The bigger council risked setting a precedent other parishes might follow, but considered the chance worth taking. As a result proposed stripping activity in the mansion was frozen in almost every direction.

The spirits learned of the decision by observation of human occupants. Antedote's followers applauded her leadership. There were those in her army who felt she was well equipped for re-entry into the human chain through a politician, so cunning and devious had been her ideas. However, they kept their views to themselves, acknowledging that her departure would have ended their freedom in the Real World.

Antedote, basking in the glory of achievement, wasn't aware of Hedstrong's presence until he twitched.

"You know I worship you," he blurted. "I would never do anything to harm you."

"Such emotion. Where does that come from? It's never been part of a spirit's make-up before."

"We've never been able to associate like this."

"There's been no problem communicating with your neighbours in the past. You've conversed with others, haven't you, even panels away when you were static?" she reminded him.

"I know, but this is different. We can actually be together – help each other."

She realised she was facing his latest attempt to share her re-charging burden, but it misfired.

"You and I as one, blending whenever you want," he tried.

"Yes, that's it. Just when I want. It's better that way," she added, closing the discourse and putting a few walls between them before he realised she was no longer there.

CHAPTER 3
POWER SHARING

As years past, Phyllis grew into what his Lordship described as quite an attractive young lady. After their initial encounter her visits to the house had continued to an extent that he'd begun to look forward to them. Now, out of university, aged 28, she was renting a small house not far from the grounds of the mansion. Archaeology took her away for long stretches of human time but, in between, she enjoyed the seclusion of her own home, writing up her research. One day his Lordship was still in the games room when Phyllis found him.

"How did you get in?" he asked, giving her a hug.

"Through the kitchen door, as usual. It's no good you having all these alarms if you forget to set them," she admonished.

"I'm pissed off with all this security. What's it for? Everything'll disappear when I go. I'm the last of the line to struggle with this old white elephant."

Phyllis would have none of it. She told him she could see into the future as clearly as she could sense the spirits that occupied his home. She predicted that one day all would come to life again and the house would be full of people. She demanded to know if he was comfortable in the small portion he still occupied and he said he was.

"Well, then," she continued. "stop being so pessimistic and enjoy what many others would kill for. It's not the pictures, the rooms, the land that matters. They will take care of themselves. It's the seclusion you've got. You can still enjoy privacy, and don't forget my friends the spirits. They live here, too, you know."

His Lordship studied the young girl, not so young now. There was a strange beauty that echoed from within her small, meticulously proportioned frame.

"You really believe they exist, don't you?"

"I can almost see them," she told him. "Don't worry, they won't harm you. They seem too busy going about their own business to bother with what you're doing."

"But why do you bother?" he asked. "Why d'you spend time talking to an old bloke like me when you should be out enjoying yourself, finding a man and…"

"And what?" she interrupted him. "Settling down? Starting a family? Being a dutiful housewife? That's ripe coming from you, the confirmed bachelor. You think that's really the life for me?"

He considered her question for a moment, then smiled. "No, you're too independent, too mysterious. What d'you get up to in that house of yours?" He paused to pick his words carefully. "In olden days anyone hearing some of the things you say would have you burnt at the stake or ducked. They'd have branded you a witch."

"Then it's a good thing these aren't the olden days," was all he got by way of reply. He didn't need any more. He knew from his housekeeper of her reputation in the village, her ability to heal where traditional medicine seemed to fail. There was a certain atmosphere about her which promised excitement, even danger. More than once his housekeeper had registered her disapproval at the meetings, on one occasion actually declaring he'd do well to stay away from her.

***

Quite a few measures passed without major incident. Hedstrong's feelings for Antedote didn't weaken, but there were times when her assumed superior attitude got the better of him. This usually ended in a war of words before she flitted off into some other part of the house. So long as she'd left him with sufficient energy, he would set out to explore the mansion on his own.

There were numerous rooms, including a very large drawing room, the well-stocked, equally large, library and even a first floor passage which led to a chapel. He'd half expected to encounter some fellow spirits in the chapel, but no amount of twitching revealed any energy at all.

It was during this period of investigation he noticed further reduction in human activity throughout the house. Shutters were left in place in most of the windows, their curtains remaining untouched. Dust began to gather and he often tried a bit of housework by wafting the small particles into the atmosphere to reveal a shiny surface or a clean floor. Others were doing the same, some using appreciable amounts of power to rattle a window here or close a door there.

Not that the Lord of the Manor was really neglecting his responsibilities. In the main he managed to keep the building water-tight and weatherproof. He did his best and, on occasion, could be seen wandering around, spending time in the large dining hall, re-arranging various items, touching the sideboard or the side oak table, or just studying himself in the mirror over the fireplace. Once Hedstrong caught him in the games room. He was fingering the snooker balls, some of which were still on the full size table with its magnificent carved legs, but, for the most part, he kept to three rooms – one where he sat and stored his favourite books, another up the still impressive, but threadbare, staircase where he slept.

Hedstrong discussed the increasing lack of human activity with Antedote. Whilst he had no current urge to leave the Real World, he felt it would not be appropriate to lose all chance of another trip should the mood take him. Having recorded that there were so few people around, he suggested the problem be discussed with their fellows and, for once, she agreed. Adopting the idea as her own she called a spiritual meeting, which was well attended. Debate centred upon the fears that there was less and less opportunity for those who decided to re-enter the human chain. They assured their leader that none of them had any immediate wish to do so, fearing that she would otherwise treat such expressions as disloyal and may deprive them of power.

With discussion failing to get anywhere, Hedstrong noticed the whole idea suddenly became his again. Antedote branded his concerns 'stupid' so he cleared off, realising the debate had left a larger than usual demand for power. Some spirits needed a boost just to return to their resting places, Antedote committed to responding to their requirements. When she next twitched onto his wavelength, he was back in his wood panel. Her exhaustion was clear to sense.

"All right, I know it's getting too much," she conceded, reading his thoughts. "If those meetings become more frequent, I admit I may need help."

"There's no 'may' about it," he told her. He stopped in surprise, realising she had taken to the panel beside him. "What's wrong?" he asked.

"I think I've overdone it," she said. "I don't seem to be able to move out of this blessed panel."

"I knew this would happen. You do realise you're no longer in control of that bunch. They're in control of you, simply using you to feed them whenever they desire."

"Nonsense. That's not true," she declared. "They look upon me as their leader."

"That's what leaders are for, to be drained dry. Surely even you can see that."

The conversation ended there, Antedote too exhausted to respond, even though, for the first time, Hedstrong had allowed his exasperation to get the better of his other new-found emotions. Nothing more happened for a measure or two, apart from the other spirits beginning to invade their space requesting power boosts. Twitching onto them, he invited them to return from whence they came, politely at first, then more emphatically when they sought to argue. To his surprise he succeeded, except for one female who drifted into a chair near him.

There was no block on her thoughts and he discovered that she hadn't been with them long. Her last human adventure had been in the somewhat forceful mother of the present Lord. Her Ladyship had actually accommodated two spirits, one a cunning creation which had given Antedote no end of trouble upon his return to Reality. Fortunately he had latched onto a local tradesperson, and was back in the human chain, no doubt causing chaos. The other, now resident in the chair, had emphasised the feminine side of her Ladyship and was altogether more caring. She claimed her power was so low she couldn't move, and had to remain static.

"Serves her right," Antedote muttered, not welcoming the wave of sympathy passed by Hedstrong to an intruder whom she considered was trespassing.

"No need to be like that," Hedstrong told her.

"Well. Fancy travelling the length of the house with so little power. What self-respecting spirit would do that?" Antedote transmitted. She had enough energy left to read right back through the history of their visitor, noting that it included one human existence in a brothel. "And she's not as innocent as she makes out."

"All I need is enough boost to get back to my door," the unfortunate pleaded.

"Well, I can't help," Antedote replied. "I haven't enough left for myself, let alone you." She sensed Hedstrong give the spiritual equivalent of a sigh.

"The freedom was good whilst it lasted," he said, settling into his woodwork.

***

Two whole measures passed during which Antedote and Hedstrong received numerous visits from spirits desperate for a boost. They came through the walls, the ceiling and some of the more stupid ones used unnecessary power to open the door. At first they didn't believe their leader had lost her energy. They thought she was just playing about for some mysterious reason of her own, intent upon keeping them in their place. Even Hedstrong was suspicious. None of them realised their doubts actually questioned the unbreakable rule that spirits cannot lie.

Demands became more and more persistent, desperation finally resulting in those who were still able to project forming a procession, which swept through the mansion to confront Antedote. They even threatened civil disobedience, but when invited to go ahead, had to acknowledge there was little they could do short of wrecking the place. Still preserving some of their spiritual intelligence which separated them from the limitations of the human world, they conceded that such action would be to no avail.

The demonstrators, totalling more than Hedstrong realised, were existing within the walls of the great house. Conversing with them, he discovered five others had been unable to join the protest - their power so reduced they were confined to their expectant Real Life resting places. Fifteen remained in the room 'bothering' Antedote, as she put it, but the female in the chair was the one who really annoyed her. She'd been silent for most of the time but, when the deputation arrived, something sparked her off and she began to champion the demands of the others. Antedote christened her 'Upstart' (forgetting to mis-spell her name in a fit of jealousy).

"I knew she'd be trouble," she complained, angrily twitching into Hedstrong's presence.

"No, I'm not," Upstart retorted, muscling in on the wavelength. "It's just that, having discovered freedom, we think you're being a little bit selfish to hog it all to yourself."

"I'm not," Antedote replied. "I share it with you all. If it hadn't been for me, you'd all have been clamouring to leave Reality in the first human that came along."

"Not much chance of that now," another complained. "Most of the place is shut up with his Lordship acting like a recluse. We can't all crowd into him. It would incinerate him, and we'd be back to Real Life before we could get out of the building, if we survived at all."

Others joined in until one of them suggested that they select a representative, or perhaps two, to absorb into his Lordship. He thought it might achieve a character change sufficient for him to open up the mansion to visitors again. The protesters enthusiastically supported the idea until some spirit asked how they would go about selecting the winners.

"We can't draw lots like humans."

"We could have a trial of strength. See who could move the objects on the dining room table furthest," volunteered another. She was asked what would happen if more than two were projected all the way and fell off onto the floor. Others suggested that the two items landing furthest from the table would herald the winners. This was about to be put to the vote when Antedote asked them how they were all going to select objects of equivalent weight from those scattered about the table and how they would be lined up. Someone mentioned a handicapping procedure, to take account of differing distances from the edge as well as the contrasting weights. This led to further debate and a proposal to elect a Handicapping Committee.

They had difficulty agreeing upon who should be on the committee and devised an appeals procedure in anticipation of inevitable complaint from some amongst them. After further lengthy discourse they reached a point at which they were all satisfied they had the basics sorted out. By that time, Hedstrong had been elected chairman of the Handicapping Committee, much to Antedote's disgust. She declined to take any part in what she declared to be a stupid idea, even when offered the job of referee, but deigned to resume recharging fellow spirits after Hedstrong had given her a sufficient boost to get her to her mains supply.

The Committee met several times and a select sub-committee retired, deliberated and came back with a set of rules to govern the game. They'd discovered that some human had been into the dining room and moved everything off the table, which had stumped them for a while, until the sub-committee chairman suggested the library. This led to books being chosen as the objects for projection, which, in turn, had led to the production of a complicated points system.

All was explained at one final meeting under the title Measured General Meeting of Competition (MGMC for short), each spirit being informed that he or she would have the opportunity to choose three books from the left hand side of the room. If they were on a lower shelf they stood to gain more points than if chosen from higher up, it being argued that the higher the missile the further, in distance away from the wall, it was likely to travel. Handicapping would also take account of weight, which would be calculated by reference to pages, the general opinion being that there were enough works of similar size and with similar paper quality to leave final thickness a matter of individual skill in selection.

When the MGMC considered the regulations, the longest and most heated discussion concerned the assessment of the distance each book travelled. There was enough pattern left on the old carpet to help, provided straight rather than diagonal distance was applied, and the chances of a human interfering by moving any of the printed works before the competition ended was considered slight. Two referees were appointed to observe from different angles, and the appeals procedure extended to allow questioning of their decisions.

In the event of a tie, there would be a penalty shoot out, each finalist projecting another book and, if there was still a tie, the relevant competitors would continue with penalty shoots until a winner and runner-up were left. The winner would have first right of human entry into his Lordship, the runner-up second.

Apart from her one outburst Antedote had remained silent whilst the debates raged, fascinated at the stupidity that surrounded her. Hedstrong, who had put a block on his thoughts at an early stage, secretly agreed with her. Having accepted the chairmanship, he took little part in the deliberations, allowing others to further expend their energies whilst he simply presided. He performed the task well - so well that when the debate ended and final decisions were successfully put to the vote they all congratulated him on a terrific achievement, showering him with praise.

Everyone agreed to start a new simultaneous measure for the games, some even asking for permission to organise a training regime and have a few practice sessions. It was only at that point that the gathering realised they were facing a major problem. Whilst they had been together in debate, they had shared each other's power, reclining in various inanimate objects about the room. Now, when they tried individual action, they again discovered that most of them had used up so much of their remaining energy they couldn't move.

At first they just stayed where they were in disbelief, but it wasn't long before the complaints started. They were mild to begin with, one asking the other why he or she had absorbed so much doing this or that. The other explained that it wasn't her or his fault, she or he had been obliged to do it in observance of a committee decision. Slowly the gathering came round to the opinion that the Rules Sub-committee should shoulder the blame for taking so long and creating such debate over the regulations. The members of the sub-committee turned to their chairman, who side-stepped the blame by placing it back in the lap of the MGMC, highlighting all the obstacles one or two trouble makers had placed in the path of progress. The troublemakers pleaded freedom of speech and the right to express their opinion, blaming bureaucracy at the top for creating too much red tape. Not long after, a vote of no confidence in the chairman left Hedstrong to shoulder the blame. He resigned.

"Getting a bit crowded in here, isn't it?" Antedote commented to anyone who cared to twitch onto her beam. No one answered. "Who's listening?" she asked. It would seem that no one was. She twitched Hedstrong.

"I heard you," he replied.

"Sulking are we?"

"No, I am not," he retorted. "It's just that you try your best, control the mob, get a result and then they kick you in the teeth."

"Glad you know what it feels like. Are we still an item?"

"I never knew we were."

"Of course we are. We have been for measures."

"It's not my feelings that've changed."

"That's good. You know that special level you use when you want us to be alone?"

"Yes."

"Switch to it now."

"If I do, it won't last long. The others will get it in a micro-measure of twitching."

"Long enough," she told him.

He did as he was told and found her waiting. Immediately he was in contact she told him how to boost his energy from the electricity supply. In his surprise he nearly forgot to block his thoughts, which attracted a caustic comment from Antedote. He asked her why she had changed her mind. She said she had developed feelings, which were for him. He believed her. Spirits couldn't lie.

CHAPTER 4
CONSUMMATION

"You don't believe her, do you." Upstart enquired.

It was a comment rather than a question, taking both Hedstrong and Antedote by surprise. They automatically tested each other's block to ensure it was impenetrable, then both replied at once. Hedstrong declared his complete faith in his dearest one's devotion. Antedote's retort was less polite.

"You'll be sorry," Upstart persisted, twitching forcefully in Hedstrong's direction. "What is *so* important you both have to try to hide power absorption from the rest of us?" Antedote sparkled with anger. " Why don't you..." she managed before Hedstrong intervened, assuring both of them there was no need to expend even more energy on unnecessary confrontation. The three became quiet, noting that the others in the room had all put blocks on their thoughts and were simply observing. After a measure, a brief one in human time, Hedstrong came to a decision.

"Which of you feel you have enough power to return to your resting places?" he asked of the room. No one responded. "Come on, you're not all without a few spare sparks of energy." Still nothing. "OK. End of conversation. You don't help us, we don't help you."

Antedote, about to react unfavourably to his assumption that he could speak for both of them, just managed to stop herself, accepting she was at a temporary disadvantage. Instead she endorsed his remark. Two more comparatively short measures passed before the deadlock was broken. First one spirit, then another, admitted they felt they could return. Seven in all confirmed a willingness to cooperate before Upstart, who had borrowed a mini-boost from a neighbour during the debate, joined in to make it eight.

"Right," Hedstrong acknowledged, "in that case, now we've got your cooperation, I think I may be able to help. I take it you'd all prefer to remain mobile, to retain your power of movement? That is if we can manage it. Just to be sure, can I have a vote on it?" He counted the spontaneous twitches. "That's unanimous, then. Now if those who can will return to their homes, all being well, I'll be in touch in a measure or two."

"Bye for now," Upstart said, deliberately choosing to pass through his panel on her way to her door.

"Bloody stuck up bitch," Antedote couldn't help flashing.

***

Satisfied that all who were able to had gone, Hedstrong gave a brief twitch to Antedote and took off for the upper floor. He wanted to practice absorption somewhere where he knew there would be no spiritual observers. Most of his companions opted for the more regal confines of the mansion, even those with human servant heritage choosing not to remain where they had once recoiled. He boycotted the main bedrooms and selected one which used to be reserved for visiting servants.

Employing what electrical knowledge he'd gained from his last excursion into humanity, he decided the only real current would be from the light switch. He contemplated it for a full measure before plucking up courage to try out what Antedote had told him. He couldn't believe it was that simple. Why hadn't someone discovered it before? All he had to do, she'd told him, was to project himself into the power exactly same way he would if he were entering the human chain.

"Here goes," he muttered, launching himself at the switch. Nothing happened, except that he passed through the wall into the corridor and nearly floated down a staircase. He went back and tried again – same result.

"It's not working," a voice said.

He gave a bolt of surprise at the realisation that he was not alone. He'd assumed there would be no presence without checking. Suddenly he recognised who it was.

"Upstart. What are you doing here?"

"I thought you might need some help."

" Well, you were wrong. You're just wasting energy. Go back to your door or whatever while you can."

"Ah, I'm afraid that's a problem. I can't." There was a pause before she added, "D'you think you could spare just a little bit of energy to get me back. It's only a short distance to Blanche's bedroom, and I can't stay in the servants' quarters, can I?"

Hedstrong thought it typical that Upstart should choose one of the main bedrooms in which to reside, complete with what the other world now called en-suite attachments. He visualised what sort of human she would be looking to choose for her next trip and forgot to block. Upstart was more careful. If she wasn't committing the impossible sin of lying, she was certainly sailing through a mist of deception and didn't want Hedstrong on the same voyage, not yet.

"Sorry," he said. "I need all my power if I'm to sort this thing out. Stay here and hope I can succeed, and watch you don't fuse yourself in the damp." With that he left, throwing all caution to the winds, and proceeded along corridors, through walls, until he eventually found himself in a dressing room to one of the main sleeping quarters in the house. He paused for a micro, looking down at the sole human occupant of the mansion asleep in his bed.

Why choose a dressing room when he has the whole house Hedstrong wondered? For another micro he played with the idea of taking a human trip, just to discover the thinking of what he was sure was this last Lord of the Manor.

Resolving that it wouldn't be worth the bother, he studied an electric bulb which, for some reason, was still alight. With his own power diminishing towards imminent static level, he made a desperate lunge at the illumination: immediate contact. So forceful was his entry through the bulb it blew with quite a bang, but he was connecting and felt power surging from the socket into his being. Only when he noticed his Lordship sitting up in bed looking at him did he realise he'd materialised.

"Go away," the elderly man said. "I'm not ready for you yet. Bugger off."

Hedstrong left, startled at the outburst, sinking through the floor in search of Antedote. His form was still visible when he got back to his panel.

"Trust you to overdo it," Antedote commented, reading his immediate past which, in his panic, he had left unblocked. Too late to stop her, she absorbed his confrontation with his Lordship and latched on to the antics of Upstart. "The sooner we get her out of Reality and back into the human chain, the better," she vowed.

**

"Well? What're you waiting for?" After her outburst, Antedote had remained quiet for a measure, but could not contain her impatience a micro longer. "Hadn't you better give me a boost. How else're you going to de-materialise or are you planning to haunt the household permanently?" Trying to visualise what a human would see, she added, "I bet you look stupid floating in that panel."

"That's not the way to treat your beloved and your saviour," Hedstrong replied, resenting her attitude, but enjoying his moment of power. "I think we should talk first."

"What is there to talk about? Just give me the boost I need so I can get on with sorting out the rest. I don't like so many in this one place with us. It's time they returned to their home bases."

"Maybe it would be better if I did the job," Hedstrong persisted. "You know, save you having to move about."

It was then that Antedote realised she had a problem. Forced to share her secret, she had surrendered her power over the house, believing it would be a temporary relinquishment easily regained upon the return of adoring Hedstrong. Only he suddenly didn't seem inclined to be so adoring. She decided it was that interfering Upstart who was to blame and allowed another measure of inactively to pass whilst she contemplated her next move. Keeping her deliberation to herself she came to a decision.

"Are you sure you can manage?" she asked. "It's not as easy as it looks… passing power from one to another. Too little and it is a waste, without effect. Too much and you could be drained and immobilised. I know you've tried in the past, but never after re-charging yourself."

Hedstrong considered what she was saying and, in the excitement of all that was going on, again forgot to block. That allowed Antedote to follow his processes: his fear that he could mess up if he tried without her; the challenge of having a go anyway; and the question whether he wanted to. She waited, listening to his thoughts until, at last, he made his decision.

"I agree," she said, not waiting for his twitch.

"It's not very polite to link in on another's thoughts," he told her.

"Don't be so pompous. You're right. We would make a good team. You and I in charge of the house. It was silly of me to take on the whole burden. We should do it together." She ended the comment with a slight twitch of affection, which worked.

"All right, then," he said. The others had been waiting patiently, trying to read what was going on between the two; not that, in their powerless state, they had much alternative.

Hedstrong and Antedote proceeded to work out a strategy. He would share his recharge with her and then they would both get to work revitalising the others in their room. That way things could get back to normal. Suddenly he felt nervous. He'd never been so close to another spirit before, least of all one for which he had somehow developed feelings and definitely not when he'd been so full of current.

"It's all right," Antedote encouraged, displaying her gentler side. "Come beside me... close." He followed her instruction. Her proximity created such a sudden, irresistible urge he lost all control, disappearing into several mircos of pure ecstasy.

"Is it always like this?" he managed.

"No," Antedote responded, also surprised at the closeness their currents were generating. "It's never been like this for me before. It's wonderful." She couldn't help herself allowing the tremors to continue and it must have been at least a measure before she was able to whisper, "Come to me. Give me power."

He came willingly, and they discovered a voltage they were convinced no spirit had ever experienced before. They were so consumed in each other that they materialised in a surging, sweeping cascade that rattled ornaments, setting paintings at an angle. Dust storms reached the ceiling to send them through wall after wall until, still wrapped in each other, they reached the kitchen and projected out into the courtyard.

Antedote was suddenly aware of the change in atmosphere. She struggled to regain control of this new, consuming emotion.

"Hedstrong, Hedstrong," she gasped. "What are you doing to me?"

"You know what I'm doing," he replied. "Are you complaining?"

"No. No I'm not," she heard herself responding. "It's wonderful. Wonderful. Don't stop." He didn't, not for several measures, and they remained in the yard materialised for all to see, except, fortunately, there was no one from human existence to notice.

Eventually the tremors stopped. Their apparitions sank back to obscurity. The two spirits became still, entwined around each other, neither anxious to move and both seeking to come to terms with their discovery. Antedote was the first to stir.

"I think we should try to separate," she suggested.

"D'you want to?" he asked.

"No."

"Me neither. I never want to be apart from you again."

"I know. I feel the same, but we must try to be sensible. We have the rest to consider." Other Real World residents were the last things Hedstrong wanted to consider. He'd blended so completely with her that she knew, if she wished, she could take every urge of power he had left and he would be hers for ever. She was so tempted, but reason slowly began to win over emotion.

"We must be sensible," she murmured again, twitching gently through his embrace. Hedstrong resisted, placing all his power under her control and, for a micro, she nearly took it.

"No. We must remain two forces. We owe it to the others. We've discovered so much in the last few measures. If we give in to our desires it will all be lost and we'll be back in our static world of boring reality."

"Give me that any day, as long as I can stay with you," he admitted.

"I know. But we mustn't and who can say we'd stay together? We don't know what forces we'd be unleashing." She sensed he was beginning to acknowledge her reasoning. She persisted, promising that there would be times in the future when they could blend and enjoy those electrifying surges they had just experienced. With one last flash, he drew away but still hovered in general contact whilst they became conscious of where they were.

"We're outside the house!" Antedote exclaimed.

"We can't be. It's not possible," Hedstrong replied.

They were so startled they each swept back through the solid walls of the mansion and didn't stop until they reached the great hall. Hedstrong found the dinner gong empty and settled in the middle of it. Antedote was right behind him and she chose the frame supporting the large copper dish.

"I don't think we should stay here long," she observed. "If a human were to touch that metal you're in, the shock would probably be terminal, and we'd have another spirit to contend with."

"Let's go back to our base," Hedstrong suggested. "We need time to work out what we're going to do. Nothing like this has ever happened to me before. And we have to recharge the others."

Antedote agreed.

"Remember to keep your block on," she warned. "We don't want them reading our thoughts before we're ready. And be prepared for the complaints. You know what they're like."

The dinner gong rocked and echoed across the hall when they left it, but the Lord of the Manor didn't notice. He was too engrossed in deciding if he had to sell another work of art. He needed cash to cover the cost of keeping the roof over his head. Whist the spirits busied themselves tending to the others, he resolved that the Turner would have to go. Keeping a deteriorating structure he had once enjoyed was almost beyond him. The effort re-enforced his resolve that, when his time was up, his family's human presence in this great mound of masonry would end. He was determined they would not have to face the problems with which he had coped.

CHAPTER 5
DEMOCRACY

His Lordship struggled to rise the following morning. On checking the time he was surprised to note it was already approaching ten o'clock. He'd agreed to receive Phyllis for what she called 'a discussion', and rushed to have a wash. The water was cold, indicating something was wrong with the boiler, not for the first time. Hastily dressing he hurried down through the kitchens to open the back door, not in the best of tempers. Phyllis was waiting in the yard holding some envelopes the mailman had left with her. She walked over to him, an attractive young lady, still with the youthful confidence he recalled from those early visits. Her smile and obvious pleasure at seeing him lifted his mood a little.

"He shouldn't have done that," he complained, not fully recovered from his early morning irritation. "You could have been anyone."

"No I couldn't," Phyllis told him with one of her smiles. "It was Arthur. He knows me. He's local."

"That's no excuse," he grumbled.

"It's not an excuse. It's a reason. Arthur knows I visit you and wouldn't abuse his trust, or yours." Phyllis put her arms around his Lordship's neck and kissed him. She felt him relax. "That's better," she said. "What's rattled your cage today?"

He took the letters off her and led the way back into the house. When they were settled in the morning room he told her of his experience with the 'ghost' the night before. He claimed it was probably a dream, brought on by the light bulb exploding and she laughed at him. He waved aside her attempt at an explanation,

38

asking what was so important that she'd needed to see him at short notice.

"Nothing too drastic," she said. "I'd just like to spend a few nights with you, now and again."

It was his turn to laugh. Why wasn't he surprised? What was it about this young woman that so captivated his attention? Was he responding to her sex appeal? She certainly had it. Was it simply that he enjoyed her company, bringing back memories of his earlier life in the army? He'd seen so many countries, so many people surviving at so many different levels. Did she want to make love to him... try her hand where so many had failed in the past?

"I don't want to sleep with you," she told him. "That's not unless you want to give it a go. Come to think of it, that could be quite interesting, but," she held up a hand, "I know that wouldn't be part of your agenda. The opportunity for producing an heir has long past."

"Correct. This part of the family line stops here," he assured her.

"And so does family occupation of the estate," she added using words he'd uttered more than once. "I think you really mean that. In fact, I know you do."

His expression, his curt nod of the head, confirmed his sadness at acknowledging the termination of generations of occupants presiding over the house, grounds and estate.

"We're of no use now," he said. "We're not even part of a community any more. Everyone's withdrawn to pursue their own separate lives. They don't need us. Most of them have more comfort in their centrally-heated, double-glazed homes. They've become as selfish as us. We haven't the influence any more, especially not at local village level."

"So can I spend a few nights here, just to soak up the atmosphere and touch a life that once served so many, before it's over?" She saw from the look he gave her and his grin that her request would be granted. "I wouldn't bother you. Let's face it, there's enough space in this old pile of rubble for me to get lost in and you may never see me."

"Of course you can," he told her. "And if you find a few moments to share with me, in between casting your spells and chanting your chants, I'd treat it as a pleasure… I think."

***

Several measures passed in the spiritual world. After administering electrical charges to their companions, with one exception, the happy couple were allowed the pleasure of just being together. The exception, still to receive her boost, was Upstart, left stranded in the servants' quarters as long as Antedote could manage.

"She doesn't deserve movement. Leave her alone and she'll infiltrate some workman or other 'inferior candidate'. That will take her away from the house, hopefully into a boring, unimaginative existence, so that on her return to Reality somewhere else she may be less bother to some other unlucky spirits."

"She hasn't really done anything wrong," Hedstrong argued. "And I don't regard workmen 'inferior'. Many are more skilled than some of the other human layabouts, such as solicitors, footballers and politicians."

"Give her a chance and she'll do all manner of wrong." With that final pronouncement Antedote took off for the upper regions of the mansion, fearing that if she didn't Hedstrong would, which was the last thing she wanted. She found the spirit exactly where Hedstrong had described.

"I thought you were never coming," Upstart greeted her.

"Did you?" Antedote replied.

"Can't we be friends?"

"Why should I want to be friends with you?"

"Because I can help you. After all, this is what you're used to. Servants' quarters. You've read my history. You know I've had far more experience of the human world than you, and achieved greater bodies."

"We don't judge achievement by bodies."

"And what does that mean?" Upstart enquired, presenting Antedote with a problem, because she didn't know herself what she meant. Spirits didn't do judging. At least they never had, so far as she knew.

"D'you want a boost, or not?" she asked, evading the question.

"We *are* in a mood. Hedstrong not dancing to your wavelength?" Upstart realised she was about to go too far and, not wishing to remain imprisoned in a neglected and deteriorating part of the house, assumed a more compliant role. "Yes, please. I would like a boost." Antedote gave her one and left before the young pretender realised she was free to roam.

***

When Antedote returned to their panel, Hedstrong having moved to join her after their burst into the outside world, he was missing. She wondered if he'd been checking up on her, but dismissed the thought. He wasn't that devious. In fact he wasn't devious at all really, apart perhaps from techniques he may have picked up on his trips into humanity. Nevertheless those techniques must have become refined. There was always a danger he could exploit them to bridge the Real World male-female intelligence gap and rise to her level.

Not so many measures ago she wouldn't have experienced such uncertainty. That was when spirits had kept themselves to themselves in static anticipation of their next journey. They hadn't questioned their position, existing in benevolent innocence. Now, thanks to her, they were all clamouring for movement and she, their liberator, was spending most of her time plotting to keep them under control. Perhaps they should all go back to their previous simple existence.

"Is that what you really want?" Hedstrong asked, drifting in through the opposite wall and twitching onto her last thought.

"Where've you been?" she asked, only just managing to project the question in gentle enquiry.

"The library," he replied. "I thought I'd test that competition we thrashed out, you know, when we all thought of a brief spell in his Lordship."

"You mean you actually shot books off the shelves?"

"Only two. I'm afraid I upset a few of the residents, who felt it was unfair to practice before the competition started. They said they didn't like the floor looking a mess either."

"Idiot. We've more important matters to consider than silly competitions. Using the Lord was a stupid idea anyway."

She lapsed into silence, leaving her thoughts unblocked so that he could latch onto them. He'd joined her in the panel and she really liked him being there. It was a comfortable feeling. Two spirits together, working for the good of their fellows.

She allowed herself to bask in the glory of their companionship. They'd been enjoying joint existence so much that neither of them had bothered to fully consider the implications of the adventure that had brought them together. Only at that mirco-measure did Antedote begin to see what they had done. In their Real State they'd actually left the walls of the house. Like the rest of the community, she'd always assumed that was not possible. But why not? After all, not so many measures ago she had assumed it was not possible, in Reality, to leave her static state, but she had. They all had.

She twitched onto Hedstrong's thoughts and confirmed that he was also struggling to cope. They could go out into the land beyond the mansion. They could explore. There were bound to be spirits out there. Would they have found the benefits of artificial electric power... currents which did not come from their inner drive? Would they be exploring too? What hidden dangers lay in wait for anyone daring to venture forth and risk being suspended in infinity?

Another thought hit them both at the same time. If they could leave the house, what was to stop alien spirits taking over their space? In proportion to humanity, they were already overcrowded in the mansion. A greater presence would be a drain on all their resources.

"We'd better call a meeting," Hedstrong suggested.

"Why?"

"To decide on a plan of action. The others may be worried and we don't want them going off on ill-prepared missions, do we?"

"Why would they do that?" Antedote asked, before it registered. She didn't even need to twitch to confirm her beloved partner had told some of them of their expedition into the outside yard. "Why did you have to go and do that?"

"Do what?" he said, blocking his thoughts whilst he sought better response to what was obviously a reprimand.

"And don't block me out. Do I mean so little to you?"

"Sorry," he apologised, revealing all. He sustained a half measure of criticism before Antedote calmed down sufficiently to come to terms with what she described as the predicament he'd landed them in. She agreed that a meeting was essential, now the discovery was common knowledge, but insisted that they have a plan of action before calling it.

"We need to keep control," she explained. "We can't have spirits wandering about aimlessly all over the grounds. It will have to be done in an orderly fashion."

Hedstrong didn't quite see it that way but was willing to go along with her ideas, especially when she implied that the alternative would be to lose their togetherness. In fact, he was prepared to follow her to the end of the estate if it meant they remained united. With his devotion evident for all to sense, Antedote achieved agreement for the first item on her Agenda. The spirits would be invited to formally adopt her as their leader and he would be her deputy. Hedstrong suggested they have a committee, to inject a measure of democracy into the arrangement. Antedote initially disagreed but was persuaded when he explained that it was a tried and tested human device for shifting the blame if anything went wrong.

"It didn't do you much good over the MGMC farce," she said, "but all right. We're not leaving the meeting to elect the members, though. The leader must be given that task. Me. I'm not having just anyone interfering in what we want to do."

With a few more matters of procedure settled between them they decided to spend the next measure contacting their fellow house spirits. Antedote insisted on one-to-one discussions with them all whilst each one was given a boost. She claimed it was a means of avoiding waste of energy during the formal proceedings. Hedstrong knew it was her way of endeavouring to remind the others who controlled the power, thereby ensuring their unanimous support. The human disease of lobbying was about to invade their world.

***

Opening the meeting, Antedote started her introductory speech by stressing that they were at the beginning of a new spiritual freedom. She convinced her audience that after generations, in human terms, of static acceptance of Reality they had been set free, thanks to her. Not only were they able to move about their mansion but, after a wall breaking expedition, risked by her and her partner, it had been proved that, with care, preparation and sufficient power, they could begin to explore a world which, until she had given them their freedom, was only open if they assumed part of humanity.

"Just twitch on this," she added. "With the power I can offer you, a new-found, virtually unlimited power, we can go abroad with full, immediate recollection. We won't need to blend with a human body, suffering the blackout of all past measures until we return to the Real World, unable to actively influence the human brain, not able to dictate when or where we might go, entrapped, not even able to escape back to Reality." She let them dwell on the message for a mirco-measure, checking some of their thought processes to confirm she had their support, before moving to the first task.

Items one and two on the Agenda went without a hitch. She was confirmed the leader, and her selection of Hedstrong as deputy was endorsed. It was when twitching moved on to the committee that things began to go astray. Initially there was no opposition. All agreed that the number of members be limited to five, and that they meet regularly. Antedote started to thank everyone for attending, attempting to bring discussions to a close. She failed. A spirit, last freed from a retired army general, with a history of habitation in army personnel throughout the human ages. led what Antedote later called the revolt. He suggested that, with all mansion spirits present, it was an ideal time to elect the committee. Antedote countered that it would be best left to the leader to select the members, after individual interview and consultation.

Others disagreed. The words 'democracy' and 'dictatorship' surfaced and emotions began to get heated. Fearing a fuseout, which could cause permanent damage to the gathering, Hedstrong attempted to calm the proceedings by suggesting an adjournment for contemplation. He reminded the meeting that if Antedote and he were left de-energised, the rest would be powerless.

"That doesn't mean we should surrender all control." It was the successor from the retired army general again, still arguing.

Surprisingly, Upstart came to the rescue. In one of her most flowing twitches, she begged her fellow spirits not to get overheated. She said she understood how they felt and that it was right and proper for them to have a say in how their community developed. Every one of them had the vast experience of many journeys out of the Real World.

"One day there will be such disruption in the superficial lives of humans following another decline in a dominant civilisation, whether you like it or not, and I know some will not... indeed most of us would not, including me, we'd be deprived of opportunity to depart the Real World for a spell of human experience. There would be no humans left. We must, therefore, prepare for uninterrupted spiritual existence."

Antedote was startled by the outburst, uncertain whether it was a gesture of support or another attempt to take over leadership. Fearing the latter she was about to suggest this mysteriously unfathomable spirit depart there and then whilst humanity existed, but a warning flash from Hedstrong restrained her.

"On the other hand, I can see how Hedstrong and Antedote feel," Upstart continued. Antedote checked her thought block to ensure that she couldn't, but remained silent under Hedstrong's urging. "They have given freedom to you all and they have done it in such a way that we have not gone over the top. Power is dangerous and their caution in delivering it has allowed you to grow slowly in strength, testing to find a way. It is only right that they should seek to control your development – to ensure you don't lose what has been gained." She paused to check reaction and was satisfied she had enough favourable twitches, so she put her suggestion. "I propose that our leader be given the right to choose three committee members. The rest of us would be allowed to select two."

It was not an instant victory. Antedote fought a strong rearguard action, using the now well established claim that the achievements to date were all down to her and that, without her, they would all be back to their static existence. She asked how they felt they could elect committee members, reminding them of what she called 'the still ongoing fiasco' when they tried to choose two volunteers to enter his Lordship.

Despite her efforts, eventually she accepted she would not win the day. And she also knew who the two elected representatives would be.

The spirit freed from the retired army general, whom Antedote immediately named Kernel, to take him down a rank or two, became the first democratic member, unchallenged. Upstart was the other, with unanimous approval, apart from Antedote, who argued that as leader she should abstain. Hedstrong succeeded in winning a measure's grace, during which Antedote was to be allowed to select the remaining three. The meeting broke up on an optimistic note allowing spirits to surge back to their resting places, charged with the belief that they had all taken another step on the road to freedom.

CHAPTER 6
AN UNCERTAIN FUTURE

He'd noticed her coming up the drive and was standing outside the front door when she arrived. She'd been away for months on one of her archaeological digs and he'd missed her company. They embraced and he kissed her. Surprised by this unusual, not unwelcome, greeting, Phyllis allowed him to guide her into the house with his arm around her waist.

"It's a nice day," he said. "Let me put on some wellies. Then do an old man the honour of a stroll around the garden."

"I'd like that," Phyllis told him. She watched him toss off his slippers and choose a pair of outdoor walking boots. "And, Richard, I don't see you as an old man."

She allowed him to find suitable footwear for her, ignoring his claim that, at 73 years of age, he could hardly be described as anything else. He wanted to show her Paradise, he said. It wouldn't be her first visit to his mini arboretum. Since her surreptitious trespassing as a young girl, nearly 30 years ago, she'd enjoyed many solitary moments amongst the trees, but never in his company.

They left through the kitchen, along old stone passages with steps down to unknown retreats. They passed the old aviary, its vertical wooden beams somehow still supporting the roof of what once must have been a beautiful little building. In fact, it still was, Phyllis thought, despite its abandoned appearance. Pausing to look up towards the rose garden, still with signs of attempts at preservation but far too much for one man to keep going, she asked him what had made him give up his army career to become the latest in a line of resident Lords of the Manor.

"I was born here. Then, in the 1970s, my mother needed help and it was my duty," he told her.

Whilst they walked on she suggested duty had little to do with it. He gave a grunt, leading off onto the grass, then a tennis court, looking as neglected as some of the other more distant parts of the garden. She told him his 'love for the place' had even outweighed his duty to what, in her time, the locals knew to be a forceful mother.

"I would never leave it," he admitted. "Certainly not now after the struggle to keep it together."

From her visits Phyllis knew the difficulties he'd experienced, the heartache he'd suffered at having to sell some of the family heirlooms; the losses he'd sustained in struggles to keep the estate viable. He'd continue to raise cash needed to keep the old place going until he 'departed this world'.

"What then?" she asked. "Who takes over then?" He'd already told her of the family conference he'd called to announce that the riches of centuries would be split. The house, the cottages, the grounds, the farms… all would be sold.

Late afternoon shadows of July followed them through the trees as, once more, he affirmed his intention, declaring that arrangements had been made. They were in Paradise. It was the area most favoured by his Lordship, and Phyllis felt his mood lift.

"I love trees," he told her. "I always have." He knew the names of each and every ancient trunk and touched some of them when they passed. Reaching almost the boundary of the formal grounds he paused, turning to look at her.

"This is where I'll be when I'm gone," he said with a smile. "Here, or in the woods above the sawmill. There's such peace below the branches, amongst the leaves, such quiet."

"No, you won't," Phyllis told him. "It doesn't work like that."

"D'you mean I've no choice?"

"The power within you will be released," she explained. "It may look like you, but it'll be much more than a ghost… an apparition."

He wanted to know what she meant, but either she couldn't or wouldn't explain. All she would say was that the so-called ghosts she saw were active and 'busy', not reflections of the dead. He asked if she could contact the dead. For example, could she summon up his mother or his father, or him after he'd gone? She told him that was a load of nonsense. If she concentrated she may be able to describe his relatives and even imitate what they might be saying if they were still around, but anything more would be simply play acting.

"What I would tell you," she continued, "would be from reading you. I can do that, just as now I believe I can see the spirits in the house. I'm certainly aware of them. But they're different. I don't think they claim to be humans, past, present or future. One day I hope we may be able to communicate, them and I."

"You really are a witch," he told her causing Phyllis to smile. "Will you come to my funeral?" he asked.

"No," she said. "What we have is between ourselves. My memories are precious, and I'm not disposed to share those with anyone. All I need to do to remember you is to be here, in the woods, or gardens, or the house. Your influence will survive longer than me and keep my memories safe."

They'd been standing under a large beech tree. He suddenly bent down and kissed her before they slowly began to walk back to the house. He seemed happy, more relaxed than she'd known during their friendship. He held her hand and confessed that, despite her assurances, he was feeling very old. He recalled the days of his early youth when the mansion had been alive with servants, likening it to a self-contained village.

"We played tennis on the court, and the lake was full. I used to sneak down here and watch the wildlife after dark. The moon would reflect off the water. It was magic."

"Have you ever thought of refilling it?" Phyllis asked.

"No, it would cost too much, and to maintain. I watched them drain it when I was in my teens. It was during the Second World

War, due to the reflection of that moon I'd so enjoyed. They said it would be like a night beacon for enemy bombers seeking the City. Mum said she'd see to it being refilled later, but that never happened. Bombs exploding nearby cracked the concrete base."

He turned to stare up at the house, recalling the nights Phyllis had spent there once he'd agreed she should. There were days after she'd gone when he'd unlock doors and roam corridors, recalling occasions when they'd been full of activity. He was glad he'd witnessed them.

"They're gone for good," he said. "I mean the servants. Our community, our village has moved out. The pop stars and footballers are the new lords of the manors, but they will never preside over the close, exclusive self-contained mansions of my predecessors. For good or for bad, that time has come and gone. Soon I, too, will be gone."

***

"I am glad to be back!"

Catching her off guard, the twitch, from an unknown source, at first irritated Antedote, who was in the middle of deciding who her loyal committee members would be. She took no notice, having projected enough negative surround to send most of her flock back to their statics, but it didn't work on him. Who was this interloper and why didn't he take the hint? She tried again, adopting the modern human phrase 'piss off' but still he remained. To her annoyance he engaged Hedstrong in twitching when her deputy should have been projecting helpful thoughts in her direction.

"Excuse me," she declared. "I'm in meditation. Would you kindly go."

"Antedote," Hedstrong tried.

"No. I won't be interrupted," she said.

"I think you should."

She was about to develop a shocking reply when she latched onto Hedstrong's wavelength, and flashed in surprise. It had happened. What they'd all been afraid was about to descend upon them. The spirit that was floating in front of her, politely allowing time for her frustrations to subside, was new, and he'd come from his Lordship. A short measure of inactivity followed whilst she adjusted to this changed situation. The news spread, causing others to drift into the vicinity.

Although maintaining a block to prevent an unrestricted delve into recent history, Hedstrong had already twitched the newcomer sufficient information to update him on the progress that had been made whilst he was away from the Real World. In return the new arrival, whilst also operating his block, had responded with a pocket book summary, going back well before his Lordship.

Hedstrong was impressed. All the same, he nipped off up to the bedroom just to confirm what had happened, not that there was any doubt. Spirits can't lie. Divert and block maybe, but not lie.

"It's true," he reported to their leader on his return. "The body's there for all to encounter. His Lordship has died, left humanity."

"Couldn't you have kept him going a bit longer," Antedote complained to the newcomer.

"Sorry. No could do. Everything was getting on top of the poor fellow and eventually we were just fused out."

"We?" Antedote questioned. "There were more than you?"

"Just one more," the hovering spirit replied. "She's gone off in another direction."

"She?"

"His feminine side I call it. Well, not actually female feminine. Humans can't usually mix male and female can they? It was all quite well balanced, considering."

"Considering what?"

"Considering that the human way of life his Lordship was trying to maintain had disappeared with the Empire, and he knew it. Just wanted to keep out of the way and do his own thing, and you know how difficult it is for any spirit to influence anyone when in human restraint."

Despite herself further discussion left Antedote developing a liking for this addition to her flock, even if some of his uttering seemed strange. His response to her aggressive greeting had been courteous, but not ingratiating. He removed his block, revealing his full history stretching back over countless human centuries encompassing worldwide experience. Reluctantly she unblocked in return and was relieved to find he had no desire to undermine her authority. There was no undercurrent of revolt. He accepted her as leader of the house. She even identified a spark of admiration for what she was achieving.

"We'll call you Lard," she pronounced, "seeing you were part of one."

He twitched a bit at that, asserting it was aimed more at fat than his stately heritage, but Antedote told him not to be so silly. She appointed him to the committee to pacify him. He thanked her graciously before declaring that he'd better find a permanent location to rest, as this floating about was beginning to drain him. Antedote gave him a boost to allow him to drift off.

"That was a bit rash," Hedstrong muttered, when Lard had left.

"What was?"

"Appointing him a member of your committee without even testing his credentials."

Never one to welcome criticism, Antedote reminded him that there'd been no attempt by Lard to put a block on his past when they'd both searched through it. She claimed they would benefit from his experience.

"I'm sure he will be very loyal to us," she added, causing Hedstrong to wonder if the force of her assurance was an endeavour to convince herself more than him.

***

53

News of the death of the Lord of the Manor spread swiftly beyond his estate and soon other members of the family moved into the mansion. Nephews and nieces of the dead human arrived and began to search parts of the old house that had been sealed away. Many had spent holidays there, especially during school years when their parents had been somewhere else. The spirits watched whilst these interlopers explored and poked into corners some had never before been allowed to enter.

The Real World observers were uncertain whether they liked this departure from the reclusive life of his Lordship. Antedote shared their uncertainty and was particularly scathing when Hedstrong suggested that more active human world presence was just what they'd been waiting for. Pots and pans were disturbed in the kitchen, books inspected in the library, bats discovered in the deserted old servants' quarters. It soon became apparent that much was about to change around them and Antedote called an emergency spiritual meeting. Lard, asked for his interpretation of the current activity, was able to confirm terms of his Lordship's will.

"Everything's to be sold and the cash split between the survivors," he announced. "This old heap's going to see new owners and, believe me, things will become very different. His Lordship's descendants in the material sense are about to share millions. But don't expect any of them to keep this place going. They'd be daft to try. It'll probably end up as flats - once they've flogged off all the valuables - or a school, or offices."

Sensing the drift of some of the gathering, Antedote warned them not to be too hasty. She suggested that latching on to the first available human that came along was no answer. Lard agreed, adding that selection of the wrong body for a trip could turn out to be a regrettable experience. It wasn't just the family poking around. There were valuers everywhere, assessing the books, the carpets, the paintings, the ornaments, the furniture, even the wood panels. A few had visited his Lordship before his demise, when he had sold the odd Turner or other work of art to pay for repairs and maintenance.

"If you knew what some of them got up to you wouldn't want to spark their presence," he said. "Remember, a bit of it will rub off into your images. And as for the lawyers, they were bad enough in Victorian times but now, well, they even try to justify their parasitical pursuits and aspire to superior respectability."

Most spirits took note although one or two closed their beings to the warnings. Fancying another trip into humanity, they were soon part of the army of greedy human 'experts' rubbing their hands in glee at the thought of handling such spoils. The increasing activity and shifting around of so many items caused Antedote to call another meeting of those who were left. Resting places were being disturbed, crockery moved, screens shifted, paintings taken down. There was even a hint that the library was about to be stripped of its books, numerous packing cases having been dumped in the centre of the room.

"You can't arrest progress," Lard told the gathering. "Let's face it, the place is deteriorating. Most of the rooms have been closed for years, with the blinds down and dust covers over furniture and things. My last human, the Lord of the manor, did his best in a sad way, but you can't defeat what idiots call 'progress'. It's programmed into human genes that if someone does better than another, that other will eventually make sure the one bettering him suffers, demanding equal rights so he can take over. Equality they call it."

Lard was in full flow, proceeding to deal with communism, branding it a different type of political force to that practised by religion - more akin to insurance companies where everyone paid about the same to be protected against disaster as long as they didn't make a claim and threaten the profits creamed off for a few. Hedstrong, as bored as the rest, apart from Antedote who, to his annoyance, was lapping up every twitch, was relieved when Lard, who would prove himself to be an astute negotiator, realised he had lost the attention of his audience. He apologised for drifting onto one of his 'hobbyhorses' and said he would 'shut up'.

"No, it's really interesting," Antedote told him. "Please proceed."

Fortunately he didn't rise to the invitation, allowing the meeting to agree his suggestion that there were more important matters under discussion. Attention returned to the major topic – how to deal with the current developments. Materialisation was suggested, aimed at frightening the intruders away. This was countered by suggestions it would encourage a separate load of experts hiking in electrical devices to look for what they called 'ghosts'. The Real World occupants may even be faced with a particularly perceptive individual arriving to 'communicate' who could actually see them and engage in twitching with them.

Again it was Lard who rescued the situation. He suggested that a programme of action be left to the committee. Antedote readily agreed, wanting to be free of all the aimless twittering that was going on around her. Apart from it not being 'conducive to positive deliberation', as she put it, echoing what Hedstrong considered the high flung, unnecessary language emanating from Lard, it was contributing to a force-field that would soon attract human attention. Paintings were getting out of line, curtains drifting, ornaments moving.

"It would help if we actually had a committee," Upstart declared, joining the debate for the first time. "I'm beginning to think Antedote doesn't want one, the time she's taking to choose her representatives."

"I've already announced one member, and I'm nearly finished on the other two," Antedote responded irritably.

"A likely story," Upstart accused.

"I really think you should decide," Hedstrong encouraged, and this did the trick. Antedote selected Baybe and Spayed, much to Lard's amusement.

"What's the joke?" Upstart demanded.

"Nothing, well, nothing important," Lard said, but still couldn't conceal his merriment. Sensing that more was expected of him he added, "Nothing like keeping it in the family." He left his knowledge unblocked, which allowed the others to discover that Baybe included in her human past a short journey to humanity as an illegitimate child, ill-nourished in human form to return her to the Real World almost as soon as she'd left it. All reading the revelation had little difficulty connecting the incident with Antedote's rocking horse experience. Spayed had occupied one of the gardeners with whom a maid had had a human liaison before she'd been seduced by high living attentions. His spirit had returned to Reality after his human form stumbled in a drunken stupor and fell down the servants' stairs.

***

It didn't take Hedstrong more than a short measure or two to grasp that the return of Lard to their presence and the last fully attended spiritual meeting had somehow changed their community. Before his Lordship's demise, they had been drifting on, mostly in their own sweet way, testing the new freedom of movement. No one had really bothered to consider where it would all lead and, in the main, had continued to do their own thing, leaving Antedote to play with her superiority almost as if it was a game.

Hedstrong, once his own force, ignoring all others and selfishly consumed with his own eternity, was now one of a group and there was a leader. That meant there were followers, which meant that there were different levels of being, which meant that one level would aspire to rise to the next. Soon, he thought, the whole community would be acting like human beings, which would defeat the whole object of spiritual existence, wouldn't it?

"What is the object?" he twitched out loud. The others had left, including Lard, and only Antedote responded from the next panel.

"What are you talking about?"

"Why are we doing all this? What does it matter if the whole place is stripped, allowed to crumble into ruin or even get knocked into flats. That's what humans do. They create things then they destroy them. If we try to interfere by preserving houses, works of art, arresting progress, we'll only create another type of body that will grow and grow until it destroys itself. Humans are primed to do that without our help. They're programmed to go on and on until they achieve ultimate destruction."

"And where would ultimate human destruction leave us if we don't try to stop it?" demanded Antedote. "In infinity," she answered, not allowing him a twitch. "Would you like that? Infinity?"

"It wouldn't be all that bad, if we could share it, would it?" he asked.

"Don't be stupid."

That was the end of the conversation so far as Antedote was concerned. She felt it was an idiotic one anyway and wondered if Hedstrong was attempting to compete with Lard. She said she had work to do, and took herself away to offer a charge to whoever wanted it.

"You're not stupid," Upstart pulsed, using the gentlest of surges and the smoothest of twitches. "You can see much further ahead than she can." Hedstrong hadn't sensed her proximity and wondered how long she'd been present. "All the time," Upstart answered, reading his thoughts. "You were busy trying to work out where we were going, and she was consumed with her own importance as usual. She's lost track of all that's going on around her."

"You think I'm right to be worried."

"Of course you are. You've discovered something about this World that the rest in this house seem so anxious to ignore, or at least most of them."

"You mean you sense it too?"

"Of course I do. And so would Antedote if she wasn't so involved with her power game. Maybe she hasn't had as much human experience as you or I, but she's had more than most. One day she'll see it. Probably when it's too late and certainly when someone else has pinched all her superiority."

Upstart had chosen her moment well. Hedstrong was troubled, and not only by the changes the coming together of the spiritual community were effecting. He was even more bothered by a feeling he couldn't identify. Upstart could, and did. It was the opportunity she'd been waiting for.

"D'you think we're all being influenced a little too much by Lard?" she asked.

"What d'you mean, 'influenced'?"

"Well, he does seem to be able to twitch onto Antedote's wavelength rather easily." She paused before adding, "I'm not sure whether his intentions are always what they should be. Remember, he has been cooped up in human suspension within a dying dynasty for a number of measures. You never know how that may have influenced him."

"You could be right," Hedstrong admitted. "I thought we were all… well, that we were all just spirits until the last few measures. But we've got feelings… emotions. We've got desires."

"I know," Upstart encouraged. "You've all come a long way in recent measures, and it's all thanks to Antedote. If she hadn't discovered the means of freeing you from your static states, you may never have made these discoveries."

"You're right."

"So we must always be grateful to her for that. But we must watch that she doesn't drift away from the main purpose of our existence."

"I agree," Hedstrong responded, not bothering to ask what Upstart considered to be their main purpose. "We must do our best for her. Where d'you think she's gone now?"

"Looking for Lard, if I read her intention correctly."

"I'm not sure that would be a wise thing."

"You're right, but she won't find him… not until he wants her to."

"Why's that?" Hedstrong asked.

"Because he's not in the mansion."

"What d'you mean?"

"He's taken himself off." She refused to enlarge upon the comment, also taking herself off.

CHAPTER 7

DEFECTION

So far as Antedote was concerned, Lard had disappeared. Her searching of the mansion and her twitchings were so persistent they eventually became a joke between the rest of the spiritual household. Relations with Hedstrong cooled. Each blocked the other to an extent that he left her to her panel, moving into one of the large upper bedrooms, where he just happened to encounter a sympathetic Upstart.

"There's room for two," she encouraged, materialising for a micro-measure in the door frame she'd selected.

"What're you doing here?" Hedstrong asked.

"More to the point, what are you doing away from your beloved?"

"She's not my beloved. Unlike humans, we don't have those feelings."

Upstart knew better than to argue. There was much activity in the house which she wanted to discuss, and romantic involvement could come later. Suddenly all the preparation for the house auction had stopped and a different human mood prevailed. She doubted if any of the others had noticed, or, if they had, whether they'd bothered to find out why. Spirits can be very thick if they tried, so she switched into Hedstrong's presence, which he hadn't blocked, to see if he was aware of the change. It pleased her to find that he was, although he hadn't sought to analyse the goings on.

"What of it?" he asked.

"What d'you know of the National Trust?" she countered.

"Not a lot."

That didn't surprise her. He'd been back for quite a time and the organisation was only in its infancy when he was last gambling a human life away. Responding further to her question he delved into her unblocked experiences, and couldn't believe what he discovered.

"You're not serious," he twitched. "Thousands? You say tens of thousands expending human energies on preserving wrecks like this and thousands more queuing up to visit them?" It was an unnecessary question, for spirits don't lie, but the vision of so many doing so much to re-create what they thought was the luxury of the past took some believing. Upstart told him not to knock it. Many a human, she said, was kept out of mischief by devoting time to this or that project. It was a fairly harmless activity as long as those in charge didn't become big-headed enough to believe they could influence governments, beat commerce or run the country.

Suddenly they realised they'd been joined by another presence. He'd been calmly drifting around absorbing their conversation in a benevolent almost superior manner. In fact Upstart considered it to be patronising and said so.

"What if it is?" Lard replied. "There's nothing wrong with being patronising and its only those who've not thought of doing it before who object."

"Your mood hasn't changed since we last met," she declared.

"Why should it?" he answered.

"Oh, do stop answering everything with a question. You sound like a human psychologist... worse, a counsellor."

Both Upstart and Hedstrong sensed the amusement floating from Lard. They were forced to admit that it was infectious, but they had no time to engage in further banter because they all felt the approach of Antedote. Lard took off back to his retreat, twitching an invitation to Upstart to join him for a more serious chat, bringing Hedstrong with her.

"He's only just left, hasn't he?" demanded Antedote, surging into the bedroom.

"Who?" queried Upstart innocently.

"You know who. And as for you…" she twitched, concentrating exclusively on Hedstrong, "you knew I wanted to contact him, yet you just let him slip through your presence without any attempt at stopping him."

"Maybe he didn't want to twitch with you," Hedstrong replied in indifferent tone.

"Who's leader here? If I want to communicate with someone, you do all in your power to ensure my wish is met. Understand?"

"How d'you suggest I do that? If he doesn't want to twitch on you?"

"You're so stupid. I don't know what I ever saw in you. Stay with your floosie for all I care." With that Antedote was off through the floor in continued search for Lard.

"She won't find him," Upstart said.

"It's not that big a house. She'll run him down eventually. She's very persistent."

"I told you, he's not in the house, so she can be as persistent as she likes." Reading Hedstrong's puzzlement, Upstart explained that Lard had taken up residence in the wooden aviary.

"But that's outside. We don't go outside," Hedstrong protested.

"You do. You have," Upstart reminded him, having noted the incident from an earlier unblocked communion.

"Yes, but that was a mistake. You know we shouldn't leave the house. It's not done."

"Why ever not?" Upstart demanded. "Of course we can go out."

In the explanation that followed, Hedstrong began to realise that Upstart was the possessor of far more knowledge than he'd given her credit for. What was more, she'd managed to block it, not only from him but the rest of the spiritual household as well, including Antedote.

"You do understand how you've all become exiled from the rest of the Real World, stuck in this old pile of rubble?" she asked him, knowing full well that he didn't. She gave a little twiggle in anticipation of the fun it would be teaching him. Antedote's loss was her gain, although she blocked that thought for fear of destroying her advantage. That was another thing he'd have to learn if they were to be part of the Lard revolution – selective blocking. "Come on, let's have a bit of freedom away from this place," she invited, and led him down through the walls into the parkland.

***

Soon after her encounter with Hedstrong and Upstart, Antedote decided on a new measure. She still hadn't found Lard and felt the best way to unearth him was to have a committee meeting. She located Spayed who found Baybe and on their way encountered Kernel. All four met in the billiard room and were annoyed to discover five humans messing about with the snooker balls. They moved to the servants' hall, where there was more spiritual presence than Antedote liked. Retracing their steps through to the hall the four ended up in the music room, non-committee spirits being told to leave.

"I say, that was a bit sharp," Kernel commented, already disgruntled at being disturbed from his meditations. The pleasure of boasting membership of the committee was to his liking, but actually having to do something was another matter.

"You can clear off too if you don't like it," Antedote told him. "Where are the others?" There was no response. "Come on," she twitched angrily, "where are they? You must have come across them on your travels."

The three each registered their ignorance of the whereabouts of the missing members, and Baybe suggested that they may have embarked on a different measure, or still be on the last one. That would make it difficult to encounter them from a distance.

"This is ridiculous," Antedote declared. "I'm suppose to be

chairman of the lot of you and it seems some can't even keep on the same measure. How am I expected to govern?"

Kernel ventured to suggest that there was no requirement for everyone to be on the same measure and it would be a little unfair to blame the others just because they were not. It wasn't as if they were breaking any rules, because there weren't any rules. Spirits didn't have them, or need them. After all, measures were always adjusted as a matter of courtesy when one of their sort encountered another. Antedote wanted to know, if there weren't rules, what had they all been doing several measures ago inventing rules to allow stupid methods of flinging books around the library just to decide who should enter the now deceased Lord?

"You see?" Kernel replied. "That goes to prove how useless rules are. They just use up power and get us nowhere."

"This is different," she retorted. "This house needs to be governed if we are to cope with the floods of humans that seem to be invading. And I've been appointed to govern it."

Kernel thought that was a 'bit steep', recalling that the only reason Antedote was leader was because she could literally give the others a charge and keep them mobile. As his view remained unblocked Antedote read it and became even more infuriated. Resolving there were enough members present to allow the meeting to continue, she told the gathering they had better settle down with her and work out some rules if they wanted to remain mobile.

***

Hedstrong was enchanted by the grounds. During his last human existence not all members of the family occupying the mansion had welcomed his character's presence. His experiences of the estate were, therefore, limited to occasional surreptitious visits his human had made up the drive into the library to gamble. Surrounding gardens had been taken for granted but, now, to drift along the broad walk, then between the trees, was an experience beyond his spiritual past. He marvelled at the simple beauty of the sycamores, beeches, cherry. Everything was looking a bit run down, and features like the walled vegetable garden and stabling had begun to assume the same air of deterioration that was beginning to grip the remoter rooms of the mansion, but it was still all there.

The presence of his guide contributed in no small manner to his disposition. Unlike Antedote, who was constantly demanding this or that and frequently criticising if she didn't get it, Upstart simply drifted at his side pointing out features she thought he would appreciate. He was experiencing an even bigger range of emotions he'd previously believed only applied to human activity.

"There you are," Upstart commented, twitching onto his thoughts. "See what you've been missing during all those past measures, static in our Real World. We've a freedom no one ever thought possible before recharging was discovered."

Talking of recharging, she felt their power was getting a bit low and led to a point where they could revitalise from the general electrical supply humans so obligingly maintained for them.

"Let me take some," Hedstrong said, preparing to attach to the current.

"No need," Upstart told him. She connected to the supply whilst he was still thinking about it. "There, that should be enough for both of us." Reading his thoughts, she added, "You didn't think the technique was exclusive to Antedote, did you? After all, it's not complex and, you must admit, sharing can be very enjoyable." She gave him a boost which stirred sensations equal to those experienced with Antedote, if not better. In fact, he found them so very enjoyable he was reluctant for the session to end.

When they were drifting back towards the mansion Upstart suggested a diversion into the old rose garden. Although surprisingly well pruned there was, nevertheless, clear need of attention, especially to the two summer houses.

"If I didn't know how futile it was to try, I might be encouraged to re-enter the human chain and experience a bit of renovation," Hedstrong admitted.

"Who was it not able to understand the idea of preserving... what did you call it? 'Wrecks', was it?" Upstart replied. "Let's pay a visit to Lard. He'll put you straight."

They made their way down to a main walk and turned to face the mansion. Upstart stopped short of the house and bade Hedstrong follow her just off the track and into a rather dilapidated, small wooden structure. Lard was expecting them and made them welcome to his 'humble, temporary abode'. When it was better held together, it had been an aviary, he explained.

"I suppose it'll be invaded at some time, when they've finished with the main structure," he continued, "but for the present it's roped off, abandoned and, therefore, exclusively mine."

"You old hermit, and there are those who say a spell in a human doesn't leave new attitudes," Upstart commented mischievously.

"You know better than that," Lard told her. "There are things that need to be discussed, away from the mansion twitchers." He forecast that it would not be long before the spiritual residents discovered that they too could flood out into the grounds whenever they felt like it. "Inevitable as human development," was how he put the prospect, expressing concern at their being let out into a world they were ill-equipped to understand. He likened them to primitive, savage humans in a jungle suddenly coming face to face with what the rest called civilisation. "Discovering spiritual mobility was a bad thing," he concluded.

Hedstrong sought to disagree, arguing that, with the many human experiences they'd all gained through the ages, it was time to put their combined knowledge to good use. When asked what, precisely, that meant, he was stumped. Lard helped him out.

"What is our purpose or, at least, what has been our purpose to date?" he began. "It's been to influence generations of humans by selective entry into their lives." He could see Hedstrong wasn't with him, so tried a different tack. "Look. There's not enough of us to go around. We can't enter every human in existence. They have this urge to keep multiplying, so we have to be a bit selective. We don't just enter any body that happens to turn up. We wait until we find the right one."

Hedstrong argued that when he had looked for the 'right one' he hadn't really bothered about influencing humanity. He'd just chosen someone whom he felt might offer a reasonably pleasurable trip or get him out of a spot rather than fulfilling any other duty.

"Exactly!" claimed Lard. "'Duty'. You saw it as your duty to keep entering the human chain. And when you got back to Reality you had more experiences to add to your knowledge which, although you didn't realise, brought more power to the individual you chose on your next trip. We spirits are responsible for the development of the human race." Lard had twitched through Hedstrong's CV and added, "Even in your last visit, when you engaged in gambling, fornication and everything that humans are inclined by their genes towards, there was an element of guidance, not to mention what you brought back to the Real World."

"Each trip gives us knowledge," Upstart contributed.

"By the impulses we add to the human brain, we influence thought," Lard continued. "They call it 'conscience' and we strive, probably subconsciously, to keep humanity in check, knowing there are only so many of us to go round and if the human populace grows too much out of control, the Real World will suffer."

"Do we do all that?" Hedstrong replied. "Even though when out of the Real World we have no recall or consciousness of Real World origins? If we do all that, we do it automatically, something like humans acting under hypnosis. I never realised we were so important."

"Neither do the rest of them in the mansion," Lard continued. "Throughout human time, how d'you think dictators developed a determination to wipe out so many of their kind in battle and execution? Who d'you think invented genocide?"

"We did?" Hedstrong questioned, still struggling. "You mean we were responsible for wars? And all the other killings?"

"Not entirely," Lard conceded, "but we have had quite a lot to do with it. Humans, being humans, have a tendency to follow their own designs now and again but, in the main, yes, we are responsible. I can't claim our efforts have been all that successful."

It was a lot for Hedstrong to take in, not the least of which was the obvious knowledge of Upstart. She seemed quite familiar with Lard's thinking, which was well beyond the scope of Antedote and her group. Her group... what was he thinking? He was part of that group, yet here he was, outside the mansion treating himself as separate, even superior to the lot of them.

"You are," Upstart told him. "You've come a long way in some short measures, but your experiences place you apart from the usual. It's time to use them."

"I can't just abandon the others," Hedstrong said. "After all, if it hadn't been for Antedote, none of us would have been able to move."

"Not entirely accurate," Lard told him. "Granted she mobilised the rest of the house but, outside, there've been greater discoveries and advances which leave those in the mansion in, what humans would call, 'a primitive state'. There's a lot of catching up to be done by them, and by others. In a way, I would prefer us not to have to encourage them."

"Why's that?" Hedstrong asked.

"Look what development's done to humanity... how humans have evolved. But, alas, there's no going back." He paused to read the thoughts of the other two before adding, "We can't neglect the house, especially now, just when it's about to be flooded with human activity. Let's descend upon Antedote and see what she's up to but, Hedstrong, keep a blanket on everything until we teach you selective blocking. An enlightened Antedote is not something I would welcome at present."

CHAPTER 8

INDUCTION

ard had this uncanny habit of drifting into a presence without being noticed. When he entered the music room, the committee meeting was still in progress, bogged down upon how to ensure everyone could be kept on the same measure. Antedote's frustration was reaching fever pitch.

"Why?" he twitched. It won him the reaction he sought from the others.

"Where have you been?" she demanded. "You were needed for the meeting. I've looked everywhere."

"You can't have done, otherwise you'd have found me. Anyway I'm here now. What's the trouble?"

Hedstrong and Upstart chose this moment to drift in through the wall, acknowledging the others. Hedstrong apologised for the late arrival and asked if they had missed much. He attracted the anticipated explosion from their leader at the futility of trying to make progress, the sacrifices she was making, plus criticism of the self-indulgent lack of interest or support. He chose a gap in the tirade to assure her they were all 'here now' before asking why the meeting had been called

"You know why. You've been delving ever since you arrived," Antedote accused. "We need to meet regularly if we are to make progress. To date, we haven't even come up with a method of keeping on the same measure."

Hedstrong resisted reminding her of their earlier attempts to solve the same problem, allowing Lard to question why there was a need to meet regularly? Indeed, why there was a need to meet at all? Antedote asked him to describe the purpose of having a

70

committee if they didn't meet, and he suggested it was an essential element of democracy. She asked him how it could be democratic if they didn't do anything?

"By being there - maintaining the hierarchy," Lard replied. "You're the leader and we all know it."

"Don't we just," Upstart twitched.

"As committee members we are the second level, and then there are the rest. That's how you want it, isn't it?"

"Don't be stupid," Antedote told him. "Spirits are equal. We always have been. You can't put one on a different level from the rest."

Lard persisted with his stupidity, questioning and prodding her reasoning until she had to acknowledge that, as leader, she'd placed herself above the rest and that this had introduced a hitherto unheard of inequality. Whilst she was trying to grasp the concept he went on to claim that, having demonstrated her leadership by using a power no one else in the mansion could match, surely the aim was to maintain that power and that her committee was there to help her do it.

"We don't need meetings. We just help keep the rest in order and that preserves our positions. They look up to us, and we look up to you."

"I like that. I must say I like that," Kernel declared. "That's the ticket. They look to us and we support you. That'll do for me. No need for all this fuss about measures, and meetings and things. Yes. I see where he's coming from. I'm with him on that."

Spayed and Baybe, both of whom had become bored with the proceedings, gave their support for a swift proposal that the meeting be terminated. It met with unanimous approval, except from the chairman. Lard expressed his pleasure at having twitched with them all, bade them return to their respective retreats but asked that they remain ever available for individual consultation.

Before Antedote was able to recover control, if indeed she ever had it when Lard was in full flow, the three departed, leaving only

Upstart, Hedstrong and him in her presence. Continuing to assess and anticipate her mood, Lard added, "Now we can get down to business. Sorry to gate-crash like that but I thought you needed help sorting out those others. They were bogging you down. I know how anxious you are to make progress." Antedote was torn between telling him she could sort out as many idiots as she liked without help from him and agreeing she was being bogged down. "You've so much energy, and you've told us how anxious you are to do the best for us. I admire that, I really do. You certainly have my support. I'm at your service. Your wish is my desire."

It worked. Antedote surrendered to the flattery and, with a brief criticism at Lard's seeming reluctance to grace her presence, allowed herself to be carried on into serious, if inconclusive, discussion upon how to tackle the inevitable invasion when the mansion became open to the public. By the time they'd finished, she was satisfied that they'd had a good brainstorming meeting to which all four made valuable contribution. She failed to realise, even after they'd departed, that she was left exactly where she was when they'd started. So inspired was she by Lard's skill, she didn't even wonder why Hedstrong had not returned to his wood panel.

***

Antedote would never know how meticulously the three conspirators had planned their coup. Before arriving at the committee meeting, tactics had been agreed almost to the last detail ensuring that the assault had worked perfectly. Her chosen two committee members had been eliminated, together with Kernel, to be used as padding if and when needed. Hedstrong was happy spending time with Upstart and, he had to admit, the opportunities the other two revealed to him seemed endless and exciting. He'd, therefore, willingly agreed to allow Lard to manipulate the full attention of Antedote and afterwards he nipped off with his new companion to explore the wonders of the outside estate.

When they were drifting between two Redwoods that overlooked the rose garden, he tried to put his recent experiences into some sort of order, aware that Upstart was studying his every thought. He marvelled at the manner adopted by Lard who, if he hadn't lied, which he couldn't – spirits don't – had certainly deviated and manipulated Antedote to the very limit of veracity. Was this something he'd learnt during his human trips, and was he, Hedstrong, using similarly assimilated techniques?

"It's bound to rub off on you," she contributed.

"What is?"

"Your human periods. Sorry to sound repetitious but we all know that spirits returning to the Real World retain emotions picked up during their travels. We can't help it. Ever since we arrived on this planet, people have been our saviours. They had the natural spark we needed." She paused for a micro measure before adding, "We've been able to mould them into our methods, to some extent, but we still haven't completely mastered the genes of the human body. The reproductive traits can be quite wayward and, when we're part of their short existences, they influence us."

For Hedstrong everything was happening too quickly. Not so many measures ago he'd been resting in a panel in a stately home, unable to travel and resigned to a wait for his next human voyage. He'd believed spirits had no feelings and were incapable of mobility in their Real World. Now, here he was, free to go where he wished, as long as he could keep within distance of his next power charge. And he'd discovered a type of excitement he'd previously thought confined to the sexual activities of humans.

"You must admit during your last trip your character did go over the top with the sex and the gambling bit," Upstart contributed, following his unblocked reasoning. "Not that I'm objecting. Male and female union is good, otherwise why would there be masculine and feminine spirits? And we do have feelings, don't we?"

Hedstrong had to agree. He found himself trying to explain how he'd been with Antedote, then contrasting the sensation to what he was experiencing with Upstart. She twitched her pleasure, suggesting they find a power supply and enjoy a joint boost.

What followed was a shared spiritual climax that surpassed anything Hedstrong had ever found in humanity. The last thing he wanted was for it to end. He said so, delighted to receive Upstart's confirmation that it was the same for her. He likened it to love, rejoiced in the discovery that it could be achieved in the Real World. Spirits had feelings. He was in love. They were in love.

"D'you realise, we've discovered the reason for existence?" Hedstrong asked. The couple were returning from buildings under conversion into a visitor reception area, having plunged the proposed shop into darkness whilst they recharged. They kept close to each other through the arboretum someone had named 'Paradise'.

"Not exactly," Lard replied. As usual he'd managed to float into their presence, reading what they were up to before they knew it. Hedstrong let his irritation show and Lard merely told him that was more evidence of the range of feelings he was developing. "But with feelings come responsibilities," he added.

Hedstrong wanted to know why and the next two human days and one night were occupied telling him. They'd returned to the aviary, still dilapidated and roped off from inquisitive eyes. More and more details were revealed to him, with pauses to allow him to grasp, first, how backward were the spiritual communities he'd entered in the past and, second, how advanced Lard was in his knowledge of the future.

For a start, Headstrong hadn't been aware that mobility had been discovered long before Antedote had found power in a torch battery balanced on a rocking horse. Upstart knew it, as did Lard, and that led to another technique which was foreign to him. They had learnt concealment. They could each block parts of their recollection whilst allowing other spirits to twitch onto the rest. His initial attempts failed and Upstart giggled whilst she roamed through his shaky defence, telling him he had a vivid imagination;

but with further practice on his own, in intervals when his general induction was adjourned for rests, he eventually mastered the skill.

"It is a matter of some regret to me that we have developed in this direction," Lard confessed, satisfied their student had grasped sufficient awareness of the progress spirits were making. Still bathing in the glow of union with Upstart, Hedstrong wanted to know why 'regret'? It was the expected enquiry to which Lard was happy to respond. "We seem to have assimilated so many traits, bringing them back into the Real World from our trips into humanity. Where's humanity's heading… hell bent upon destroying itself through greed and ignorance?"

"But we have a knowledge they will never achieve," Hedstrong argued.

"That doesn't make us safe. Look at Antedote. The moment she tasted power, she wanted to keep it all to herself. She still does so she can enslave her fellow spirits. She doesn't ask where it is leading. She doesn't wonder what might happen when humans go too far so, again, a planet's civilisation dies, or disappears in one big bang. Electricity sustains us just as much as food does them. We still rely a great deal on them for our power and they aren't too many measures away from extinction, but d'you get Antedote asking what comes next? Of course you don't, and she has even yet to rediscover sex."

"You're wrong there," Upstart contributed. "She can do sex all right. She had Hedstrong in her grips without much trouble. How d'you think she managed that?"

"All right, she's mastered the human trait of sex, but using it to maintain power she doesn't really comprehend what she's doing. It's just a tool to feed a self-indulgent appetite."

"You don't like her," Hedstrong suggested.

All three laughed at his statement of the obvious. Lard stressed that the worst part of her character, so far as he was concerned, was the ease with which she could be attracted to control and the appetite she had for devouring it. He'd used pure human techniques to bait and manipulate her, dangling in front of her a superiority she craved. She wouldn't rest until she was satisfied she had absolute control: something Lard claimed no one ever had, either in humanity or in the Real World.

"And that's the trouble," he explained. "Now I shall be pursued by Antedote until she's satisfied she has control of my being and can move on to the next target."

"She won't get you," Upstart said. "I know. I've tried."

"But you had the strength of mind to move beyond the lust for control," Lard told her. "Antedote will continue to be a minor irritation I could do without."

Whilst discussion travelled further along these lines, Hedstrong again had to acknowledge how naïve he'd been and how backward were the spiritual communities he'd inhabited throughout his planetary measures. What did it all mean? What was all this evolution about? He didn't block his thoughts, selective or otherwise, and both Lard and Upstart were switched onto them.

"You need to grasp what is happening to you," Lard said, "because it is happening to spirits planet-wide. There are communication experiments that have been going on for many measures. I've been in and out of the family in the mansion since it rose to prominence some human centuries ago. Got into a doctor in their 17th century when he was unsuccessfully tending a patient down south from here. For some reason the only cure for everything at the time seemed to be blood letting. How they thought removing the lubrication of a body would solve functional problems without even knowing how to replace it or treat the result, was beyond me… but I digress."

Lard went on to expand his strange progression of human entries, confirming that he'd deliberately jumped in to the next family member almost as soon as the former had expired. Hedstrong had never considered being part of a dynasty. Lard told him that in between, during brief periods in Real Life, he'd been mobile enough to debate with other similarly advanced spirits.

"A quick exchange of twitches, and we each had the other's knowledge before the next journey," he explained. Unlike Hedstrong, he'd been determined to add to his learning and it was just before his latest human ride he'd discovered how far fellow spirits had advanced. Listening to him Hedstrong realised that the negative and positive currents he'd experienced when viewing a potential human were part of the spiritual early warning system. He'd tried to enter several bodies in the past, only to change his mind sometimes at the last moment.

"That's because they were already full," Upstart told him. "You know what happens if too many of us occupy one poor human? Sometimes we do, having ignored and overridden the negative forces, and we're into what humans call murder, madness and a whole lot of other crimes."

"Have you tried that?" Hedstrong asked.

Upstart actually managed to project embarrassment when she admitted she had, for a dare, when she'd once been established in a prostitute. A cavalier had fought a roundhead for the favours of her human host, the result being the deaths of all three of them. Several spirits found themselves back in the Real World together and, probably still under the influence of the human fight, persuaded her to jump with them into a merchant who happened to be in the brothel at the time.

"It was such a struggle. He already had more than one entrant," Upstart explained, "but we just carried on trying, regardless of the negative vibes. Somehow we made it, and drove the poor human potty. First he robbed his customers, then he organised a gang of thieves and eventually he was eliminated on the gallows. We felt a bit guilty about it and the moment his neck broke we floated in opposite directions to select more normal successors amongst the crowd."

Hedstrong was about to ask why he'd not twitched onto all this when Upstart had first floated into his presence, then remembered and marvelled at her skill in selectively blocking. She'd had all this knowledge before she arrived at the mansion. She'd kept it from the meeting and had been fooling Antedote all along. Twitching onto the unblocked thoughts of his new-found love, he received confirmation he was right. She'd deliberately chosen him to be the one to share her knowledge. Although she could recharge herself, she'd let Antedote and Hedstrong, and the rest of the house spirits, believe she couldn't.

"Not a lie," she explained. "I just let her make her own assumptions and concentrated on you. I knew you'd respond. Your feelings were already developing in your association with Antedote, but she was never enough for you. Admit it, she soon started to frustrate you with her ignorance and pretences."

Hedstrong didn't admit it… not immediately. In fact he was beyond admitting anything after so many revelations. All he wanted to do was fade into the background and rest; another feeling he'd never known he had. He was tired.

CHAPTER 9

REVELATION

"Let me introduce you," Lard commenced. "This is Compresser. He travels extensively and has come to report."

Headstrong, having arrived in response to an urgent summons, delivered surreptitiously by Upstart and charged with the duty to ensure that his departure was not missed, especially by Antedote, acknowledged the presence of the stranger. He awaited an explanation for all the secrecy.

"Because we have to be careful and only choose those capable of progressive understanding," Compresser told him, reading his thought. "After all, we don't want to end up like humans, do we?"

"Is there a danger of us ending up like humans?" Hedstrong asked.

"Of course there is. We're halfway there already, aren't we?"

Hedstrong wanted to know what he meant and Compresser was happy to begin what turned out to be quite a lecture. First of all he touched upon Hedstrong's feelings. He asked for a list of emotions that had developed since the mansion had been introduced to independent mobility. He asked how many of those feelings were of spiritual origin and how many he thought had rubbed off from his journeys into the human conscious. He wanted to know if any of the house occupants had thought of what, if they materialised, humans would make of their attire, sometimes in the mode of an earlier age, sometimes not. They weren't questions requiring response, just Compresser's manner of speaking.

By the time he'd finished Hedstrong was exhausted without even having had a chance to utter a twitch. The other two also acknowledged some fatigue, although they'd heard most of the detail before and were used to the spirit's rather strange method of approach. Compresser confessed to being puzzled at their reactions. To him, what he'd been saying was no more than common sense. He failed to comprehend why, at a first induction, indeed at any induction, his audience should experience such a drain. The fact that almost every sentence he projected ended with a question mark was, to him , irrelevant.

"There you are, you see, don't you?" he concluded. "Another human emotion, isn't it? Stress. I'm off now, you understand? Professer will be along in a measure or two with your tasks – you're ready for that? And that's another thing, isn't it, if you care to consider it… even if you don't? Why have we adopted this custom always to spell our names wrongly? It's universal, you know. We all do it, instinctively, don't we? So you see, we have instinct as well, haven't we?" With that final declaration he departed with such speed and power that, for a moment, he materialised.

"Is he always like that? What's he look like to humans?" Hedstrong asked. Human comment, observed by other spirits enabled them to build an image of each other. He was a six foot tall monk, clad in brown from head to toe, Lard confirmed.

"So much to tell so many in such short visits he often forgets to control his power. The monk's uniform has lasted for a number of human centuries, is accepted and avoided by most people. Humans place monks in a special category apart from the rest, and Compresser is, therefore, less likely to cause panic if he suddenly appears by mistake.

"D'you mean he could choose what he looked like in materialisation?" Hedstrong asked.

"Of course, even though none of us, including him, can see the result." Lard noted that the meeting had caused a drain on most of Hedstrong's power, so intense had been his concentration. Nevertheless, he was satisfied he'd selected well and this new recruit would be a valuable member of their secret inner circle.

"Why don't you and Upstart take a drift down to the visitor reception area for a recharge? I think we've had enough revelations for this measure."

Hedstrong didn't want to go. He wanted more discussion but with the inviting influence of Upstart he assented. Further enquiry could wait. The couple made off along the walk through Paradise, amongst the hundreds of humans who were beginning to invade the ancient estate now it was open to the public.

***

"I'm not quite sure what's happening to me," Hedstrong admitted. He and Upstart had just gathered sufficient electrical input to revitalise each other, thoroughly enjoying the sensation. For a micro-measure they'd placed the National Trust shop in darkness, much to the annoyance of volunteer helpers already angered by a visit from a self-appointed busy-body who had tried to tell them how to do their job. Amused, the couple retired to a dilapidated summer house in the rose garden.

"One measure I'm awaiting my next human trip, and the next I'm experiencing all sorts of emotions and cruising around places I thought I'd never visit, except when I wasn't in the Real World."

"Never mind, darling, at least you've found me. Am I not worth a few emotions?" Upstart asked.

"That's what I mean. I've got emotion. I've definitely got feelings. Desires even." He pictured the visit they'd just made to the shop and the sensation he'd experienced the moment they'd shared that electrical surge. Upstart twitched onto his pleasure, confirming that she, too, had enjoyed the joint impulse. He said he felt different when he was with her and she said that was good.

"We'll make a good couple," she told him.

"Are we a couple? How can we be a couple? We're spirits, damn it, and this is the Real World. We're not meant to experience desires; that's a human affliction."

"Oh, Hedstrong, you've so much to learn and such a short time to do it in. I'm glad I'm with you and that I've got you as my partner. We'll achieve so much together."

"So we are together," Hedstrong concluded. "I get the feeling all this was designed to happen. That your arrival in the mansion was intentional and that you deliberately chose me." Upstart agreed and again Hedstrong felt power draining from his being whilst he struggled to cope with what was happening to him. Sensing his problem, Upstart gave him a boost and he groaned in ecstasy.

"I could take more of that," he twitched. "D'you know what it does to me?"

"Of course," she replied. "And you can do it to me too, but not now. We have another meeting to attend."

"Do we have to?"

"We do. Professer will be waiting."

***

Professer was, indeed, waiting and none too pleased at that. He twitched an atmosphere of irritation at the young couple the moment they drifted into the aviary. So forceful was the reprimand that a young human boy, about to creep under the barrier to explore forbidden territory, felt the full force and quickly rejoined his sister who was digging into the grass with her heel on the other side of the main path.

"Now, now," Lard twitched back. "No need to be like that. If you want to blame anyone try me. It was I who sent the two love birds off. You forget, our new recruit is being asked to learn a lot in a very short measure."

"All right. All right," Professer replied. "But you must understand, there's so much to do and little real time left to do it in. I haven't the measures to mess about waiting whilst… "

"You've been saying that for many a measure," Lard

interrupted. "If time is so short you'd better get on with it, hadn't you?"

Hedstrong's being was still in a sort of dream world which caused him to question if he really was still in Reality.

"And you can get that sort of idea right out of your system straight away," Professer told him. "How can I indoctrinate you if you think like that?"

Hedstrong experienced another emotion – anger. He didn't want to be indoctrinated; he was all right as he was, thank you. Who was this stranger called 'Professer' and why was he surging around the aviary in such an agitated wound up manner?

Lard attempted to come to the rescue, exercising a diplomacy which had no doubt rubbed into him during one of his expeditions through humanity. Well known to Professer, he had sufficient authority to tell him to 'shut up'. Addressing Hedstrong he told him he'd been chosen as an advanced spirit, capable of assisting in the development of their world. He said the opportunity offered was a mixture of duty and privilege, plus a touch of adventure for good measure. Somehow his calm, carefully phrased, approach succeeded in reducing Hedstrong's objection and Professer's irritation.

"I'm sorry," Professer apologised.

"So am I," Hedstrong responded. After a few micro-measures of triviality, the next stage in his education began.

***

By the time Hedstrong returned to the mansion his being was slowly spinning at the enormity of what he'd been told. Never again would he have the luxury of reclining for a while in the Real World before another human trip. He'd been selected for a mission, given an understanding far removed from his simple existence. Professer had made that abundantly clear. He'd accepted it, encouraged in no small manner by the promise of constant company with Upstart. She'd definitely assisted in his manipulation into this position, but he didn't care. It was worth it, although he was still unsure of her feelings for him.

After reaching his old panel, he set about sorting the information the Professer had given him, taking care to protect his deliberations from whoever might be eavesdropping. To his surprise he'd mastered the partial blocking technique quite easily. An angry twitch from the adjoining panel broke into his thoughts. It was Antedote. He'd almost dismissed her from his mind and her demand to know where he'd been surprised him.

"Keeping out of your way."

"Why?"

"You know why."

"No I don't. One minute we're a couple, sharing everything, and the next you come all strange on me. I thought we had something going together."

That was typical of a female, Hedstrong thought. Ride roughshod over a male, in or out of the Real World, doing whatever she desired, and then happily banish it from her thoughts as if everything was the man's fault. He was about to say so when he realised he'd started to respond like a human. Professer had warned it may happen and taught him how to stop the moment it began.

"Trask, trask, trask," he twitched. It was meant to discipline himself, but the expression was sufficiently unblocked to reach Antedote.

"Pardon?" she demanded.

"Nothing," he replied. "Just letting off steam."

"We don't do steam."

"I know. Just a saying."

"We don't do sayings either. That's for humans."

"Oh shut up, Antedote. Go and give someone a boost or something. I'm tired."

The shock at such a reaction from a spirit she thought was

totally under her control rendered Antedote twitchless. Torn between anger and surprise, she disappeared in a flash to the upper floor to seek counsel with more submissive others. Realising she'd gone, Hedstrong was able to relax. For the first time for so many measures, he was alone. Only then was he able to begin to sort out with why he'd been selected to join what Lard called the 'inner-council'.

He supposed that, compared with some, his travels in human mode had been extensive, although he'd never really considered it in that manner. So had been the human emotions he'd shared in the situations to which he'd been subjected. But it was still difficult to accept some of the definitions Professer had come out with, especially when he likened the spirits in the mansion to a lost human tribe, buried deep in an equatorial forest.

Professer told of current experiments into how to drift into and out of humans when Real World occupants chose, not having to await death to be released. Apparently the procedure was at an early stage, and not all humans were suitable vessels. Then there was travel. Methods had been perfected which allowed world exploration. The revelations opened up an exciting new existence Hedstrong had never visualised. He'd been keen to take advantage of the knowledge until the Professer began to explain the downside.

Although there was still sufficient power around, except for a few backward pockets, all, like the spiritual inhabitants of the mansion, had caught the desire to travel. So many had mastered the ability to recharge, they were quite content to remain in the Real World. There were never enough spirits to occupy humans in the first place, and the new reluctance meant that thousands, perhaps millions of earth beings were left without infiltration. Humans were consuming more power themselves, not into their beings, but for incidental, irrelevant activities such as artificial lighting, radio messaging, vehicle movement, television and computing. All sorts of complex theories were being applied by uncontrolled minds in the guise of progress. So many developments which may have taken the human brain generations to resolve were being revealed to them in micro-measures.

Professer's examples were very convincing. Travel between the continents was now taking human hours when it once took many of their days. Messages between one part of a country and another, and one country and another, which first relied on word of mouth, then written word, were communicated instantly. The result, he'd claimed, was an ever increasing rush to disaster. What was more, with the current level of human communication, Professer said that, whereas disasters in the past had simply eliminated one human species in favour of another, the trend was towards planetary extinction. Wars had been local affairs. Now they threatened to be global conflicts and that would result in planetary disintegration.

Apparently most of the spirits weren't really bothered. They saw no reason to interfere in annihilation of humanity, until asked how they thought there would be enough power to go around when the people of the planet stopped producing it. Even then many were happy to contemplate return to static form, intent upon enjoying the pleasures of movement while it lasted. That was what the inner circle were fighting against, and Hedstrong suddenly grasped the enormity of having just been enrolled as a member of their council.

He wasn't sure whether to take it as an honour or a burden. What he had to admit was that the greatest inducement to participate had been the promise of continued association with Upstart. For another mini-measure he wondered if she'd been the bait? Whether once he was caught up in the whole process she would drift away in search of other simple-minded idiots, gullible enough to be taken in by her charms, ready to submit themselves to the experiments the Professer had talked of, but had not been inclined to describe in detail? Despite the closeness, she remained a mystery; an attractive, irresistible mystery.

Further deliberation was prevented by the return of Antedote through the ceiling.

"Look," she began. "I think we should twitch."

"What about?" Hedstrong asked.

"Us."

"I didn't know there was an 'us.'"

"Of course there is. It's been you and me ever since we shared that power together. You enjoyed that, didn't you?"

"Yes," he admitted. "But since then you've gone off on your own. We've drifted apart."

"I'm sorry if it's seemed like that. I didn't mean it to. It's just that there are so many responsibilities involved in keeping control of all of us in the house. The demands of the others keep growing and I don't know if I can keep up."

"Why bother?" Hedstrong asked. Antedote didn't understand and asked him to explain. When he suggested she teach them all to take their own power instead of relying on her, she thought he'd gone mad and told him so. She wanted to know how else they could keep control and when he suggested they needn't that was the end of the twitch.

CHAPTER 10

CONSPIRACY

I t would never be the same again now he was gone. Phyllis hadn't been to his funeral and kept away from the turmoil of sale followed by the National Trust takeover. But the estate was like a magnet to her: the paths, the woods, grounds known since her childhood trespassing, then later with visits to his Lordship. She couldn't help herself getting involved, gritting her teeth to go through the rigmarole of application and ingratiation to become a volunteer. Now the public were swarming in and she was in charge of the shop, fitting shifts in with the work she was doing on her latest book.

That morning she'd spent a few minutes in Paradise before the gates opened. She'd felt sadness as she passed the trees the last Lord had told her he'd loved. She still had difficulty using his Christian name despite his insistence when he was alive. She'd sensed he'd had a difficult life, full of obligation, short on emotion. Only during their final meeting, when he'd kissed her, had he shown the deep feeling she felt could have been released if the right person had turned the right key at the right time. In a way she'd known they wouldn't meet again. Afterwards she'd realised that somehow he'd known too, and she wasn't surprised when news of his death leaked out into the village… but sad at the loss of a secret friend; the end of her contact with an ancient, departed way of life.

If anyone had asked her, she'd have described her decision to join the increasing force invading the estate as a whim. Perhaps it had been but soon it had turned into a determined interest in the spiritual goings-on she'd noticed. They seemed to be getting more intense, no doubt a response to the human activity. She was back in the shop and shrugged her shoulders as if to dispel her melancholy mood. The tall female visitor at the end of the converted building needed watching. With such a large bag capable of concealing several of the books she'd been fingering, she may be their first shoplifter. Fortunately the building seemed surprisingly free of spirits, so offered no distraction.

"Can I help you, madam?" she asked the tall lady, convinced a hardback copy of a history of the mansion was about to disappear into the large bag.

"Just looking," the woman managed, replacing the edition on the shelf. She left shortly afterwards without buying anything and Phyllis relaxed.

***

"We have ideal specimens with which to experiment," Professer told them. "Then we can link with the other units and compare notes."

Hedstrong had only just joined the group and didn't immediately grasp what was being discussed. Upstart and Lard were already in the aviary and all three waited for him to register that the specimens referred to were the mansion occupants.

"Wait a moment," he said. "You can't treat my fellow spirits as specimens."

"Why not?" Professer asked. "They're backward in knowledge, remote from outer suggestion and anxious to develop. In fact, they're desperately wanting to be free of the control of the female." He went on to suggest they would be only too anxious to cooperate in return for their liberty. "I don't advocate putting them all through the same experiment, or targeting them all at once."

"I'm sure that'll reassure them," Hedstrong told him.

Professer twitched annoyance at the sarcasm and asked if he wanted to be part of the team or not. In his customary manner Lard intervened, attempting to diffuse another developing situation. He was given a lecture by Professer upon the waste of time taken up in fruitless argument and the inability of those who didn't want to see grasping what was patently obvious. It took a micro-measure break and some persuasive twitching from Upstart to convince Hedstrong at least to listen to what was being proposed. Whilst she was performing her task, Lard was handling Professer and the result was an uncomfortable truce.

Still grumbling at the waste of time, Professer explained what he had in mind. Experiments already afoot elsewhere, to discover a means of leaving a human being without awaiting death, had stalled. 'In their automated, ill-informed way' (Professer's words) the humans were moving towards artificial regeneration of organs which could prolong their lives. Therefore, a spirit entering their chain would be deprived of Real life for longer. Other research had proved that, whilst spiritually occupied, humans often performed differently, to the benefit of the Real World, if not their own.

"So you see," he concluded, "if we're forced to occupy them for their longer lifespan, they will progress further and swifter and the whole thing will get out of hand. We might all get perpetually stuck in bodies and, as yet, we haven't perfected a method of actual human control. We can only influence them, so when they annihilate themselves, as they certainly will, we shall be doomed."

"Why?" Hedstrong asked, totally confused. "If they're daft enough to eliminate themselves, we'll be released… free to enjoy the Real World."

"I thought you said you'd chosen someone with a modicum of intellect," Professer retorted, aiming the twitch at Lard.

"I have."

"Then how come he's so stupid?"

That was it. Hedstrong was off. He surged out along the path and through Paradise, down onto the cracked concrete of the drained lake. That was where Upstart found him. Glad of a spiritual audience, he wanted to know what right an outsider had to enter their domain and treat him like an imbecile? Who did he think he was, and what good did he possibly believe could come from meddling with a system that had been ticking quite satisfactorily for countless measures? His annoyance was so consuming he said he felt like finding the nearest human and entering, just to get away from 'this lunacy'. He eyed a young boy who had run down to play at the lake, but the lad was too far away – even further when he fell into it and would probably have drowned if there'd been any water in it. Giving a final flash of discontent Hedstrong took refuge in a tree. Upstart allowed him a few micro-measures before she settled next to him.

"That was a lot of emotion for a spirit who, not so long ago, didn't think he had any," she said. No answer. "D'you really want to abandon what we both have in exchange for another human trip?" Still he remained silent. "Would you like me to depart?"

"No. No, I wouldn't," he blurted out. "I love what we've got, but that idiot is just confusing everything. I've never even thought of trying to influence my human hosts. I've let them get on with their lives. Make their own mistakes. He's no right to meddle."

"I think he has," Upstart said gently. "In fact, I know he has."

"How d'you know?"

"Because the council gave him the right at the last meeting."

"What council?"

"The Planetry Council. The one to which you were elected." Upstart went on to explain that there were representatives from all over their world who met every so often to discuss their spiritual future and decide upon united action. Hedstrong asked why, if he was a member, he hadn't been to any meetings? "Because there haven't been any since your election. They don't happen often. No one has yet perfected a swift method of getting all the representatives to the same destination on the same measure, so someone has to travel round gathering everyone up. You're the last on the list."

"Because I've just been elected?"

"No, because the meetings will take place here in future."

It was happening again. Hedstrong was being pitched into something he didn't understand and felt ill-equipped to handle. Upstart read his reaction. She twitched that she sympathised, and apologised for his having to grasp so much in such short measures. She explained it was because there was so little time left, in human terms. Hedstrong wanted to know who had suggested there was little time left, and she told him it was Professer?

"It had to be," he declared. "He's mad."

"That's a human emotion we could do without," Upstart responded lightly. "I can think of much better ones." She refused to be miserable, and gradually coaxed him to relax and concentrate more on her than the future. "Compresser will be back soon and he'll give you a full explanation. Would you like a little power to be going on with? I've got plenty."

Hedstrong couldn't resist. Soon he was drifting in unison with his beloved. He was convinced he was in love with her, and she, twitching onto his unblocked emotion, did nothing to discourage him.

***

Something was going on. Phyllis could feel it. Every time she left the shop to take a look around the grounds she was drawn to the old aviary. She detected movement. She pretended to inspect the rotting woodwork still supporting the roof but concentrated on identifying images. She could see shadows, but they were vague. She knew they were communicating with each other, but she couldn't join in. If only she could discover a way of conversing.

At that point she was interrupted by a little man, requesting details of the history of the structure she was examining so intently. He'd noticed she was 'official' by examining the badge on her chest, using his scrutiny, she suspected, to enjoy a study of that part of her anatomy. He seemed harmless and, noting the thick lenses in his glasses, she felt she might be being unkind – not that she objected to a show of appreciation for her carefully maintained attributes. A moment later she had to apologise for mistaking him to be a visitor.

He explained he was engaged to assist in checking the many timepieces in the big house. After several dusty hours wrestling with a grandfather clock that didn't show any signs of cooperation, he'd decided to take a break and do some sightseeing. It was his first venture into the grounds, his pleasure at being involved in such a large undertaking demonstrating an almost childish excitement that appealed to Phyllis.

She obliged him with details of the aviary, even suggesting she'd show him the grounds if he wished. They walked slowly past the path to the rose garden and down over the tennis court to the arboretum, her favourite location. She found herself explaining her last visit, and was surprised at the sense of loss her recollection stirred.

"Last time I was with a very dear friend," she said. "Just before he died."

The clock repairer expressed sympathy for her loss, adding that he too had recently suffered a bereavement. His mother had passed away last year and he was only slowly adjusting to a new way of life. They both agreed solitude can have advantages although Phyllis suspected that, whilst she treasured the seclusion she'd created around herself, he still had to come to terms with his. She was tempted to take him under her wing, knowing he could easily be moulded into an ardent admirer. She rarely had difficulty in achieving success in that direction, but decided against making a move. There were so many other interesting pursuits available to her in her current busy life.

On their way back to the path they encountered a well-proportioned religious figure clad in traditional monk's clothing. He nodded at them benevolently. The clock repairer seemed not to notice his passing. When Phyllis drew attention to him and they looked round he'd gone.

"Must have gone down into the trees," he commented, before continuing with an explanation of his work on the grandfather clock. Phyllis kept her thoughts to herself as she gently prized herself away from the lonely little man, explaining she had to return to her duties. She took a circuitous route back to the shop but there was no sign of the monk, just a shadow of a figure close to the little man as he trotted back towards the house.

***

Hedstrong and Professer had been kept apart until Compresser came back to explain the basics at a meeting convened by Lard and Upstart. He told of the growing fear amongst the more seeing occupiers of the Real World that the human race was getting out of control. He talked of greed coupled with a craving for change upon change, which meant each discovery was treated as old almost before it was new. He warned of use of global wireless power to an extent that gravity would soon be challenged. Atmospheric pollution was moving to a density that could eliminate human form.

"Why not let humans develop themselves into extinction?" Hedstrong asked.

"Because we need mobility, don't we?" Compresser explained. "And how do we achieve mobility? By ensuring that humans maintain a system of electrical power sufficient to keep us charged up. Where d'you think we'd be if electricity wasn't so readily available for our boosts? We'd be back to static state, and there'd be no humans to enter to give us travel experience, would there?"

"So what?"

"So we would simply exist, statically, doing nothing until another life form comes along, don't you see?"

"Maybe that's our destiny," Hedstrong suggested.

Compresser said that if he, Hedstrong, believed that what was he doing messing about with the council when all he had to do was to return to his jungle existence and shack up in a panel?

"Maybe I should," Hedstrong replied.

"Aha, aha," Compresser twitched at him, reading his immediate thought before it was partially blocked. "Feelings. You've discovered feelings – emotions – haven't you? You've got emotions, haven't you? You know if you regress, you'll lose Upstart, and you can't do it, can you?"

Hedstrong thought of flashing an angry disparaging emotion back at Compresser. He objected to his private thoughts being aired. In humans wasn't there a law against that, ineffective though it was? Again he forgot to block. "And that's another thing. Laws. We've got to have them and quick. Otherwise the Real World will become as chaotic as human existence, wouldn't it?"

"But isn't it a load of stupid laws that's destroying humanity?" Hedstrong demanded.

"Precisely," Compresser concluded, as if his point had been made.

Lard and Upstart had been silent during the debate, having attended the induction of other spirits into the workings of the council. Upstart also recalled hers and the weird way Compresser always told it, leaving her thoughts unblocked in sympathy with Hedstrong. Compresser read them too and invited her to take over if she felt she could do better. Her indication that she might just do that stimulated Lard into exercising his usual calming force, and the session was brought to an abrupt end.

***

Whilst Lard took off to side-track Antedote before she noticed Hedstrong's absence, the two loving spirits retreated to the rose garden, settling in their favourite summerhouse. Upstart gave Hedstrong another mini-boost, not because he needed it, but because she wanted to. He gave one back and they spent time sharing the togetherness it stimulated.

"Professer would accuse us of waste," Upstart twitched gently.

"Then he'd be wrong," Hedstrong replied. "He can't have it

both ways. Either we have emotions or we don't and, if we do, there's no law against sharing them, is there?"

"Not yet," Upstart told him. "But there are laws, and there's no telling what the council might come up with next."

Hedstrong wanted to know what if they did, how did they think they could enforce them? "Spirits can't be controlled," he said. "We can't be punished."

"That's another thing Professer and his teams are working on," Upstart told him. "He's into control in a big way, not only testing restraints but also claiming elimination for the most serious contraventions."

Hedstrong wanted to know what was considered a serious contravention and Upstart told him nothing at the moment, but the council could easily come up with something. "Once they've discovered why we are here," she added.

"We know why we're here," Hedstrong told her.

"Do we?"

"Of course we do. To infiltrate humans, whilst they do what they are here for."

"And what is that?" Upstart asked him.

"To reproduce and maintain their existence."

"What for?" she asked.

"For us, of course," he replied, almost automatically. Then he realised what he'd said. "Aren't they?" he asked.

"Perhaps that's what we're destined to find out."

∗∗∗

Further education followed before Hedstrong was dispatched back to the mansion. He took his time. There were still questions to which he needed answers, and still elements of the outside Real World he didn't understand. Gradually he'd been persuaded to accept that changes were being made, that they were inevitable and, without them, the Real World was in danger of total stagnation. He'd also accepted his first mission: to distance himself from the mansion residents, including Antedote.

When he reached his usual wood panel he detected Lard's presence. Sensing Hedstrong's return Antedote greeted him, but there was none of the superiority or confidence in her reception. Lard graciously excused himself.

"Always the true gent," Hedstrong commented. "His human trips must have been a great influence on him."

"Humans can't influence us," Antedote retorted, "just as we can't influence them."

Hedstrong didn't argue. He wondered if spirits like her would ever accept how wrong that statement was, carefully blocking the thought so as to avoid arousing her natural suspicions. He gave an angry twitch when it dawned on him he was beginning to question matters in a manner which would have won the approval of Professer. He didn't want or need that approval. In fact, if it hadn't been for Upstart, he would have told the self-opinionated boffin what he could do with his experiments. Antedote had detected the twitch if not its cause.

"You're in a funny mood," she said.

"So are you," Hedstrong replied.

"I've had a lot to think about."

"D'you mean 'think about' or 'discuss with Lard'?"

"Both." Hedstrong noted defiance in her response and wondered if he should mention it. There was no need. "You've been avoiding me," she continued. "It's no good you denying it, you've definitely been avoiding me."

"How could I deny it?" Hedstrong answered. "Spirits can't lie."

"They can have a good try. Ever since you got what you wanted, you've been avoiding me. It's been remarked on."

Hedstrong wanted to know by whom. At first he failed to achieve a satisfactory answer, but persistence enabled him to gain the admission that only one had 'remarked' on it and that one was, of course, Lard. There followed the expected enlargement of the claim that he had rejected her from the moment she'd given him the ability to recharge. He'd failed to support her against the others and had even conspired in forcing her to suffer the burden of a committee of idiots who did nothing but obstruct. This had, apparently, increased her problems of leadership to a point where it had become intolerable.

Whilst she continued, Hedstrong began to detect words and phrases more akin to Lard's art of conversation. By the time Antedote paused to test reaction, she'd convinced herself that, however innocently, Hedstrong had betrayed her trust in him and treated her extremely badly. As a result, she said she couldn't rely upon their special relationship. She had therefore decided, unfortunately, that she was forced to consider him no more than a normal member of her committee, and that he was to cease to be her deputy. She said she was sorry, but she had to look to the future of their community. She would miss his companionship, but there it was. Perhaps it would be better if he were to relocate, somewhere away from the room they had shared, so they could continue their separate existences.

Hedstrong asked how she would manage without a deputy to help her in the day to day chores, more to camouflage the simplicity in achieving his first mission than to extract a response.

"Lard has kindly agreed to assist," Antedote replied.

"So he is to be given the technique of recharging so he can answer the needs of the inmates?" Hedstrong prodded. "Have you already told him the secret?"

"That's none of your business."

"I think it is. How else am I to know what to do when the others ask me for a boost? If I'm just a simple committee member, am I to give it to them, or refer them to you? Remember, it was you who decided you couldn't cope on your own."

"The problem won't arise," Antedote told him. "Lard and I have discussed it, and we've decided that it would be best to allow the others to recharge themselves."

"You've decided. Both of you. What about the committee?"

"They'll agree, I'll see to that and, after the way you've treated me, you're not in a position to object."

Hedstrong didn't try. He had to hand it to Lard. The spirit had achieved exactly what Hedstrong had been delegated to do; precisely what had been discussed with Professer in the aviary. All spiritual occupants of the mansion would be able to charge themselves in readiness for the experiments and Hedstrong had been released from any obligation to them. He was free to assume his place in the greater advancement of their kind and, of more immediate attraction to him, he was able to enjoy the company of Upstart. He expressed his sadness to Antedote at how things had turned out between them both, sustaining the characteristic pronouncement from her that he only had himself to blame. He left the sanctuary of his panel to join Upstart in the billiard room where she awaited him.

"What an idiot Antedote is," Upstart told him when he arrived. He'd left his record of the conversation unblocked so she could be fully informed. "And there was a time when you thought all spirits were equal."

CHAPTER 11

THE EXPERIMENT

Baybe was selected for Professer's first mansion experiment. Hedstrong's responsibility was to ensure she 'volunteered' for a trip back to humanity. He latched onto her whilst she was testing her power gathering, having been amongst the first to receive Upstart's basic, grudging tuition. Much to his amusement, she was messing up the trial recharge to an extent where she materialised, just as he had in the late Lord's bedroom. Although unable to see her, the excess pressure waves were unmistakeable, confirmed by her giving one of the National Trust volunteers quite a shock whilst she floated along a corridor. Fortunately that person was where he shouldn't be, sneaking a look at forbidden parts. The hapless human fled back downstairs, and didn't dare mention what he'd witnessed, nearly convincing himself it was a trick of the light.

"Careful," Hedstrong twitched. "We don't want to scare our humans away."

"I can't quite seem to get it right," Baybe replied.

"You will. It just takes a little practice. But might it not be better to choose a less exposed location to try?"

"I thought this was one," Baybe responded.

"I can show you a better one."

The puzzled spirit willingly followed Hedstrong on a tour of the mansion to use up some of the power she'd acquired. They amused themselves dodging Antedote and Lard, who were still both intent upon delivering the secret to the rest. When Hedstrong was satisfied they'd consumed enough energy, he positioned Baybe alongside the main electrical cable into the house. Explaining that a recharge at that point was not likely to increase the house bill and cause suspicion, he gave her a much clearer description than she'd received off the impatient Antedote. He wondered if others would do the same, but decided the amount of activity on the part of the new owners would probably mask anything they did anyway. Following his guidance she managed the task without further difficulty.

Although his tuition had required him to share with Baybe in the electric activity, he noted that participation didn't afford the same sexual satisfaction he felt when joining with Upstart. I'm glad, he thought, although he had to admit, as a spirit, Baybe was not without attraction, probably more so than her image, if it was as a newborn baby after her last trip..

"Pleased to twitch it," Upstart declared, referring to the sexual bit, not the attraction. Her undetected arrival caused him to flash in surprise.

"Where did you come from?" Baybe demanded. She'd been enjoying the sharing experience and rather resented Upstart's invasion.

"From the garden."

"That's not possible. We're not able to leave the mansion."

It gave Upstart pleasure to contradict her, amusing Hedstrong at what he took to be a hint of jealous possession transmitting from his beloved. Soon Baybe was being shown the grounds by them both, overcome by the new freedom and drifting in dreamlike manner from one feature to the next. It was the time of day when the public were allowed to roam around a small part of the stately home, and quite a few humans were making their way from the car park along the path to the house.

"I haven't seen so many of them for measures," Baybe twitched. "Life is certainly going to change in the mansion now."

"That's what we wanted to talk to you about," Hedstrong started.

"What d'you mean?"

"Well, you must have noticed how different the planet has

become since we arrived." He'd read her past which, during the tour of the grounds had remained unblocked. Despite the rather disastrous last short journey into the ill-fated baby delivered from Antedote's human, she'd previously chosen well. "After all, your history reads like a religious procession through the ages, even during sacrificial times." It was unusual for someone in this section of the planet to have had such experience, stretching back to the ancient civilisations that once dominated South America and other parts of the human world. He hadn't had enough mirco-measures to fully investigate the details of her story and would have liked to learn more but Baybe made it clear she was in no mood to oblige. Having started to cope with this new life, she found time to register objection to his inquisitiveness, proceeding to put a stop on everything.

"We'll have to teach you partial blocking," Upstart commented. "There's really no need to be quite so secretive."

Baybe was about to reply when they encountered Professer. He was in his usual agitated mood and demanded to know what had kept them. He didn't allow opportunity for reply but, assuming she'd been fully briefed, proceeded to explain Baybe's task to her. Hedstrong and Upstart were as surprised as she was at what was planned.

***

Whilst all this was going on, Lard was enjoying himself. It was always flattering to have fellow spirits paying homage to his superiority, and here was Antedote virtually swooning in his presence. Whatever he suggested, she endorsed. Wherever they went, she twitched his praises, sometimes to an extent that, if they'd been in human guise, the other spirits would have been physically sick. Her antics were beginning to convince the community that, with their new found freedom to recharge, treating her as their leader may be inappropriate.

When it was Kernel's turn (in fact being a committee member he was out of turn because they'd had difficulty locating him) they eventually discovered him slumbering in a dormant grandfather clock and none too pleased to be disturbed. At first he suspected he was being summoned to another meeting and started to grumble that he wasn't sure if he was cut out for 'this committee lark'. Antedote suggested if that was how he felt he should do 'the other', as usual without precise definition of 'other'. She followed this with an invitation, to summarise her words, to take himself off somewhere else if he didn't want to learn the secret of independent living.

Detecting Compresser's arrival, Lard moved away to converse with him, unnoticed by the others. Antedote was still developing her theme on his return but, at that very micro-measure, a human chronologist, the repairer, began fiddling with the mechanism of the clock. Moving both hands up to midnight it suddenly began striking the hour. Perhaps it was a combination of the human invasion of his privacy, his confusion at Antedote's insults, his irritability coupled with the resounding, echoing chimes (which incidentally had nothing to do with the actual time of day); whatever the cause, Kernel was electrified. In a flash he was 'off' and the other spirits sensed in awe as he materialised before inadvertently merging with the clock repairer. Compresser quietly faded away from the scene.

"I've never been that close to unmeditated human entry before," Lard said. "Quite fascinating."

Antedote was shocked. She said she hadn't meant to drive him out of Reality. All she'd meant was to... and there she paused. She realised she hadn't bothered what she meant, or what trauma she might cause the target of her outburst. She'd simply vented her annoyance at someone who got in her way. About to offer another explanation to avoid being placed in a harsh critical light, but prevented because spirits couldn't lie, she blocked everything and advocated they look for the next recipient.

Lard suggested the time had arrived for a break, and conducted the self-appointed, still startled, leader back to her panel. He remained in her company for a mirco or two, noting that she automatically twitched to check if Hedstrong was installed in the adjoining panel. He wasn't, of course, and she remembered why. She'd driven him off. It seemed she was getting rather good at that sort of thing.

"Don't be hard on yourself," Lard consoled her. "You've done your best and none of us are perfect... well, not quite, anyway, I think." The partial blocking of his last thought was not quick enough and Antedote picked on it.

"You think you are, don't you? You think you're perfect and better than the rest of us. Don't you?" she demanded.

Denial was impossible so Lard attempted a fruitless explanation that perhaps he had had more experience than most. Almost before the twitch had left his being, he knew his honeymoon period with Antedote was over, an impression immediately confirmed by her condemnation of his attitude. Delivered in her traditional form, he hastened to give his apologies for any unintentional offence he'd caused, suggesting it might be better for him to retire.

"Piss off, and take your high and mighty airs and graces with you," Antedote flashed before sinking into her panel and blocking out the whole of the spiritual world. This suited Lard. The mission he now had to accomplish was becoming ever more urgent. With a polite 'goodbye' to his erstwhile companion, which was ignored, he was off.

***

Lard made his way back to the aviary with the speed of light, creating a brief glow along the path. Humans were still steadily, expectantly, trudging from Paradise towards the mansion in anticipation of their organised exploration of what was now described as a National Treasure. Some experienced, rather than saw, a warm pocket of air, one or two of the more aware commenting upon the sudden rise in temperature, unusual for early spring. A little boy claimed it was a ghost, adding that he had actually seen a man turn off and disappear into the aviary. His mother told him not to be so stupid, explaining to an old lady being pushed along in a wheelchair that her son's imagination would get the better of him one day. They nodded to a monk who was passing by, and Compresser nodded back, proceeding to take a circuitous route into nearby bushes before de-materialising.

Professer, already agitated with Upstart, Hedstrong and Baybe by the lack of preparation of Baybe for her task was awaiting his arrival. The monk reported that having faithfully followed the clock repairer since the man's meeting with Phyllis, on his re-entry to the mansion he'd handed the task over to Lard. Still recovering from his scorching dash, Lard chose that moment to try to smooth things over in his usual manner.

"You can stop that for a start. It won't work. How am I to achieve results if everyone around me is so ignorant?" the learned spirit demanded.

"By calming down and acting with some responsibility, can't you?" Compresser told him.

Professer might have done if, in unison with the others present, he hadn't just twitched onto Hedstrong's unblocked comparison of him with the conceited superior attitude demonstrated by Antedote. Both Hedstrong and Upstart had been hovering around, unsure after safe delivery of Baybe, whether their presence was required.

"You think I can calm down when he compares me to someone with the intelligence of a being as backward as those jungle idiots prancing around the mansion?" Professer stormed.

"She knows no better. You should," Hedstrong told him.

"I don't see the point in going on with this. What's the use? Why should I bother? I think it's best if we abandon the whole project.

What could I possibly get out of this ignorant, objectionable backwater?" Professer had worked himself up into such a state that he momentarily materialised. If a human had been present he would have seen a being that looked like a professor too, squat, slightly overweight with wild white hair and eyes to match.

"That's a pity, isn't it?" Compresser told him. "Just when I'd discovered a new target for experiment, haven't I?" The suggestion, worked upon a little more, helped diffuse what could have become an impossible situation. Slowly Professer calmed down and the two spirits discussed how they could keep track of the young boy who had seen Lard dashing back to the aviary. "He obviously has talent which should be developed, doesn't he?" Compresser urged.

It was agreed Compresser should track the family until the boy's home location could be ascertained. Just before Compresser went on his mission, he paused.

"Oh, by the way, you're going to have difficulty with your current experiment. You'd better ask Lard to explain, hadn't you?" He was gone, taking Upstart with him, before he could be questioned further.

"What's he mean?" demanded Professer, twitching towards the others.

Lard sought time to contemplate upon how to break his news, allowing Professer more opportunity to complain at the ill-equipped nature of Baybe, who had not even mastered the simple task of selective blocking. Then he wanted to know of Lard where the target human was. Lard played for even more time by seeking to describe the complications of keeping Antedote occupied whilst moving on to tackle the assignment passed to him by Compresser.

This inspired further tantrums, the Professer complaining that the target had been shadowed for several measures, as he well knew, and was obviously active in the mansion. Eventually, after more prevarication, Lard was obliged to admit that, unfortunately, there had been a distraction.

"I'm dealing with a load of idiots. I've had enough," Professer declared, about to take off to hunt down Compresser when the monk suddenly materialised in their presence.

"Sorry, I should have told you, oughtn't I?" he apologised to no one in particular. "Thought I'd pop back, shouldn't I? Had to leave the boy a while to get Upstart to keep an eye on the main target, didn't I? Thought that's what you'd want, isn't it? In the circumstances? We've found him and she'll report back if she thinks he is about to leave the premises, won't she? He's still working on the clocks upstairs, isn't he? But there's a problem though, isn't there? Lard will explain, won't you? Must drift, can't afford to lose the boy for long, can we?" and he was off again.

With the rediscovery of the chronologist: the human target for the experiment with Baybe, Professer became surprisingly calm whilst Lard explained the incident with Kernel, now lodged in the clock repairer. There was a silence whilst the allegedly learned spirit deliberated. The others awaited the inevitable outburst, but it didn't come. Instead Lard was asked to recount in minute detail exactly what had happened. Professer was especially concerned to establish Kernel's intent at the point of human entry.

"You are sure it was the shock generated by the striking of the clock, combined with the idiotic attitude of that tribal leader which caused the entry?"

"Certainly," responded Lard. "I'm convinced he had no intention of leaving the Real World at that mirco-measure."

"You'd better be right. And if you are, then all is not lost. We just advance to the next stage. Let's go find the human." Professer was already moving when, almost as an afterthought, he added, twitching at Baybe, "Oh, by the way, we won't need you now. Hedstrong will sort you out." With that he left the aviary, accompanied by Lard.

Baybe, still not fully aware of what had been planned, let it show that she thought they were all mad. She'd heard enough to know it would not have been to her liking whatever the intention and took off back to the safety of the mansion.

***

Professer and Lard had some difficulty finding the clock repairer. The unfortunate man, now being under whatever influence Kernel might be having on his human character, was becoming noticeably less decisive in his work. Lethargy, one of Kernel's attributes, was taking over. He resolved upon a longer lunch break than usual and, followed by Upstart, wandered out into the grounds to eat his sandwiches. The two searching spirits eventually tracked him down to a stone seat at the end of one of the walks. Upstart was hovering uncertainly in the background and expressed her relief at their arrival. Professer wanted to know where was the pepper?

Needless to say, neither Lard nor Upstart knew what he was talking about, which stimulated the return of the usual state of agitation in their learned colleague. They both remained floating whilst he ranted and raged at the shortcomings of a system within which he was forced to work. He would have probably reached materialisation had not the clock repairer finished his food and stood up.

"What about the café?" Upstart asked.

"What about it?" demanded Professer.

"They're bound to have pepper."

"Then that's where we must go. Which way?"

Upstart told him, warning that it was only in the early stages of construction and didn't yet offer a full range of food. The learned man wanted to know what interest that was to him, as long as they had pepper. He was advised, quite primly, that it would be of interest if the pepper wasn't liberally distributed about the place in pots and was actually sealed up in little packets which even humans had difficulty opening. Twitching veiled threats at all who may be in range Professer, nevertheless, took off towards the makeshift café, followed by Upstart and Lard.

"Aren't we forgetting something?" Lard ventured.

"What?" Professer demanded.

"The victim?"

"Isn't he following?"

Upstart checked and reported that not only was he not following, but he was heading back to the mansion, away from the catering facilities. She also sought to suggest, rather sarcastically, that there was no way she knew of communicating with the human brain to influence the direction in which the host body moved. To reduce the inflammatory nature of the remark Lard tried a diversion by pointing out an unruly family he'd noted picnicking on steps which led out of the formal garden towards the house. Usually the clock repairer, heading in that direction, would have found a route round them, but with the influence of Kernel he considered it their duty to give way.

The picnic was a complex one, prepared to cater for the excessive appetites of mother, father and two children. A large Cornish pasty, acquired from the local supermarket, fell far short of the level of seasoning to satisfy the head of the family. He'd already drowned it in salt and was brandishing a pepper pot when the clock repairer came to a halt in front of him. Being of cowardly nature, and being confronted by a worker wearing an official tag which, with Kernel's influence, made him look important, the father struggled to his feet.

It was a simple task for the returning spirits to summon up enough turbulence to agitate the hand held pot and ensure that a resulting cloud of pepper drifted up the nostrils of the clock repairer. The result was instantaneous and alarming. Whilst most humans would simply have sneezed adding a cough or two, the clock man first clutched at his throat, then collapsed on the ground in a contorting, choking bundle of agony.

The spirits hovered back to watch, and suddenly, there was Kernel beside them.

"I've done it," twitched Professer. "It works. It's the breakthrough. Quick. Back to the aviary. I need to do a full examination."

Carried forward by his enthusiasm, Lard, Upstart and Kernel

followed the great man back to the small, dilapidated bird house. Professer started his debriefing of Kernel immediately, wanting to know, in micro-detail, everything from the moment the clock chimed until he returned to Reality.

Lard tried to raise a point, but was silenced by an impatient twitch. The interrogation continued with Professer becoming more and more excited. When he'd exhausted all his questions, which had almost drained Kernel, he was ecstatic. He couldn't help explaining the results of his experiment. Two victories in one, he claimed. The first was perfection of the casual mode of entry. The spirit had to have no intention of permanent invasion of the human form, and Kernel had achieved this admirably. The fact that it had been a mistake, and one in which Professer was not involved, seemed not to matter. It had happened, and that was good enough. What was even more striking was that Kernel had returned. Apparently it had been Professer's pet theory that, if a serious allergic human reaction could be induced, then a spirit would be expelled to regain the Real World without the death of the human. Earlier research by Professer had revealed that the clock repairer was allergic to pepper, or at least the concentrated wave aimed at him by the spirits.

"Don't you all see the implications?" he cried. "Just think how we can progress. All we have to do is identify humans with serious allergies and we will be able to get in and out of them at will. I've cracked it. I've made it at last." He asked what it was that Lard wanted to say.

"I was just wondering if your theory would be defeated if the subject human was dead?"

"Of course it would. That's the whole basis of the experiment. The human lives. All the being has is a violent human reaction. Surely even you can understand that?"

"Yes, I think I can," Lard replied, "only the clock repairer looked very dead to me when we left him."

CHAPTER 12
THE INVASION

Allocated one too many to assist in the shop, Phyllis took herself off for the estate office to sort out the rotas. She passed in front of the mansion at the very moment of confrontation between the clock repairer and the picnic family. Able to make out shadowy figures, she was convinced they were behind what was happening, especially as she experienced an increased glow the moment the poor man collapsed.

All hint of ghostly activity had evaporated by the time she reached the steps. Ensuring the emergency service had been alerted, she knelt down beside the prostrate figure, ignoring screaming children, a wailing fat mother and a father telling them all to 'shut up'. She used skills she'd learnt over the years, some perhaps justifying her more mysterious side, and managed to restore life into the little worker. By the time the medics arrived, he was breathing again.

Turning her back on the family protestations that it wasn't their fault, she followed the stretcher to the ambulance and witnessed a moment of consciousness. The man opened his eyes and recognised her.

"I saw your monk and some others," he said, before drifting back into oblivion.

"D'you know him?" one of the medics asked. Phyllis said not, apart from a brief encounter whilst he was taking a break from his clock work. "Seems like you've given him a chance of survival," the medic observed. "What did you do?"

"Just the usual," she said, sidestepping further questioning by undertaking to have someone contact the hospital with his details.

As the ambulance drove down the drive, she wondered if there was anyone who would care… whether there was a next of kin, or friend, now his mother was dead. If the village ever found out that the poor creature was the second man to face death after a visit with her to Paradise, that would set tongues wagging. Her reputation hadn't diminished over the years, one or two locals never reluctant to give voice to their views in the village public house.

***

Hedstrong again had to force himself to acknowledge he was in the middle of fundamental change. The world… his Real World, the one he'd known for so many measures, had suddenly disappeared. The sheltered existence of regular retreats from humanity was gone never to come back. He knew that and, with so much developing so swiftly, he wasn't sure he liked what was happening. Values were slipping.

He was in the aviary with the rest when a new arrival entered their midst. Jenius – he discovered later that was his title – echoed his thoughts by suggesting all present, except him, were heading into an abyss as equally terminal as was forecast for the humans upon whom they depended. He'd latched onto Professer's claimed success for his experiment. He'd also observed the event, staying on at the scene, undetected by Phyllis. The clock repairer hadn't died, but he had suffered a major physical arrest, only reversed by the attentions of a human woman. The newcomer demonstrated no affection for the learned spirit and only reluctantly conveyed details of the human's survival.

"No doubt they'll find something wrong with him, shove a few tests through him to disturb his static balance and send him on his way," was all Professer said when given the news. "Pity we can't have him back here to see what effect it all produced on him – whether it disrupted his sanity. Not that we could tell if it was our technique or their tests which did the damage."

"That's typical of you," Jenius told him. "Always so impulsive. Never a thought for preparation and clinical accuracy when you go blundering off into the unknown."

"If I waited for the likes of you," Professer replied, "we'd never get anywhere. We need progress, and we need it quickly."

What was apparently a familiar argument between the two of them was allowed to take its natural course. Jenius objected to the risk of human life in experiments for the spiritual world. He claimed there was no need for such excessive speed. Professer countered by asking how he knew what time was left when, in their ignorance, greed and stupidity, these mortals could blow themselves to smithereens or succumb to some plague or another. He claimed the sacrifice of a few here and there was totally justified. He added that the concern of Jenius was no more than a mask for his regret that he had not the ability to experiment, or the intellect to comprehend the results.

"I'm off," he concluded, leaving with a burst of energy along the main path to the mansion which caused several visitors to chase across the grass after lost head-gear.

In the aviary Jenius allowed peace to return before addressing Lard, Upstart, Kernel and Hedstrong. What he had to say eliminated any chance of Real World life reverting to how it had been in the mansion. First of all the main house was to be adopted as the spiritual centre of meeting for the council. It would be the administrative headquarters of the inner-council and would house the full planetary gatherings whenever they took place. Secondly, Jenius, who was apparently the appointed Head of Planetary Council, would take up residence within the estate. There was some discussion upon how the move was to be achieved before Hedstrong suddenly twitched a question, aimed at no one in particular.

"What right do we have to decide this?" he asked.

"Planetary right," Jenius replied. The others automatically offered the spiritual equivalent of a nod, as if that was the end of the matter.

"What 'planetary right'?" Hedstrong persisted.

"Doesn't he know anything?" Jenius demanded almost adopting Professer's attitude. Lard explained that he was a new recruit and had not yet been familiarised with the governing structure.

"I wasn't even aware there was a governing structure," Hedstrong complained.

The rest of the measure was spent bringing him up to date. He learned that the discoveries Antedote had pioneered in the mansion weren't really discoveries at all. Spirits throughout the planet had been well ahead of her and had been drifting around all over the Earth. Needless to say this had caused complaint some were trying to pinch territory off others. There'd been conflict, giving rise to emotions closely akin to human reaction, leading to a need for government. Some spirits had been more adept at organisation than others, with campaigning eventually leading to the formation of the Planetary Council.

One of the declared aims of that august body was to seek independence from the need to rely upon humans for power. It was the only aim upon which they all agreed. To date, precisely how to go about discovering such a technique had escaped them. The arrangement of full council meetings had proved such a problem that the inner-council had been formed to investigate and report, despite more suggestion they were simply following human habits.

Jenius had secured the position of supreme leader. With others either bored with the whole concept or exhausted, he'd been left to choose the members of the inner-council. Matters had progressed quite rapidly. From time to time there'd been objection to his high-handed attitude, but when a dispute became too electric to handle he'd simply moved onto something else, leaving a sub-committee to deal with it.

***

Later, in the rose garden with Upstart, Hedstrong claimed Jenius had obtained for himself the dictatorial power to drift around all over the place ensuring that his demands would be met, whilst some obscure group somewhere on the planet had been too idle to stop him. Upstart agreed, but suggested that it would be less than diplomatic to mention such radical twitchings. They'd both just received authority to act as another sub-committee to organise the mansion ready to receive the spiritual influx.

"Perhaps later, when things have been arranged, we could try a little reforming," she encouraged.

Meantime Hedstrong enthusiastically agreed they should share a boost of power in anticipation of the task. The couple took off to the gift shop, one of Hedstrong's favourite locations, especially when manned by volunteers and crowded by tourists searching for over-priced bargains.

***

Kernel had stayed in the aviary with Lard and Jenius after the other two had left. He'd been compelled to repeat details of his last human entry experience. Jenius was even more exacting in his questioning of events than Professer had been, paying great attention to the period after the return out of the clock repairer into Reality. Had Kernel detected the presence of any fellow spirits in the human being? He hadn't. Had he been aware of his separate Real existence from the human brainwaves? He hadn't. Did he try to direct those brainwaves away from human intent? He didn't. It was a tiring episode, although Kernel surprised the others as well as himself at the vigour with which he rose to the occasion.

Nevertheless, when offered, he welcomed the opportunity to return to the more familiar surroundings of the mansion, under instruction to keep everything blocked until Hedstrong and Upstart completed their assignment. Jenius had decided not to teach him selective blocking in case he got it wrong. When he'd gone, Lard asked why he'd been so specific in his interrogation?

"Part of our ongoing experiments," he said. "I've got a number of teams perfecting temporary entry techniques, others exploring methods of return and also, for the past few measures, several groups assessing whether this type of human entry experience has any effect upon spiritual character."

"And what did you discover from this latest, perhaps fortuitous, episode?"

"Interesting," Jenius replied. "For a start, Kernel seems more lively than his history suggests. Until the involuntary entry into the clock repairer, he'd chosen mature, sedate individuals, higher in the echelons of human hierarchy but never reaching their pinnacles, probably due to laziness. Would you say that was how you read him?"

Lard was obliged to agree, recalling that in the past the spirit had been happy to accept office as long as it didn't mean he had to do much. "But I'm still not convinced it'll be more than a temporary change. You've twitched his history," he argued, "wouldn't you say his spiritual character existed even before his first human entry? I know it's a long way back, but does one entry change all that, especially an unanticipated one?"

"Good point," Jenius conceded. "I think we've established that spiritual being is not without individual character, but what I also suspect is that it can be massaged through human contact. In fact we've all but proved this. What we don't know, as you rightly question, is whether it's a temporary or permanent feature, and whether it's automatic or subject to spiritual intent."

"This is getting a bit too complicated for me. I think I'll stay in control of organisation and leave you to the pioneering stuff," Lard concluded.

"Don't put yourself down," he was told. "To suggest you don't understand would be an inaccuracy, and I know you can't do that, yet. But you must acknowledge that with our emancipation, everything must be scrutinised, including the belief that spirits can't lie. There's so much to do and that idiot Professer is right: we don't know how many measures are left to do it in. Even if humans fail to annihilate themselves, there's bound to be an asteroid bashing into the planet sooner or later. We need to be prepared for that."

Lard suggested he leave Jenius to familiarise himself with what was to become his headquarters for the foreseeable future. He was to take over the aviary and wanted to establish a spiritual exclusion zone surrounding it, to avoid unwelcome callers. Lard embarked upon a trip into the main house to 'see how things were going'.

***

Hedstrong and Upstart spent some time in the gift shop. They both knew it would be many micro-measures before they might again enjoy the privacy of their own company, and resolved to make the best of it. The staff were trying to close up for the day and the couple had been playing tricks on them. A brief spark here or there had caused chaos with the electronic cashing up. Adding to that a few books falling off shelves, and an ornament suddenly slipping from one poor victim's hands to smash on the floor, left the two assistants accusing each other of incompetence or worse. Only the intervention of Phyllis had saved the day, by which time Upstart had enticed her lover into another intimate sharing of power.

"We'd better get on," she twitched whilst they rested in each other's presence. "We've work to do."

Reluctantly Hedstrong agreed. With one last spark at the cash computer, which started to cough out receipts until it was unplugged, the couple took off. Travelling at some speed alongside the trees and through the drive, they entered the manor via the chapel. Drifting to the ground floor they located Kernel and charged him with the task of gathering all the residents into the games room. Then they found Antedote in her usual resting place.

She'd only recently returned from a power consuming search of the building, trying in vain first to find Lard and then Hedstrong.

"Where's Lard?" she twitched.

"He's on other business," Upstart replied.

"He's no right to be on other business. I need him."

"I'm afraid he has a right," Upstart told her.

"Nonsense. I'm in charge and I say what he has to do. He's getting too big for his shroud. I've had enough of this. He's fired." Antedote turned to Hedstrong. "I'm re-appointing you as my deputy. Go find Lard and tell him he's fired."

"There's no need," Lard replied, having drifted in on the twitching in his usual surreptitious manner. "And I'm afraid you're not in a position to fire me. In fact, you're not in a position to do anything unless my two fellow spirits direct."

Antedote was twitchless whilst she fought to decide which announcement to condemn first. Upstart expected her to materialise but discovered she had insufficient power to do so.

"Would you like a small boost," she offered, "so that you can regain your composure?"

It had the desired effect. Antedote's temper got the better of her to such an extent that she flashed around the room twice before collapsing in her panel, exhausted.

"Get out, all of you," she twitched. "That's an order. Get out."

No one moved. They simply waited for her to calm down before Lard began his explanation. After a diplomatic interlude, during which he praised the manner in which she had organised her group, the control she'd kept over dissident voices and the personal sacrifices she'd made for others, he said her good work had achieved one of the greatest of honours. Sufficiently mollified, Antedote relaxed and thanked him for his consideration, which, she claimed, was much more than she was receiving from the other two. So taken was she with Lard's golden words she said he could be her deputy again before even asking what it was she had achieved.

"This manor-house has been chosen as the Planetary Headquarters for our movement," Lard announced.

"What movement?" Antedote twitched. Lard endeavoured to explain. "You're mad," she told him.

"No, he's not," Hedstrong intervened. "And what he says is correct."

"I've had enough of this," Antedote twitched. She tried to depart through the wall, but she didn't have the energy. "Give me that boost," she demanded of Upstart.

"Sorry," Upstart replied. "It's too late for that."

"I order you to give me a boost," Antedote twitched.

"I'm afraid you can't order me, or anyone else. You've no authority." Upstart, with her usual deliberation, failed to block the pleasure in her twitch, enjoying the result, whilst Hedstrong, who still had some feeling for his ex-comrade, tried to intervene.

"Things have changed," he told her. "There's a lot you don't understand. We have to adapt to new circumstances."

"She's got you just were she wants you, that's for sure. And don't kid yourself. She's as vindictive as ever. You just can't see it."

Hedstrong twitched onto Upstart, seeking in vain for support for what he was saying. Upstart was being vindictive, and she was enjoying herself. She told him so, reminding him how vindictive Antedote had been in the past.

"If she could, she'd be fighting me with as much force as she could muster. But she can't. We've got her where we want her. She can't escape or even move from her panel unless we let her."

"Oh, yes I can," exploded Antedote with a final flash. Unfortunately Phyllis, having closed the shop, was passing to join a volunteer and staff meeting in the morning room. She experienced a bolt of lightning and waited for the roar of thunder, which never came. Aware of three beings watching her she shrugged to regain her equilibrium.

"You all right?" asked Bernard, one of the permanent staff. He put his arm round her waist and for a moment she allowed it to stay there.

"Fine, thank you," she replied as they entered the meeting. "Just adjusting to the gloom in here after outside."

Unaware that Antedote had become merged in her being and was now a part of her, she gratefully took a seat. Could she really see images from the next world, even understand? And was one of them the double of her late departed friend, his Lordship? It was obvious no one else was aware of them, so she would have to postpone investigation until she was free of human presence.

CHAPTER 13
BUREAUCRACY

Hedstrong's thoughts were in a whirl. He'd retired to his panel to try to sort out his emotions; the panel he'd occupied before his Real World was turned upside down; before he'd developed feelings he once thought spirits didn't possess. He was alone. The others had gone.

Where would all this lead, he wondered? For a while, he longed for the past with everything ordered and simple. Why was there need for a sea of emotion, of experimentation and of government? This was what humans were for. Why did spirits need to get involved when they had a perfectly peaceful, organised existence? He knew the answer almost before he'd asked the question. Spirits depended on humans. That's how they travelled through… through what? What exactly were they doing on this planet and where were they going… if anywhere?

"It's a lot to learn," Upstart twitched. He hadn't realised she'd returned or that he'd kept his thoughts unblocked. "But you're special. You've seen so much and travelled so far. We need you with us to lead the rest."

Hedstrong couldn't believe he was special. In his mind he was just another spirit and it always puzzled him when he twitched onto expressions that, somehow, he possessed something others didn't. Upstart noted and accepted the puzzlement. Although she'd never experienced it herself, she knew it existed and not just in the Real World. It was also a human trait which had, in the past, annoyed her. Since her association with Hedstrong she had come to see it in a different light. She rather liked it. At first she'd treated the battle with Antedote as a challenge, and won, but in the winning had she

121

begun to experience something else? Perhaps that was what the experts had been working on. Perhaps there was something to be discovered; that they weren't just messing about for the sake of messing about, pleasant though it could be… with Hedstrong.

"Thanks a bunch," Hedstrong twitched, having read her thoughts.

Upstart giggled. "I haven't heard that expression for measures. Not since my last human trip."

"You have done a human trip, then?" Hedstrong enquired sarcastically. "I was beginning to wonder whether you were like the rest of us, or if you were on a higher plain, treating us savages as playthings for your amusement."

"You were right to wonder. But, yes, I have had human trips, you know that. We all have, but you have to accept that some of us have advanced a long way beyond the remote world Antedote controlled in the mansion." Upstart was serious now, no attempt at criticism or fun. "That's one of the difficulties we're facing. So many different groups at so many different stages of advancement." She reminded Hedstrong of the travels he'd completed in the humans he'd chosen. They'd taken him half across the planet, into deserts and jungles, where he'd encountered beings, some of which had never seen an aeroplane, or a car. They'd all had the basic desire: to survive. "I know we're not like humans… not in many ways. We don't have to bother with time or survival and we don't die. At least I don't think we do. I've never witnessed the end of a spirit, have you?"

"How could I have witnessed such a complex thing in my backward world?" Hedstrong replied, still sulking from Upstart's earlier comments.

"I love you," Upstart twitched suddenly. The admission had bubbled up from nowhere and bounced out with a flash. "Sorry. I don't know where that came from," she apologised.

"Is this another of your tricks?" Hedstrong's response was full of suspicion, although it did lack some of his earlier aggression. His spiritual being was experiencing an electrical surge which he was having difficulty controlling. They both remained quiet in the panels for several mini-measures.

"Look," Upstart began after the pause. "Can we begin again? I'm sorry if I offended you and for the way I treated you. This hasn't happened to me before, not since I arrived on this planet. I didn't know there were such feelings and I still don't know how best to express them. I suppose that's why I blurted out a human emotion."

"Don't be sorry," Hedstrong told her. "I've had feelings too. It's just so right to be with you. I don't know why and I've tried to dismiss them, but… I can't."

"What about Antedote?" Upstart asked.

"She introduced me to feelings, I have to admit that, but everything was a confrontation. Nothing had to interrupt her surge for power. She would sacrifice anything if she believed it would increase her control." He paused, before adding, "With you, it's different."

**

A meeting of key spirits was held in the library at Jenius's request and he took the chair. Present were Lard, Kernel, Baybe, Spayed, Upstart and Hedstrong. Professer was back as well, sparking away in usual manner, and there were three others who, at first, kept quiet, lodged in several encyclopaedic volumes on the third row by the door.

"We know you're there," grumbled Professer. "Declare yourselves, for infinity's sake. It's no good trying to hide. I know how to locate you."

"Leave them alone," Jenius told him. "They're just doing their job."

"What job? All they do is go around spying on unsuspecting spirits. What real contribution have they ever made to our progress? I ask you, what contribution have they made?"

"If you'll just shut your twitching for a moment, I'll tell you. At least I'll try in the hope that, for once, you'll listen instead of going off into one of your usual stupid experiments."

"They're not stupid. I'll have you know…"

Lard interrupted. He caught Professer offguard by asking how he'd learnt the technique to establish whether uninvited spirits were present at a distance greater than the usual close awareness. Thinking he was the only one with power to do so, Professer willingly embarked on an explanation, proving the technique by revealing that, apart from those already identified, there were five mansion residents, one in a volume of Shakespeare and the others between the dusty pages of editions of *Strand*. Lard located them, gently persuading them to move out of the room with a promise that he personally would explain what was going on in a measure or two. He suggested they might gather the other spiritual residents in the chapel and managed to impress upon them that they had been given a mission and a responsibility. They left convinced that the successful performance of their task would not be without reward.

Jenius thanked him for his diplomacy whilst the Professer complained at the use of yet another humanistic ploy to offer everything and give nothing. The gathering then settled to discussion.

For those whom he suggested might not be fully informed, Jenius described the inner-council, made up of 19 individual spirits from across the globe, all appointed by him. He confirmed that these, which were called Thrillators, were regularly consulted when he required to resolve major matters of policy. There was one present amongst them, he said, and to Hedstrong's surprise, confirmed that it was Upstart.

"Her speciality is to gather emotional data and use it to advise on spiritual feeling," he said. "And I am now appointing, from the full council, Hedstrong as the twentieth Thrillator. There is a bond between him and Upstart which I know to be genuine on both sides and which I believe will make them a team to give valuable service to the movement."

He touched upon the experiments that were being carried out, adding that even Professer was contributing to development of an independent force capable of survival without recourse to humanity. Professer objected to the 'even' and the verbal twitching that followed offered a comic interlude to the proceedings. Lard intervened with enough diplomacy to restore calm and Jenius, in thanking him, confirmed him to be the council's general secretary.

"For the first time, I am creating a planetary council headquarters which will, from now on, be our base," he announced. "This mansion is to be it, and Lard will be in charge of the administration. That brings me onto the next topic: how we are to progress without falling into traps that continually seem to ensnare humans. A small group will observe and report upon the demonstration of spiritual behaviour. Unless we can define feelings, they will get out of control. Therefore, the three I have chosen will be based here but will have my authority to travel where and when they wish. Their job will be to report to me upon any trends of behaviour which they consider to be damaging to our community. I have called them the Thought Processing Team. They're the three, as you know, Professer, reclining on the third shelf."

The announcement attracted a negative flash from Professer. He was still arguing with Jenius when the gathering broke up to drift their separate ways, the three Thought Processors having faded into the background.

***

In recognition of his promise, Lard joined the mansion residents in the chapel, taking Hedsdtrong and Upstart with him. Only house spirits were present, Professer having eventually disappeared to find Compresser and, hopefully, he said, the next specimen for his experiments. Jenius had adjourned to the aviary to plan something else and no one quite knew where the three Thought Processors were.

Some of those attending found it difficult to grasp the enormity of what Lard had to say, especially when told of Antedote's departure. Hedstrong tried to reassure them, explaining that it had taken him several measures to come to terms with what had been going on elsewhere on the planet. Kernel endeavoured to assist, touching upon his clock repairer experience, which confused the rest even more.

Property opening time arrived, with several members of the public touring the chapel as part of their visit to the ancient estate. Several puzzled spirits, troubled by what they were being told, stuck to the old-fashioned remedy and departed the Real World to enjoy another human adventure, perhaps never to return to the same location. When two found foreigners who would be travelling back to their home part of the planet, Hedstrong realised he was growing a greater sense of awareness, because he actually registered their departure. He could single out the humans they had entered.

"You see?" Upstart encouraged. "A measure or two ago, you wouldn't have noticed. Now you're tuned in to what's going on around you."

Lard was similarly aware of the spiritual departure and annoyed that he was losing what would otherwise have been helpers. He asked if any more felt like going, suggesting that this was the time for them to say. Receiving a negative response he went on to outline how he visualised the mansion would be used for planetary headquarters' activity. It was an ambitious scheme which involved education of the house residents into differing skills and also rules of behaviour. The suggestion of personal restriction took all his diplomatic prowess to win acceptance, but eventually he was able to convince those remaining of the need for a certain conformity. Reluctantly they signified they were prepared to accept the situation, for now.

Every Real World house occupant was charged with the task of monitoring the presence of outside spiritual visitors. When one was detected, they were to report to Lard or, if he was not available, to twitch onto Hedstrong or Upstart, who were designated house host and hostess respectively. The new arrivals were to be treated as guests and accommodated in a panel, shelf or work of art commensurate with their status. Only planetary council members would be installed in the library, with the chapel pews and adornments designated first choice for others. The house spirits who had used the library shelves in the past were allowed to return on the understanding that they would undertake hosting activities when required. The return was made out to be their reward, presented in such fashion by Lard that they were convinced it was their promised prize for having called residents to the meeting.

Spayed and Baybe were appointed commissioners, to protect the dining room when taken over for council and inner-council meetings. Spayed moaned that he didn't see why he had to be a 'bouncer' but Baybe thought she quite liked the idea. Lard described it to be an important position, especially as they would have to work with experts to perfect a way of ejecting troublemakers. Kernel was afforded the task of information officer which he accepted with pride. It didn't carry any specific duties, which was just as well, for the vigour he'd inherited on his return from the clock repairer seemed to have worn off and he was ready to resume his semi-active, self-important state.

Lard, having consumed most of his power, willingly accepted a boost from Upstart before leaving the premises to seek out Jenius.

"There's no need to be like that," Upstart told Hedstrong, who hadn't been too comfortable about her linking up with Lard. "It was only a boost and he doesn't turn me on. Not like you do." She suggested they spent the rest of the measure enjoying themselves, and they retired to the shop where it took no more than a shared flash of power to satisfy his desires. Hedstrong, being in one of his favourite places, was about to embark upon a game, disrupting the human volunteers, when he suddenly recognised one of them.

"That's the woman who was in the house when Antedote left," he twitched. "It is, isn't it? The one she entered when she left the Real World."

"So it is," Upstart agreed.

They watched, fascinated, whilst she went about her business. Two other volunteers were with her and she was instructing them what to do whilst they began to close the premises for the night. She'd obviously assumed charge, demonstrating her impatience when one or other of the assistants failed to comply with her wishes or took longer than she felt appropriate. In the end she suggested it was time for them to knock off, bidding them to leave the rest to her.

The two spirits had been fascinated by her attitude. Upstart described her as a perfect match for Antedote. Hedstrong agreed, proposing that they have a bit of fun with her. He did his usual trick with the cash till, then drifted back to his lover whilst the paper roll surged out of the machine onto the floor. Suddenly he realised the woman was looking straight at him.

"Don't think I can't see you," Phyllis said. Hedstrong checked to confirm he hadn't materialised by mistake. "I know your sort. Think you can make a fool out of me just because you're in the next world. Well, it won't work, so stop it right now, or I'll start a few chants." Upstart read his thoughts and they both made their way out of the shop. "That's right. Off you go, the pair of you," the woman shouted after them.

Concerned by the incident, they called in at the aviary where they encountered Jenius and Professer having one of their usual arguments. Lard was there, too, but for once was letting them get on with it.

"And what right do you have to interfere?" Professer demanded, sensing their presence.

"We're not," Hedstrong told him. "We wouldn't waste the power."

"You've got plenty to waste," Professer retorted. "You've both been having spiritual sex again, haven't you?"

"Don't be crude," Upstart told him. "We were just doing a bit of recharging at the shop."

Hedstrong, irritated by the learned man's attitude, nearly changed his mind but eventually told of their encounter with Phyllis. Professer immediately became interested. In a complete variation of mood he asked if she was still there?

"She is as far as I'm aware," Hedstrong answered.

"Oh good. A witch. A halfway human, right here in our midst. I mustn't miss this." He departed through the flimsy wall with such speed that, for a moment, it smouldered and the others prepared for it to catch fire. Fortunately it didn't, leaving some black marks where the heat had been greatest.

"We really must try to control him," Jenius said. "One day he'll cause a real disaster."

"Hasn't he already, more than once?" Upstart asked. "Perhaps he'll get wrapped up with 'the witch'. Just think. Him and Antedote in one human. A recipe for spontaneous combustion if ever there was one."

"Don't," Lard begged. "That's just what we don't want. A sensation which would bring all the human cranks from the planet to interfere, with their gadgets and tantrums. It's bad enough having a human who can identify with us."

"You think she really is one of those?" Upstart asked.

"Sounds like it. She won't have a perfect technique. None of them do, but they're a nuisance, all the same," Jenius said.

"Not another complication," Hedstrong muttered. "Trust Antedote to be at the bottom of it."

CHAPTER 14

CONFERENCE PREPARATION

O n his way to the shop, Professer encountered Compresser who, for some reason, had materialised and was stood in the middle of the walk.

"What you doing here like that?" Professer demanded, sensing but unable to see the monk, visible to the human eye..

"Looking for you, isn't it?"

"Can't stop. On a mission."

Compresser had gathered that much from Professer's unblocked intention and, knowing the impulsive nature of his companion, was resolved to do his best to abort the mission. He started by suggesting it was time to commence detailed work on the boy. The idea was dismissed as if Professer had never heard of it. Compresser tried to describe the care he'd taken and the research of the young subject he'd completed, but was told that was part of his job.

"So you're just going to barge in on that woman and cause chaos are you?" he finally accused.

"Certainly not," Professer retorted. "What gave you that idea? I shall simply observe and assess. How did you know about her?"

"I didn't, until I felt you approaching at your usual impossible speed and you didn't block, did you? So intent on your mission, weren't you? Not that you'd taken any time to work out what you were going to do, had you, after you'd 'observed'? I'm coming with you, aren't I?"

Professer was already on his way, and Compresser had difficulty keeping up with him, having to stay materialised until he could disappear from home-going humans, before resuming his spiritual presence. He accelerated after his associate, catching him a micro-measure before the shop entrance. Phyllis had just locked up and was making her way to the car park. Professer was behind her.

"Don't do anything daft, will you?" Compresser twitched.

"Shut up."

"Charming, isn't it?" he twitched indignantly.

"Charming indeed," Phyllis said. She turned round to confront the two spirits. They were both about to take evasive action when she was joined by another human; one of the managers employed to govern all the volunteer individuals. "The decor," she added, waving vaguely at the nearest newly decorated wall. She hoped it was a suitable explanation of what the manager might otherwise have considered an unhinged expression voiced into clean air.

"Phyllis, there are times when you are a complete mystery," he told her.

"And you find that attractive," she suggested. "In fact, you find it irresistible, don't you?"

"I wouldn't go that far," he complained.

"You just happened to be passing this way at this precise moment, did you?"

"Well, no, I can't say that. I was waiting for you." The man paused. "I was wondering if perhaps we could have dinner together?"

"You inviting me on a date?"

"Well, yes. Yes, I suppose I am."

"I accept."

"You do?" He couldn't believe what he was hearing. "That's great. Yes, that's very great. Great indeed. Shall I pick you up at your house later?"

"Seven thirty," Phyllis told him. "And don't be late." He assured her he wouldn't and sped off to prepare. "Idiot," she muttered under her breath before continuing to her car. The two spirits followed, hovering behind her in mid-speculation upon whether she'd detected and addressed them or whether she was just a bit unhinged.

"And don't think I can't see you two, because I can," she told them over her shoulder. Reaching her car she opened the door, got in and was soon speeding away towards the exit.

***

The two spirits were still arguing when they returned to the aviary, Compresser suggesting Phyllis should be left well alone, shouldn't she? and Professer inviting him to depart in another direction, taking his meddling intervention with him. The spiritual boffin was hell bent upon gaining authority for a full scheme of research, but his blustering arrival at headquarters found Lard and Jenius none too pleased to be interrupted. The head of planetary council made his feelings abundantly clear. He needn't have bothered, for neither Professer or Compresser took any notice. Professer told the monk a decision had to be made and Jenius had to make it. Compresser said that was a load of rubbish. When asked, in that case, why he'd bothered to 'come along' he twitched he'd decided it was the only way he could think of to stop development of a mad, ill-conceived, idiotic idea.

"What's happened now?" Lard enquired wearily.

Both spirits twitched at once and, although knowledge transference could be assimilated from several direction at a time, Jenius chose to reject the opportunity, principally in an attempt to slow matters down.

"Don't you try that with me," Professer told him. "Just give us a ruling. That's what you're here for, isn't it?"

"I don't think it's for you to threaten the leader, is it?" Compresser said.

"It could be taken as an insult," Lard contributed.

"And if it is, what are you going to do about it?" Professer demanded.

"That's one of the things we were discussing until we were rudely interrupted," Jenius told him.

"Really?" Professer was immediately interested. "You were discussing punishment? I've been considering that for some time. You need me in on that. Glad I made the meeting."

"Nothing will be finalised without full council agreement," Lard told him.

"I know. I know. But there'll be a need for experiment. That'll be my contribution. Stop blocking me off. Let me twitch where you've got."

Jenius decided it was probably best to let him in on the discussion, if only to divert him from some other mad-brained scheme. He flashed a partial unblock, enough to whet Professer's appetite, and agreed he could stay. The discussion continued, concentrating on how to implement regulation. For many measures enforcement had always fallen down on how to punish any infringements. Compresser knew one day they'd find a way, but he didn't want to be any part of it. He gave the equivalent spiritual rendering of a snort and departed.

To the Professer, the remedy was simple. Send them for a trip to humanity. He said so, any idea of tracking down Phyllis the witch having been discarded in favour of this much more fascinating opportunity.

"We managed to get that far ourselves," Jenius twitched angrily. "If that's all you can contribute to the debate, kindly keep quiet."

"Oh, but it's not. You both know the stumbling block. How to enforce human entry. I'm nearly there on that."

"Explain," Jenius commanded.

"Confinement. I've been working with the Thought Processors. Between them they can maintain enough power to confine any spirit and not only confine. They can propel a dissenting voice into a chosen corner and keep them there until the criminal pleads for human entry."

"Imprisoning them is not sending them into humanity," Lard twitched.

"I know that, but it is a form of restraint. A deprivation of liberty. Isn't that a punishment in itself, especially if the entry into humanity was the only alternative to infinity?"

"That would take quite a force to maintain," Lard argued.

"So? There's enough willing to join the Thought Processors. What's wrong with an army of enforcers?"

"It's a possibility," Jenius conceded.

"You'd just be copying a human idea," Lard said.

"So? They do sometimes come up with a good one."

"Judging by the prison population in this part of the planet it's not proving much of a deterrent," Lard argued. "That is what we are aiming at, isn't it – a deterrent?"

"Maybe also a chance for an experiment or two?" Professer suggested. "I could do a lot if there were a few groups of captive spirits around to work on."

Experimentation was not an idea that held much attraction to Jenius. Letting a spirit as eccentric as Professer loose in a prison would promise immediate disaster. However, the opportunity of an army of Thought Processors, to enforce his laws, was attractive, especially if they were under his control. It was a suggestion that should at least be placed before the inner-council, and he said so, instructing Lard to add to the Agenda for the next meeting.

"Compresser's been doing the rounds. Members should be turning up soon and we'll be able to make some progress. I only wish we could get everyone on the same measure then we could speed up things," Jenius added.

"Aha. I've some ideas on that as well," Professer contributed.

Lard had difficulty blocking his despair.

***

The first inner-council member arrived soon afterwards, encountering Kernel who, needless to say, failed to recognise him as an outsider. It was only when Spayed happened to drift by that his presence was discovered. The visitor maintained a total block on his past when challenged, partially relenting when told he would be escorted to the council leader.

"Good. That is what I want. I'm expected."

"No one's told me," Spayed complained.

"I'm not sure I am favouring your attitude."

"Tough, mate. I don't like yours, but I'm prepared to put up with it. Look at it my way. I got a job to do. I don't like that either, but I'm doin' it. You won't tell me who you is and I don't know you. What would you do?"

The visitor suggested that he would twitch a lot more politely and stop using silly human dialect. Then he gave way by revealing he was a member of the inner-council. Spirits don't lie, and with the admission being offered in unqualified fashion, backed up by partial unblocking, his status was accepted. Spayed, with continued bluntness, still managed to enquire why he hadn't bothered to mention the fact in the first place.

Hedstrong and Upstart arrived in time to witness the confrontation, and Spayed happily delivered the guest to them.

"You can take him to Jenius," he twitched. "It's about time you did something instead of just swanning around like you owned everything."

"Whilst I am in admiration for the effectiveness of your security," the visitor said, "perhaps a lesson in politeness might be of assistance to your colleague. I'm Frenco, by the way."

Upstart, who had met him at previous gatherings, welcomed him as their first inner-council guest, apologising for the rough reception he'd received. He was conducted to the library and introduced to two of the permanent residents, charged with and still willing, despite what they now felt was Lard's duplicity, to accept their spiritual duty to act as hosts. They offered Frenco the choice of several volumes on the second shelf on the left, leaving him to recover from his journey before providing a recharge of energy for his meeting with Jenius.

"Perhaps we should find Spayed," Upstart suggested. "Tell him to be a bit more courteous next time."

"D'you think it would do any good?" Hedstrong asked. "He's doing a job he doesn't want for which few will thank him. If we push him too far he'll be off. Would you like his responsibilities?"

Upstart conceded she would not but was still vibrating at the suggestion that she was doing nothing. She considered the accusation to be grossly unfair. Hedstrong agreed 'grossly' was inappropriate, but suggested 'unfair' wasn't entirely inaccurate – not from where Spayed was twitching.

"Because I like my job, especially my partner, perhaps we might do a little more 'swanning around' before our duties as mansion hosts really begin to demand our attention," he suggested mischievously.

It wasn't long before that attention was needed. Compresser had performed his rounding up well. Somehow all the inner-council members, or Thrillators, as they were called, arrived within the measure. Most of them were spotted by Spayed, who had taken up residence as outside doorperson, coupled with frequent circling of the whole building. Experienced spirits didn't always have the courtesy to bother with main entrances, a habit which irritated him and guaranteed his customary greeting. They were quickly rescued by either Hedstrong or Upstart, or both.

Upstart did try to take Spayed to task, suggesting that he could be a mirco-measure more polite, to which he confirmed Hedstrong's prophesy by replying that if she thought she could do the job better she was welcome to take over. She would have persisted except she suddenly realised most visitors saw no objection to his style. In fact he was becoming quite a celebrity in his own way, and beginning, secretly, to enjoy himself.

"They say it adds character, which is what they'd expect in

such an ancient mansion," Upstart told Hedstrong when the two were alone together.

"No accounting for taste," he observed, "which I'm learning, in our Real World, seems to be as diverse as in humanity."

***

Lard made a mansion inspection whilst the guests were settling in. A report from the library revealed some initial minor difficulty when it was discovered that different guests from different parts of the planet had developed differing methods of re-boosting. Fortunately Professer came to the rescue, introducing them to the wiring and indicating power and light points where they could help themselves. He'd abandoned another project to spend time studying the different techniques, explaining to all who would listen that it was a significant barometer of higher levels of development. No one bothered to enquire what he meant.

Spayed was asked to confirm he had security organised to ensure that the inner-council meeting could be held in secret.

"Don't be daft," he twitched. "How the hell d'you expect me and Baybe to patrol the whole place? It's a lot of good us protecting the dining room doorways when anyone can come through the floor, the walls and ceiling."

Jenius had joined Lard and explained it was a problem that had been experienced elsewhere. When there'd been need to discuss matters of extreme secrecy, which wasn't often, the Thrillators had been gathered in a large open space, surrounded by an exclusion zone with sufficient depth to distort any twitchings. Extra guards had been commissioned to ring the outer perimeter.

"If we need to, there's plenty of space in the grounds. That's one of the reasons why we chose this place," he explained.

"And who'd be responsible for finding enough volunteers to circle you lot?" demanded Spayed.

"Don't worry, that's left to the Thought Processors. They'll always be available when members of the council meet… not that you'll often sense them. They'll be about in or around the dining room, so you and Baybe can just hover by the doors if you like. Until they're familiar with the place, it's surprising how few gatecrashers realise they needn't use the usual entrances and exits. There's always a chance of flash-fusing with a hidden power supply, and we all know what that can do."

None of those within twitching distance had the temerity to admit they had no idea what it could do, but most resolved to be more careful in their wanderings in future. Flash-fusing didn't seem something they would enjoy. Spayed likened the Thought Processors to secret police and threatened to go straight out into humanity if they got in his way. It was left to Baybe to pacify him and, whilst she did so, more than one of the mansion residents noted that the proximity demanded by their 'bouncing' responsibilities seemed to have created what might be described 'an amorous bond' between the two.

"I shouldn't be surprised if they didn't enjoy a quick recharge together now and again," Upstart twitched to Hedstrong when they were alone in Paradise.

"Real life's getting really complicated," he replied. "Every measure I seem to be coming up against more difficulty." Again he began comparing their Real World discoveries with humanity, asking if there was any true difference. He felt that too many emotions were creeping in and could possibly destroy it.

"You've also come up against me," Upstart suggested. "D'you call that a difficulty?" She proceeded to prove it wasn't in the only way a female spirit in the Real World could.

CHAPTER 15

CONFRONTATION

C ompresser was having a day off. He'd worked hard to assemble the 20 Thrillators comprising the inner-council and the meeting was over. All the visitors had left for their customary abodes elsewhere on the planet. He visualised them reporting to other gatherings who would further deliberate amongst themselves. He knew they would complain about the activity, or lack of it, object to being kept in the dark whilst decisions were being taken, suggest that they were being singled out for victimisation, or ignored whilst their problems increased, wouldn't they?

He'd materialised as he often did these measures. It was a sort of comfort, and the concentration needed to keep his form in contact with the surface took his attention away from more spiritual cares. That was how Hedstrong sensed him, wandering through the grounds of the mansion between the trees. He, too, was taking time off whilst Upstart did something or other in the walled garden. Jenius wanted a report for further implementation of what he claimed came from one of the inner-council decisions.

She'd asked Hedstrong to accompany her until she read his unblocked thoughts. Then she suggested it may be better if he kept his distance until her project was over. The openly displayed opinion of her lover that the whole idea of civilised progress was no more than a desire of Jenius to impose his authority might well have proved inappropriate.

"Those were dangerous views, aren't they?" Compresser twitched, also having caught the thoughts in an earlier unblocked moment.

"Yours aren't always entirely loyal," Hedstrong replied.

Compresser's immediate agreement was a major surprise. The big man, checking no human was near enough to create a fuss, dematerialised to allow the two to drift on together, consumed in their own world. It was Compresser who twitched first.

"You don't think you're the only one who wonders where we are going, do you?" he continued. "I'm not so sure all the effort to centralise everything is working, you know. After all, it's what the humans are trying, isn't it, and can't you see where it's getting them? Disintegration of local communities, lack of responsibility for anything bad, isn't it? I do believe that, one day, they will end up with the whole of their planet population bogged down in mechanical domination, except for one little man. You can see him, can't you, working away, and the rest would be organising him, wouldn't they?"

"Why a man? Why not a woman?" Hedstrong wanted to know.

Compresser expressed surprise at his even raising the point. "There was a time," the monk expanded, "when women chose to remain in the background, promoting an image of male superiority, didn't they? At least they gave the impression the male humans were the stronger of the two, physically and mentally, didn't they? Now women even challenge that, openly taking control, aren't they? Can you see one of them allowing the rest of the human world to organise them? No. It has to be a man, isn't it?" The monk's greatest fear seemed to be that human women, having been superior to men from the start, were obsessed with reducing themselves to a male level, which, in his view, meant that they then drove their masculine counterparts to a lower level before endeavouring to follow.

"That's the sort of thing we should be investigating, don't you see?" he twitched. "When we enter them, we don't even know how great our Real World influence is upon them, do we? Let's face it, we haven't even discovered why we do have males and females in the Real World, have we? At least in humanity it's the device to allow survival, by breeding, although, the way they're going, even that won't be necessary for long, will it? But we don't need to breed, do we? We're here and, barring conflagration, we're here for infinity, aren't we?"

"What's conflagration?" Hedstrong wanted to know.

Compresser expressed further surprise he hadn't come across it and was happy to explain. He'd actually witnessed it with Professer, who had, for once, then completed a well presented study on it, although even that raised more questions than it answered. They were conducting a routine operation involving one of their companions. She'd decided to try to bridge the sex gap and launched herself into a man in a somewhat artificial manner. Whilst human males could support a female side, the method of spiritual entry had been too drastic, the reaction so electric that the human had simply burnt out. The combustion had been from within, which meant that there'd been little left of skin and bone, apart from charred remains. The poor man's garments had been untouched by the inner fire.

"So far as we know, the reaction consumed our fellow spirit as well and, you know, she ceased to exist, didn't she? At least, if she didn't, we can't find her, can we?"

"So you think that's why we have male and female spirits, for female and male humans?" Hedstrong ventured. "I must admit I've always gone for human men and assumed others have done the same."

"It's not quite that simple, is it? Some have tried the cross gender route and there's nothing to suggest it hasn't been successful, most of the time, you understand?" Compresser said. "What it does to the human is still the subject of several of our investigations, isn't it?"

The two continued their discussion on a telepathic level instead of twitching, neither willingly admitting they didn't know the answer to the questions thrown up by their debate. So engrossed were they that eventually they had to leave Paradise in search of a boost to replace lost energy.

"Let's try the shop, shall we?" Compresser suggested. "We may discover our friendly human witch and we can have a bit of enjoyment, can't we?"

"You've investigated her, then?" Hedstrong asked. "How d'you know she's friendly?" He failed to receive an answer whilst they accelerated through a few trees towards the walls of the converted farm buildings housing the shop.

***

Both spirits had virtually completed their boost before it dawned upon Phyllis that there was a presence. She had a shop full of customers, all elderly, and all of whom had staggered in from a coach trip. Whilst two volunteers took money in return for books, postcards, photographs, jam, drinks, trinkets, and the other odd items of merchandise typical for stately home visitors, Phyllis wandered about trying to spot thieves. It took concentration to identify the spiritual gatecrashers and, when she succeeded, Compresser was about to interfere with the electronics of the till.

"Don't," she told him.

For a moment he didn't know where the instruction came from. None of the humans seemed to respond, and it took a few mini-measures more for him to grasp that Phyllis had not used the spoken word. She'd actually twitched at him. He was sufficiently startled to suggest to Hedstrong that the shop was perhaps not an ideal location for their sport. Again Phyllis twitched, inviting them to stay.

"You can help by spotting the shoplifters. They cost us a fortune."

Hedstrong detected what he felt was the influence of Antedote and conveyed the thought to Compresser who agreed.

"Madam," the monk twitched imperiously, "it is not for us to do your work, is it?" Whilst they were taking their leave he added, "but you might remind that old bloke with a beard that his limp, impressive though it may be, does not justify his staggering out with an unpaid for walking stick, does it?"

Light refreshments were being served in the temporary facilities across the yard and they considered a bit of interference with the food preparation before they became aware that Phyllis had followed them, chasing the old man, who was also moving in the same direction.

"Thank you for your assistance, but if that's all you can do, why don't you clear off to your own world and leave us alone?" she demanded.

"This is our world," Hedstrong told her.

"No it's not. It's ours."

"We share it," Compresser ventured, forgetting to turn the remark into a question.

"Stuff and nonsense," Phyllis snorted. A number of visitors looked at her and she realised she'd transferred from twitching to actual speech. "It's what we call the two cats that hang around. They were his Lordship's favourites," she explained, waving vaguely in the direction of the house. "They've probably gone off to the chapel. That's where they usually stay these days. We shouldn't really encourage them and we're told not to call them or draw attention to them, but they're so cuddly."

"You tell us not to mess about, and then you do just that?" Compresser twitched at her, "and you lie?"

"Feminine prerogative," she twitched back. "Now run along, there's good boys, and leave me to deal with this thief."

"You see? Did I not tell you how the female humans are behaving?" Compresser declared. The two spirits did as they were told, speeding along the drive to follow a small group of visitors into the chapel, still in the hope of entertainment. A volunteer, delegated to ensure no one stepped over any restraining rope, concealed the real reason for his presence by offering a short history of the place to anyone who might wish to listen plus several who would have preferred not to.

He was puzzled by some surreptitious whispers of 'Stuff' and 'Nonsense', especially during mid lecture, when those in the audience thought he wouldn't hear. Being highly strung at the best of times, he greeted with derision the explanation it was simply in search of cats named 'Stuff' and 'Nonsense'. His enquiring whether they thought he was born yesterday led to further escalation of the confrontation, assisted by Hedstrong who managed to dislodge a candle on the alter. The hapless volunteer demanded that all visitors clear the church and visitors, being visitors, lodged complaint. That reached the ears of the local National Trust management, who immediately reshuffled the voluntary pack, restocking the chapel with a sturdier member of the team. The confused, aggressive former incumbent was relegated to car parking duties.

"So predictable, isn't it? See what we can do?" Compresser twitched to Hedstrong, the two having hovered about to witness the conclusion of the incident.

"Except we didn't inspire it, that human female did," Hedstrong observed. He again wondered how much influence Antedote was having upon Phyllis the witch.

"Don't let Professer get wind of those thoughts, will you?" Compresser warned whilst the two were travelling through a few walls in search of a now much needed booster point before returning to headquarters.

***

Back at the aviary they found Lard and Jenius still involved in deep twitching. They were not alone. Compresser detected the presence of a Thought Processor the moment he entered through the roof, and alerted Hedstrong, who was following

"It's no good you taking that attitude," Jenius told him, reading the twitch. "They've a job to do and they do it well. And it would be of benefit to the Real World if you two stopped playing about with humans. It's so childish." He thanked the Thought Processor for his report and dismissed him. Compresser, who couldn't believe he'd missed detecting the spirit who'd obviously observed them in the shop, made sure he'd left their presence before moaning at having spies monitoring his every move.

"You know it's not like that," Jenius twitched back, irritably. "He was performing a task for me and just happened to witness what was going on."

"And just happened to surge back here and tell you, didn't he?" Compresser grumbled. "It's coming to something when a spirit has to watch his every move for fear of details sneaking back to base, don't you see?"

Lard assumed his usual task of pacification, explaining that the description of activity of Compresser and Hedstrong had been no more than a casual remark within a detailed record.

Compresser wanted to know what was being reported upon and was told that Professer had been in the vicinity. He was being trailed to discover why, but had detected the Thought Processor's presence and cleared off in another direction. Apparently there was some concern that, despite an order from Jenius to keep away, he'd been observing Phyllis the witch.

"What of it?" Compresser demanded. "Why shouldn't he observe her?"

"Because she's to become the subject of specialised research," Lard told him, "and you know how haphazard Professer can be."

Compresser enquired why the Thought Processor had been involved in trailing Professer when a simple twitch in his, Compressor's, direction would have been sufficient.

"I am perfectly capable of keeping him under control, don't you know," he argued. "If he's found out he's been under observation by them, you know what that will do, don't you?"

"As it happens I don't, and I don't want to," Jenius replied. "Anyway, you've more important things to attend to."

"Such as?"

Jenius explained that they'd been working on details of

increasing the number of Thought Processors which, it was considered, were now required to enforce the regulations he was introducing. Compressor wanted to know what regulations and was told they were intended to achieve some spiritual conformity in the Real World. With prompting from Lard he'd accepted that approval of council members should be obtained before the new contingent could be put in place, so Compresser was needed to do a tour to obtain inner-council votes. This would be a swifter, simpler method than having to call an actual meeting.

Compresser asked if it was wise to seek such one-to-one authority without first allowing the opportunity for full communal discussion. He was told it was in the interests of expediency. He asked what he should do if a number of members objected and demanded a full meeting? At first Jenius tried to suggest he could overcome any reaction simply by using his tact and diplomacy. When this didn't work he threatened delegating the Thought Processors to accompany him to ensure he achieved his purpose, and when that resulted in Compresser offering his resignation he had to rely upon Lard rescuing the situation.

In his usual manner, the newly appointed council general secretary sought to assure Compresser that they had full confidence in his ability to perform the task and, of course, to suggest a Thought Processor was needed to accompany him was just one of Jenius's ways of teasing. By voicing it as an opinion he was able to avoid telling a lie and, with more placating platitudes – which stretched veracity to the limit – he managed to bore Compresser into submission.

"I'm not doing it on my own, d'you understand?" the monk declared.

"Take Hedstrong," Lard suggested. "It will give him some experience of the rest of the planet."

Hedstrong was shocked at the idea of leaving the safety of the Estate without embodiment in a human, but he liked Compresser. He was warming to the proposal when Upstart joined them, complete with the information Jenius had required from the walled garden. She checked Hedstrong's thoughts and endorsed his embarking upon the mission, provided that she went too.

***

A full measure of preparation passed before the three declared themselves ready for the journey, mostly due to Compresser's attempt at organising Professer into an activity which might keep him out of trouble until they returned. At a meeting in the aviary, Professer objected to Compresser's interference, declaring he would pursue his own devices, thank you. Jenius warned that he was in danger of forcing Thought Processor intervention, causing further friction and ending up, despite Lard's diplomatic attempts, in the learned spirit accusing Jenius of high-handed, doctrinaire, dictatorial despotism.

With Professer surging off into Paradise, chased by a Thought Processor, Compresser followed, telling the rest of them his mission would have to wait until he'd sorted things out, wouldn't it? After a search through the grounds, and a fruitless visit to the shop, which earned him a sharp rebuke from Phyllis still having trouble with elderly shoplifters, he eventually discovered the disgruntled academic in the mansion games room, trying to influence a red ball to move along the snooker table into the middle pocket.

"Why are you doing that?" he asked.

"Why not?" came the reply. "Is it another offence? Another regulation introduced for the good of Reality?"

"Don't be daft. Jenius is just trying to bring about some conformity and centralisation into our world, isn't he?"

"You know as well as I do where that will get us. He's become obsessed with his own importance. Thinks he can do just what he likes."

"How can you twitch that when he's just delegated me to seek an inner-council decision before he acts? That's democratic, not dictatorial, isn't it?"

"That's window dressing and you know it."

"If you think so, come with me and make sure it's democracy, won't you?" It was Compresser's final attempt to ensure Professer didn't fall into the hands of the Thought Processors, aware their unguarded twitching would be fully reported to Jenius.

"All right I will," Professer decided.

"Good, then let's get back to the aviary and tell the others, shall we?"

Professer was already on his way leaving Compresser and the Thought Processor to follow in his wake. None of them had taken note of the two eavesdroppers who had been drifting quietly in one corner of the games room, possibly because their signal had been muted. They were sorely in need of a recharge.

"That were interesting," Spayed twitched to his companion.

"What d'you think they're up to?" Baybe responded.

"Don't know, but I'll bet it's nothing to keep our freedom. It won't help the likes of me and you, that I can tell you. Professer's right. We got a dictator in our midst. Look at all that's happened since he arrived."

"We happened," Baybe reminded him. "That's not bad, is it?"

"You knows it's not, but we would've happened anyway. It's natural."

"There was a time when it wasn't. But let's not worry about something we can't do nothing about. Come on, it's time for a charge."

They too, having found the thrill of sharing an electronic surge, dived onto the nearest power point and were soon swooning into each other's presence, blissfully unaware they were breaking another regulation Jenius had just introduced – using an undesignated point of power. If discovered, they would be subjected to punishment, if only their leader could find a method by which he could dish out punishment.

CHAPTER 16

EXPEDITION

t took all Compresser's skill to persuade Jenius that Professer should join his mission. He described it as a valuable opportunity for the learned spirit to add to his knowledge. Jenius told him the suggestion was no more than a device to keep his friend out of trouble, a view Compresser could not deny. Lard intervened to suggest both might be accurate and Professer declared he didn't care what they all thought, he was going anyway. He cleared off before the others could clarify whether he was referring to the mission or something else.

Jenius said that, if Professer joined the group, he would have to let one of the three Thought Processors go with them, but, surprisingly, Upstart managed to calm things down by claiming her presence would be good enough. She was a Thrillator. Surely she could be relied upon to report back without Thought Processor help.

"After all," she said, "in anticipation of a favourable vote from the rest of the council, you will need all three Processors to work with you to formulate the training programme. You do intend to train new recruits, don't you?"

Although stressing it was not a final decision he'd taken, Jenius acknowledged that it had occurred to him to give the proposal his full consideration during the delegation's absence. Upstart pressed home her point. It seemed the research she'd carried out for him in the walled garden was relevant to his formation of an enforcement squad, and she suggested it would only be natural for him to take some preliminary steps. She felt his desire to instigate an initial provisional recruiting of personnel ready for instruction, should the Council approve his idea, including how they would be trained and where the recruits would be accommodated, would be better explored without the worry of others around him.

"I take it you will have the force based here. That was why you wanted my detailed description of the walled garden and orangery, wasn't it?" she twitched.

Jenius said it was not her business to question his motives in requiring reports. With skill and simplicity Upstart registered offence and disappointment at his attitude. Compresser frequently claimed it was one of her typical womanly attributes, or dangers, whichever way you looked at it, don't you? She won an apology upon which she worked to achieve the leader's agreement to her part of the mission. All three Thought Processors would remain within the mansion grounds as valuable assistants in the preparation for recruitment and indoctrination of the anticipated security force.

That motivated Compresser's withdrawal of another untwitched but, nevertheless, apparent threat of resignation and Hedstrong went in search of Professer. He found him in Paradise, lodged in one of the larger trees, contemplating a human family of five who were having a picnic. A few more mini-measures and Hedstrong knew he would have been gone, embarked upon another human trip.

"That would be an admission of defeat," he twitched.

"What makes you think there's a war?" demanded Professer.

"You do. You can hardly conceal your Thought Processor feelings."

"Why should I? They're nothing but interfering, self-righteous, opinionated busy images who've got nothing better to do than get in the way." The strength of Professer's response was so great it shook the whole tree, showering the family he'd been studying with several small branches. "They'll be the ruination of the planet if they're not stopped. Jenius can't even see that. He thinks he can create and control an empire. He's ignoring the total human evidence around him. It's all right for their sort. Humans can often succeed in controlling the masses by force for one or two of their lives, but we're dealing with infinity. He can't do it. It's lunacy."

"He hasn't got approval yet," Hedstrong suggested. "Maybe a majority won't agree."

"And you think that'll stop him?" Professer created another shudder, but the human family had moved away and the falling branches missed them. The effort and emotion left him deprived of electronic strength, Hedstrong, after gaining an assurance that he would not pursue another human entry and would join the travelling party, not now to be shadowed by a Thought Processor, gave the learned being a boost.

***

Meanwhile Compresser and Upstart had moved away from the aviary to prepare for their journey, not that there was anything to prepare. They didn't have to pack like humans, because spirits didn't have belongings. They didn't have to cancel newspapers, turn off the gas, water the garden, tell the neighbours, check the car or book tickets.

"That's for humans," Upstart twitched, reading Compresser's unblocked thoughts.

"I know, and that's what regulation is for... for humans. Why do we need it?"

"It's progress?" Upstart ventured.

"No it's not, is it? It's just blind ambition by one being to control the rest of us, don't you see?"

"Some of us could do with a bit of control . Take Professer," Upstart suggested. She went on in her gentle, sometimes flippant, manner to speculate upon what the learned spirit would get up to if it wasn't for the likes of Compresser restraining him. Give someone freedom, she argued, and they'll immediately want more, soon wanting more than everyone else.

"You can't stop experiment, can you?" Compresser told her. "Wouldn't you like to be free of humans?"

"Not especially. I liked taking a human life holiday before we latched onto their artificial energy."

They were joined by Hedstrong and Professer, on their way back from Paradise.

"What a stupid comment," Professer declared. "If they weren't creating energy they wouldn't be there and we wouldn't be here. How can anyone be so stupid. Don't you realise," he continued, twitching directly at Upstart, "humanity won't last for infinity? They're well on the way to annihilating themselves already. If we don't find a substitute supplier of power, directly or indirectly, we'll be finished too."

"No we won't," Hedstrong told him, seeking to defend his loved one. "We'll just return to our normal static state."

"And do what?"

"Wait, I suppose, for the next power source to come along. Destruction of humanity won't see the end of us."

"And you'd prefer to be stuck wherever you happened to be at the time, immobile. That's what you'd be faced with?"

The debate carried on for a while before Compresser got fed up with it and told them it was time to make a move. Hedstrong had no idea what to expect. He gathered that the others, including his beloved, were experienced expeditionists and asked where they would be heading. Being told it was first to the south-east of England he wondered how many power points they would need for recharges on the way.

Upstart, noting his predicament, explained that to use their own propulsion would call for too frequent boost stops. They would, therefore, latch onto human transport for most of the journey, only expending their own energy when absolutely necessary. All needed a bit of this before leaving the estate, but were soon through the trees, across the fields, beyond the hedge onto the adjoining public highway. Several vehicles were passing and Compresser opted for a large saloon, telling the others to follow. Hedstrong nearly missed it when it accelerated to overtake a slower vehicle but just managed to latch onto the rear fender before progressing through the back to join the others. Professer told him he'd have to be quicker than that if he wanted to keep up. Upstart told the Professer to have some consideration and to try explaining a few techniques instead of always being critical. She also told Compresser not to be so impulsive in selecting the transport, stressing Hedstrong hadn't done any of this before. Compresser didn't take kindly to the criticism, arguing that Hedstrong had travelled the planet whilst embedded in his human choices and should be able to keep up but, in an effort to maintain solidarity, promised to try.

Only after this initial exchange of emotion did the spirits begin to take note of their current surroundings. It was a comfortable limousine with the back vacant, allowing ample room for the four to settle and save power. A male and female, who occupied the front seats, were involved in an enthusiastic argument, so were totally unaware of any change in atmosphere.

The man was trying to explain that they had acquired the particular type of vehicle he was driving precisely to enable him to complete the manoeuvre he had completed with safety. The woman said that was not why they needed it. They required it as a status symbol. How else were they to demonstrate their success to their neighbours? If he didn't stop handling it so aggressively, she was going to get out and walk. The man responded with a burst of acceleration which took him past a lorry, but narrowly missed a police car travelling towards him.

"That's it. Stop the car," cried the woman. "I've had enough. You're going to kill us."

The Professer was speculating upon whether there may be any of their spiritual kind lurking within the human bodies, and whether they were about to be released back into the Real World, when the vehicle underwent a violent swerve into a car park.

"If that's the way you want it, we'll take the bus," the man said in a controlled voice.

153

"I intended to anyway," his companion replied, "but don't think I don't know why we're in here. You know that police car will be after us and you just hope they won't find us in here."

It was a large park with several hundred cars all uniformly arranged around a central turning circle. The man found a space and, whilst they alighted, the couple heard the police siren wailing its approach. They stood and listened until it faded into the distance.

"All right," the man conceded. "I shouldn't have done it."

"No, you shouldn't," the woman replied. "Come on, the bus will be there in a minute."

"What next?" Hedstrong asked.

"We catch the bus," Compresser replied. "This is a 'Park and Ride'. They park their cars and ride on the bus."

Hedstrong was just recovering from the experience of an up-to-date motor car. To him, if his recollections were accurate, a bus meant something noisy, dirty, open at the back with a driver up front and a conductor ringing bells and collecting money. During his last human trip it hadn't long replaced four wheeled structures drawn by horses but he was beginning to doubt his recall; another strange emotion.

They left the back seat of the Jaguar to drift over to the stop, and he was amazed by the number of cars scattered around the place. There had been a few in the mansion car park; quite a few in fact but nothing like this.

"What's that?" he wanted to know, twitching towards the large double-decker bus trundling into the pick-up area.

Upstart explained whilst they made their way towards it and entered through the roof. He wanted to explore so they drifted downstairs where there were more passengers. The couple they had travelled with were at the back, still arguing. He went to the front to watch the driver. Gradually he sorted out his recollections to recall his earlier bus experiences, some with two decks, but most unreliable, draughty affairs. They often flashed their way through city streets, many restricted to rails and most driven by electricity taken from lines hanging overhead to which they were connected by rods.

"They were trams and trolleys," Upstart told him, reading his projections. "They've gone now except for a few. But they may be back. You know what humans are like."

The two spirits drifted onto the windscreen from which Hedstrong could watch the driver and marvel at how easily she guided the big vehicle through traffic - hardly any effort on the steering wheel and no shuddering gear changes. He recognised the route from his last human experience and settled down to await a view of the dockland before they reached the city centre.

"Where's all the ships?" he twitched, when they were nearest to the waterside. "They've gone. It's all houses and offices. I can't see a boat anywhere, except that... it's an old one but it's all decorated and looks new, never like I remember her when I was in a human."

He was amazed at the changes, especially the blocks of flats where once had been dirty old warehouses, the neat pedestrian ways and roads where once cobbles and grime had survived the horse-drawn era. Then they were in the city centre where, again, new tall buildings towered above the old squares. Twitchless, he allowed the windscreen to point him at new view after new view. Buildings and traffic seemed to dominate each scene, pushing humans into a background within which they toiled, and hurried, and worried, and were seemingly oblivious to what was going on around them.

"It all seems so impersonal," was his only comment, repeated several times.

Upstart waited, reading his thoughts and allowing him the opportunity to grasp how much had changed in so few human years. During the time he'd spent secluded in the mansion much about the human order of life had evolved; a lesson it was important for him to learn before they began to work seriously upon their mission. Although there would be more for Hedstrong to face, nothing would leave an impression greater than this chapter in his first Real World journey beyond the grounds of the stately home where his enlightenment had begun.

**

At about the time the foursome were embarking upon their south-eastern journey, Phyllis was enjoying one of her customary moments of relaxation in Paradise, recalling visits she'd made to the estate in the past. From the first encounter with Richard, the Lord of the Manor, to the last occasion, just before his death, she'd cherished their time together. Despite the obvious deterioration of the house, she'd understood his determination to keep it going, leaking roofs, frayed stair carpet, rodent infestation and all. In fact, he'd explained that control of vermin was far better during his occupancy than in previous generations, when no one worried at the scurrying sounds behind the panels or under the floor boards. They accepted such goings-on were part and parcel of the life of the time.

She was wishing she could go back to the days when he would suddenly appear to catch her wandering between the trees… when there he was, standing just down the hill from the oak where she sat. He was watching her, waiting for her to spot him before he drifted up to join her.

"This is weird," she said out loud. He bade her hello. No voice, just an awareness he was addressing her. She knew he wasn't human. He was one of the apparitions she'd recently begun to see clearly. She changed to the newly acquired technique of twitching.

"You look just the same," she said.

"Maybe, but you know I'm not." He studied her for a moment. "I'm in a different world. I'm not the Lord you knew, although I can recall the times you two spent together. He cherished them. They were highlights in what was often a disappointing period of his human life." Lard paused again. "This is very strange, talking to a human, although you are a special one. You know that, don't you?"

"I'm not quite sure what I know," Phyllis told him. "But it is interesting. I'd like to know more."

She was about to ask a question, but Lard was gone. She thought of trying to follow, perhaps seeking him out in the mansion. She was sure that was where he would be heading, but no. The time would come, and she could be patient.

***

Many more surprises greeted Hedstrong upon the way to the south-east. He was so occupied with the sights before his eyes, he didn't even ask why they were destined for that part of the country. All four used human transport wherever possible, taking the train to the capital. This, again, was an experience for the struggling spirit... no first, second and third class carriages with side corridors, and no cramped compartments, each sealed off from the next to hold a maximum of eight humans. Gone were the windows that had to be hauled up and down manually by a leather strap, with the usual arguments when the steam from the engine fumed in, laced with the acrid smell of the burnt fossil fuel. One occupant, he remembered, always one occupant, would complain by motions rather than words that he was too cold or she was too hot.

There were still the same attitudes. Human sitting next to human ignoring each other in usual rehearsed, well practised way, but now the corridor was in the middle of the open carriage; windows remained shut and the atmosphere, he detected, was regulated by an artificially controlled temperature. Many of the humans were fiddling with electrical devices, pressing keyboards, talking to implements that gave off waves that interfered with spiritual atmosphere. There was no engine to the train either, just a streamlined nose, which forced out a greater pollutant.

"Don't be daft," Professor twitched, having studied his thoughts. "Of course there's an engine. It's diesel, fed automatically from liquid fuel. Surely the combustion engine was about when you were last away from the Real World."

Hedstrong confirmed it was, but not on railways and not refined to an extent that it could pull a trainload of people with an efficiency this journey to London was demonstrating. During his last trip, embodied in his human, there were engines, with drivers protected from the elements by no more than a sort of canopy which also housed dials, wheels and the levers he used. His mate shovelled coal from an open tender to burn at a temperature sufficient to keep the boiler producing the steam power. Oil and coal dust, essential elements of their job, had impregnated both driver and mate. His outburst caused Professer to take Hedstrong through to the modern cab to emphasise the contrast.

"You see?" he twitched, "another sedentary job. No need for use of muscles flexed in the past. Just more evidence of deterioration of the human form. That so-called driver'll have to waste time exercising if he wants to keep fit, but he won't. Few do, for long."

Hedstrong thought the comment a bit harsh, the Professer again wondering, unblocked, why a spirit so backward in experience had been allowed on their mission. The learned man was immediately reprimanded by Upstart, who'd joined them. She stressed the importance of having someone who could at least highlight the changes. How else, she demanded, could they continue to assess how long before humanity increased its speed of life to the extent that it ground to a halt and expired?

"She's got a point, hasn't she?" Compressor twitched. He too had arrived to make up the foursome in the cab.

"No, she hasn't," Professer countered. "Only an idiot would fail to note the stupidity of humans. I really don't know why I bothered to come on this trip. I should be getting on with other things. Exploring means of dispensing with humans… testing, experimenting."

"There we have the silliness of spirits," Upstart twitched to no one in particular. "So independent they just go off on their own, exploring the slightest whim with not a thought for how they may be wasting valuable measures or corrupting what others may be doing."

The learned member of the team was too far out of range to grasp the remark because she had ushered Hedstrong back through carriages into a toilet. He'd used up a lot of energy just floating about the train exploring and she wanted to be sure he was able to complete the journey across the capital to the next form of human transport. They latched onto the train's electrics to top up together, which was a mistake. Alarm bells rang, activating systems which automatically applied brakes and brought the express to a halt.

Human minutes were spent trying to find out who had done what before the journey resumed. As a result, the train arrived late in the capital and started a knock-on effect which took controllers several human hours to sort out. Passengers from numerous destinations moaned, first, that they were late and, secondly, that no one had told them why. Professer, discovering the cause of the chaos, complained at what he conceived to be another demonstration of spiritual ignorance but was told by Compresser to treat it as evidence of how humanity could be disrupted should the need ever arise.

Departing the train just before it reached the station, the four did some sightseeing. Hedstrong noted the increased influence of motor vehicles on Hyde Park - ever more an isolated, shrinking island - and remarked upon how clear the pedestrian walks were of prostitutes.

"You would notice that," Upstart twitched.

"It's mostly under cover now, isn't it?" Compresser told him. "A human trait you know. When it's hidden it can be ignored, and those organising it can specialise in greater depravity leading to higher profit, can't they? I understand there's a move to make the whole thing legal which would do no end of harm to the black economy which runs this part of the planet. Until someone developed some other form of forbidden excitement, isn't it?"

"They've already got it," Professer told him. "They drug themselves with herbs and then can ignore everything. It's easier than the sexual act and they can crawl into a corner on their own and live out their fantasies and their lives. I've seen the result. We're trying to analyse how it affects any of our kind who happen to be imprisoned in the human form at the time."

" Surely it has no effect," Hedstrong ventured.

The Professer ignored the twitch having already written off conversing academically with someone of such ignorance. Anyway they had to concentrate upon following Compresser when they sensed he'd materialised and was simulating a strut round the Serpentine Lake as a monk.

"Why does he do that?" Hedstrong demanded.

"It's his therapy," Professer replied, "and because he can," forgetting for a moment that he had decided against meaningful conversation, "but don't you try in your last apparel." Hedstrong wondered how Professer had discovered what his last apparel looked like.

"Simple," the learned gent replied. "I haven't, but I can guess from the time you were last in humanity."

"That's something else that puzzles me. Why, if we materialise, do we always have to appear in the same clothes and style as the last human we entered and why can't we see each other?"

"Does it now?" Professer twitched. "That's the first intelligent observation you've made since we started. Keep enquiring and you may become useful."

Compresser dematerialised and came to the rescue. "Now, now," he began, "let's keep things civil, shall we? We have a mission to accomplish, remember?"

"Some mission," the Professer retorted.

Hedstrong was about to respond when he was suddenly aware

how close Upstart was. She gave him a quick boost and the sensation eliminated all other feeling. He really enjoyed the moment and it was just as well he was captivated by his lover's electronic embrace and didn't latch on to Professer's disapproving twitch.

CHAPTER 17

INNER-COUNCIL

L ard had little trouble selling the idea of what he called 'Co-ordinator' to Kernel. Painting it as promotion for past services, he soon had the spirit drifting in military fashion round the orangery, inspecting the adjoining walled garden and checking points of power. It was a simple task. Declaring himself satisfied whilst Lard hovered nearby, he paused, uncertain what to do next. He'd grasped the importance of the project and the significance of his role in it, but wasn't sure exactly how he fitted into the scheme of things. Not that that mattered too much, provided others acknowledged his position and title.

"It won't be long before the force begins to build up," Lard told him. "They'll need co-ordinating into a squad and preparing for training."

"Right," Kernel replied. "Right. Er, exactly what sort of training?"

Lard told him not to worry about that. Jenius would be arranging the training. What he had to do was to have the squad ready and waiting. He likened it to one of Kernel's human military trips, having him picture men and women lining up, standing to attention, in uniform, awaiting inspection."

"I get it," Kernel responded. "You want me to get them on parade, ready for drill, army style."

"Exactly," Lard told him.

Kernel wanted to know if he was to be expected to drill them and was relieved to hear that he was not. He asked if he was to greet them and arrange their accommodation but was informed that nothing else was expected of him. The three original Thought

Processors would allocate permanent locations in which each recruit would be expected to reside unless called to duty. Authority with little call for active responsibility; that fitted in well with Kernel's reacquired state of being, the one to which he had returned after a few measures of vitalisation following his brief human encounter with the clock repairer.

Next Lard tackled Spayed and Baybe. After the departure of the inner-council members, their bodyguard routine had lost impact. Boredom had set in, leaving them with nothing to do except play tricks on human visitors to the mansion – frequently verging upon materialisation each time they indulged in joined power surges. There was one occasion when they actually appeared at the front door, Spayed in gardener's guise, Baybe drifting appropriately in his arms, her last trip having, of course, ended whilst her human was still a day or so old. Reaction from the Trust volunteers confirmed they looked like visitors but were forbade entry of unsuitable footwear. Lard offered them membership of the TPT.

"What's that?" Spayed enquired, managing to make his twitch echo suspicion, caution and aggression in one combined flash.

"You needn't be so confrontational," Lard replied. "It's the Thought Processor Force."

"Then why's it called TPT?" Baybe wanted to know. "What's the second 'T' for?"

Seeking to avoid being placed at a disadvantage Lard blocked his thoughts until inspiration hit.

"Team," he twitched casually, recalling earlier debate on the subject. "The 'T' stands for team, because that's what it is, a 'Team' building operation."

"That don't seem like fun to me," Spayed complained. "I think we'll stay as we is thank you, if you don't mind." Even in his time away from the Real World the spirit had always gone for a particular labouring type of human which had afforded him substantial experience in how to do nothing, convincingly.

Lard explained the alternative: staying in the mansion, with constant reporting to and from the aviary several times a measure under the close surveillance of Jenius. Spayed began to weaken. He agreed to see if he liked what was available in the Orangery, which was at least a quarter of a mile from the House and Aviary.

Partial blocking enabled Lard to conceal the fact that the couple would be answerable to the three original Thought Processors and would be organised by Kernel. He considered it best to stress the positive before facing up to the negatives. This he mentioned to Jenius when he reported back to the aviary.

"Don't worry. Those three Processors know their job. They'll have all the recruits softened up and under control before any become aware what's going on, and then they won't have any option but to stay. They'll take orders all right. That's what they've inherited from their human trips. Without someone bossing them they'd have nothing to complain about."

"We do seem to be more and more influenced by our trips into humanity," Lard twitched. "It should be the other way round. We should be influencing them."

"We've got enough trouble controlling Reality without bothering about humans," Jenius replied, leaving Lard with the quickly blocked impression that their leader might just be drifting a little from the original purpose of their existence, whatever that was.

***

It was a day off for Phyllis. She spent a large part of it just sitting, or strolling about in her garden, thinking. Much was going on at the mansion that she didn't understand. Somehow she'd inherited a new energy and this had enabled her to detect spiritual presence more effectively than ever before.

She could see into and communicate with another world. She wasn't sure what world or if it was one she would ever join. At times it was becoming embarrassing, like the occasion when she had been forced to invent 'Stuff and Nonsense' to explain her conversation with the spirits. She would have to be more careful, otherwise she may lose her position and that would deprive her of easy entry to the mansion. A good job Bernard's smitten, she thought. He was well liked and trusted to hold down a responsible job on the estate, even though she could never quite establish what he was supposed to be doing. She resolved to ask him when they next met, which was in less than an hour.

Whilst she put the finishing touches to her appearance, arranging her deep black hair so it flowed loose over her shoulders, she considered how the relationship was developing. There'd been a break since the last man in her life and it had taken her a little while to adjust. She was fond of male companionship, on her terms. She was attractive, she knew that. Men admired her and she kept her figure in order although, perhaps, it had spread a little, for her height. She'd confessed as much to Bernard and he'd made the mistake of agreeing, fortunately adding that it was only in the right places. He'd meant it to be a compliment but, on their first date, he'd come close to guaranteeing it was their last.

Easing into her high heels, she lifted her summer dress to study her legs in the full length mirror. Yes, they would do. Encased in black stockings they remained one of her greatest physical attributes and she was using them to good advantage with her current conquest. He was the type she preferred. Uncertain, inexperienced in relationships and thrilled at the chance of being with her. He would do. He could be moulded and, perhaps, just perhaps, she would let him into her secret life. But not yet. There were several hurdles to negotiate first and it was time for her to lead him to the next one.

After that first date, they'd dined out together. They'd been to the theatre. They'd surreptitiously met in the grounds of the mansion and she'd let him kiss her in Paradise. At first he'd been hesitant, their lips barely touching. She liked that. It gave her a chance to keep the initiative, gently encouraging him. When they'd reached an extra quiet spot, hidden from the main view, he'd suddenly responded with an urgency of desire that had surprised her. It always surprised and excited her when a man became aroused in her company. She'd let him press her tight against a tree, hold her in his arms and secure a lingering passionate kiss.

They'd remained entwined for several minutes, hugging each other, and she'd allowed him - indeed encouraged him - to explore her body, guiding his hand until the message registered, exciting him even more. The sound of an approaching lawn mower had saved her the trouble of terminating the interlude before things went too far. They'd crept back to the reception area, she to resume control of the shop whilst her conquest disappeared about his business.

Now he was coming to dinner. It was time for the next step. She heard the crunch of car wheels on her gravel drive and, with one last check to ensure that the bedroom was ready, she went downstairs to meet her guest. The table was laid, food prepared for a final microwave touch in the kitchen whilst the lounge-dining room awaited, decorated with what, to the inexperienced eye, might appear to be a host of gently burning perfumed candles. They offered just the right level of incense she needed. A wave of enchanting aroma followed her to the front door to greet him.

"What a wonderful smell," Bernard couldn't help himself saying, allowing his eyes to become accustomed to the darker hallway. Then he saw her. "You look beautiful," was all he could manage, but his body language expressed a sufficient cocktail of admiring, lusting, loving, devoted emotions to confirm to Phyllis that tonight was definitely the one to tackle the next hurdle.

***

Yet again Professer's patience was wearing thin. Several useless measures had passed whilst the team awaited response to

Compresser's message, issued to an inner-council member. Hedstrong had previously tried to question why they were static in a coastal town when he'd thought they would be doing a one-to-one tour of bases where each of the Thrillators resided. His enquiry had been met with a disgruntled response from Compresser. If Jenius thought he, Compresser, was about to tour the planet to talk to each individual he was mistaken, wasn't he? Anyway it wasn't necessary, was it? He, Compresser, had had words with the inner-council members following the meeting at the mansion and agreed they hover along the coast down here until he was in touch, hadn't he? Lard wasn't the only diplomat, was he? and where would they all be without the monk's calming administrations? Did anyone think the Thrillators were happy with the 'goings-on'? Wasn't it better to have them on hand, yet well away from Jenius's clutches?

Professer's intended endorsement of his annoyance at the delay was arrested when he suddenly sensed their foursome had been joined by others.

"Why the hell didn't you twitch your arrival?" he demanded irritably. "How are we to know you're here unless you tell us?"

"If you weren't so busy moaning, you'd have realised they were here, wouldn't you?" Compresser told him.

The gathering was in the main living room of a vacant third floor flat in the south coastal town of Eastbourne, dotted about odd pieces of furniture. The spiritual monk had known of the presence of the eighteen Thrillators the moment they entered, but he'd waited, allowing them to make the first twitch. The members of the inner-council, apart from Upstart and Hedstrong, had obviously got together beforehand and, after Professer had acknowledged their presence, Compresser enquired why? They explained that they wanted to present a united front.

"What does that mean?" Compresser asked. It was Frenco who replied. He seemed to have been elected unofficial spokesman.

"There is a lot going on that we are unhappy with," he

twitched. Pressed to enlarge upon his complaint, he said his fellow members of the inner-council felt that decisions were being taken without their participation. They felt they were often kept in the dark, and simply used as a rubber stamp to endorse policies that had already been adopted. Communication with the outside planetary representatives making up the whole council showed that these spirits felt they were even further from the controlling body and were becoming disillusioned, especially when their inner representatives couldn't give them answers to key questions. "And what is this TPT business?" he finished. "It seems to us that Jenius is trying to gather an army of personal bodyguards around him and he has begun to do so without consultations at all."

Compresser, after somewhat sarcastically complimenting them upon their access to updated head office information, tried to assure them that this was not so; that Jenius had despatched him and his colleagues to test the views of the inner-council and, of course, through them, other planetary members first, before implementation of the proposed reforms.

"Without even an inner-council meeting? No discussion, just a 'oui' or 'non' vote," Frenco countered. Compresser tried to suggest that if there were any doubts then, of course, Jenius would call a full formal meeting of Thrillators. This may have begun to pacify the guests had not Upstart left her thoughts partially unblocked. Perhaps it was an error on her part, Hedstrong tried to convince himself, although, observing how the meeting progressed, this seemed unlikely. Frenco immediately latched onto her unguarded moment which confirmed to him that she had completed a report to Jenius upon the suitability of a base for the force. He also discovered, thanks to her available recollections, that she believed the leader was already embarking upon his scheme. This backed up his previously gathered intelligence.

"They're only preliminary measures, isn't it?" Compresser tried, having read Frenco's intentionally unblocked response. "They can easily be reversed if you all disagree, can't they?"

"How is it that they can?" Frenco demanded. "He has already got the three Thought Processors around him. Once you have set them up there is no stopping them. They will perform in any manner he wishes so long as he is in control. They love it when they can exercise control. I think it is time that we took a break and us selected representatives have a discussion on our own. And that is not to include the two of you from the head office."

There was a mass exodus of eighteen Thrillators through the French windows, off the balcony, down into the garden square outside. It was so emphatic that it caused, what was later described in human Eastbourne circles, a minor hurricane. No real damage was done, except to the plants and bushes in Howard Square, but it was good for local interest. The incident won a report in the evening news bulletins with a few self-appointed experts grabbed off the street to explain the phenomenon. The spiritual head office team, abandoned by the Thrillators, had drifted down in the block to an occupied flat where they watched the news on a television screen.

To their amusement they heard an expert explaining that the sudden contrast in temperature, confined to the Square by the surrounding buildings, produced an anti-clockwise surge. Another favoured the idea of turbulence created by the high tide, or an aircraft or helicopter flying too low. Some residents complained of lack of warning, demanding a public enquiry which motivated the local mayor to promise that the matter would be fully investigated. He was countered by the opposition political party arguing that it was another example of bureaucratic inefficiency and bad planning.

To save cost, the programme producer ended the report with a piece from a feature several weeks ago. This had his 'correspondent' rounding matters off by questioning whether the emergency services were properly prepared for swift response and asking if lessons would be learnt to guard against a future similar happening, although, this time, she claimed, people were not injured and lives were not lost failure to fully investigate the incident could have devastating future results. So amused had been Compresser and Professer that they didn't immediately sense Hedstrong was not with them.

"He's gone after the other Thrillators," Upstart twitched.

"He's no business to..." Compresser started, before he acknowledged that having been appointed the twentieth member of the inner-council, he had every right.

"I'm too close to the enemy and you're only officers," Upstart reminded him. "He's a selected representative. It'll do him good."

"I'm not an 'officer'. You leave me out of this," Professer told them. "In fact, I've no idea why I'm here. Why am I here?"

"To keep you out of mischief," Upstart told him, and just saved one of the usual outbursts by adding, "and to help us prepare for the revolution."

CHAPTER 18
REVELATION

They seemed a likeable lot, not averse to a bit of mischief especially where humans were concerned. In addition to causing the mini-hurricane in Howard Square, the Thrillators swept though Eastbourne's streets. They whisked a hat off a father's head just when he was about to reprimand his young child for some minor misdemeanour, spilt a pint of beer in a drinker's lap because they thought he'd drunk too much, and interfered with vehicle electrics to cause a traffic jam in the centre.

With what they called their relaxation activity consuming a lot of energy, Frenco led them to an amusement arcade on the Pier for a recharge. Their final act of devilment was to all link onto the pier mains supply at the same time, causing chaos with the gambling machines, many of which coughed up their jackpots to the delight of unsuspecting players. Finally they gathered on the pebbles underneath for their conference.

Instantly they became serious, first establishing that nineteen were present, including Hedstrong who had located them simply by following their trail of mischief. Frenco assumed leadership and bluntly asked the 'mansion' spirit why he thought he should be accepted as one of them.

"Where did you stood in the scheme of things?"

"What d'you mean?" Hedstrong twitched.

"Where is it that your loyalty lie? Are you with us, or them? Who do you support?"

They were questions Hedstrong had not considered, and he found it difficult to formulate a reply.

"Take time," Frenco told him. "We will wait."

So began the next phase in Hedstrong's education. He decided to be straightforward and removed the partial block he'd begun to practice almost unconsciously, so revealing all to the meeting. His fellow spirits were impressed. Some reciprocated by removing theirs. Frenco was more cautious.

"We can see that you got a lot to offer, and you are certainly not cluttered with any thirst for power," he observed. "But there is this thing with Upstart. It could be what is called a distraction."

"It's not a distraction," Hedstrong twitched. "It's a recognition that there can be genuine feelings between us. I once believed I was meant to be on my own, moving in and out of humans without any recognition of what the Real World had to offer. Upstart has introduced me to a new sensation. I've come a long way since then, and…" Hedstrong paused in the realisation that he was on the brink of a major discovery. "I think there is some meaning to our being on this planet… that we are to achieve something."

"Welcome to the Real World," Frenco commented. "That still does not answer the question. Are you with them or us?"

Hedstrong admitted that he had not been aware that there was a 'them and us'. He asked for an explanation. The twitched responses revealed that there wasn't really a division; or at least there hadn't been until the Thrillators had created it. What they and members of the full council were concerned about was the organisation of Real lives in such a way that leaders emerged, seeking to control the rest. This had led to criticism and confrontation. From reading his unblocked history, they likened it to the measures Hedstrong had experienced with Antedote, only on a planetary rather than local scale.

"We have all had similar experiences," Frenco explained. "We are just a lot further along the line than you. Those who now seek control have made divisions. This way no one else has backing to challenge their leadership."

Hedstrong learnt of the conflicts that had begun to escalate, in manner similar to human behaviour. This had led to creation of the council. It had been heralded as an antidote to anarchy, promising Real World unity.

"The trouble is," twitched Frenco, "when you go for unity, it has to be organised. And you can see where that has got humans."

Hedstrong couldn't immediately see, needing more explanation before he began to get the picture. Spirits all over the place were beginning to form groups which were then electing smaller groups to introduce order into their lives. These smaller groups employed others to administer reforms. These employees assumed that they had licence to experiment with their own ideas, safe in the knowledge that for any mistakes they made they could explain they were only carrying out the policies of others who employed them. Those employers then passed the responsibility to those who had elected them and so things went on, with no one ever responsible for anything.

"It has become a disease with humans," Frenco explained. "At every level of their being you can find these groups – in politics, in business, in religion. Everyone always has someone else to blame for everything. It is always 'them' that is fault and 'us' that suffers. We worry our world go same way. We think Jenius go that way. He take control. He believe he bigger than us, thinking he can do what he likes."

Hedstrong still couldn't grasp the comparison with humanity until he sustained some more detailed twitching. He suggested that as they had only one council, which covered the whole planet, and only one administration, which the Thrillators were chosen to oversee, that was completely different from the humans who created many groups all over the place. He, as one of the chosen ones, was happy to accept responsibility for the actions of the Spiritual World Council.

"So you think we control Jenius?" Frenco pressed. "How?"

"Because if we disagree with his methods, he can be replaced as leader," Hedstrong argued.

"How? By whom?" he was asked.

"By those who elected him," Hedstrong twitched, but had to admit that he had no idea how he'd been elected, or by whom. He was reminded that he himself had been 'selected', not elected, and by Jenius. He was told so had all the other Thrillators, all chosen the same way, by Jenius. "But what of the other council members? Those who are not Thrillators, whom we can call upon for support if we need them?" Hedstrong asked. "Who selected them?"

"It was us," Frenco replied.

"So we can call upon them to meet and vote down anything we don't like, such as Jenius's idea of a Thought Processor Force," Hedstrong persisted.

"How?" Frenco asked.

"By having a full council meeting and having them express the views of the planet." Hedstrong was puzzled by the clearly transmitted amusement coming from the others. Controlling their mirth, they proceeded to complete Headstrong's induction into the workings of the planetary council.

It transpired that, over the measures, individual Thrillators had each been charged with the task of selecting a handful of candidates to make up the full council. Their recommendations had been communicated to Compresser who, in turn, had transmitted details to Jenius. Some nominations had been accepted and others rejected. Finally one hundred nominees had been established, each Thrillator being made responsible for a group of five or six. The selected general council members had then been charged with finding humans likely to visit various other parts of the planet, so they could enter them and then could return to the Real World in due course with sufficient knowledge to claim they represented that part of the planet.

"That must have taken some measures," Hedstrong observed.

"It is still going on," he was told.

"So some of these council members are still out there?"

He was told they would probably stay 'out there' without any means of transport back if their human happened to expire in a remote region. He asked how often the full council met and was told they had never met. He asked how the Thrillators had travelled to find representatives from these remote parts and was informed that they hadn't. They'd each simply selected a handful of willing spirits close to their location of existence, called them a representative of one 'country' or another, and sent them off.

"We've used human geographical listings, such as New Zealand, or Africa, or China," another inner-council member explained.

Hedstrong couldn't believe what he was hearing. The council members selected by the Thrillators all came from France, or Spain or Italy. They'd simply embarked for the various destinations, always having to gamble upon their carefully chosen human actually reaching there. Some had come back almost straight away. Others were still navigating the globe, still ensconced in their respective non-real word individuals. No one knew quite where, and only those spirits who had somehow found their way back had kept contact with the Thrillators.

"Travel is getting better," Frenco explained, "and spirits are getting better in selection of humans for trips. More council members return to Real World. They tell of visits to places, sometimes even where they should have been."

"It's a bit hit and miss, isn't it?" Hedstrong twitched. "The council is claimed to represent the planet and we are supposed to represent the council yet no one seems to know what's really going on in many parts of our Real World or the humans' world. It's a sham. A lie," he declared.

"It cannot be that," Frenco reminded him. "Spirits cannot lie."

"It seems they can distort the truth."

"Not quite," Frenco responded, but went on to concede that they were skating close to the borderline. "Jenius argue that we doing our best to represent whole planet, and we have no knowledge of anyone else doing same, so we are entitled to say we do. We suspect elsewhere, beyond what the humans call the 'developed nations' there may be others of us who organise, but we don't know. You know what means 'developed nations'? They is those groups of humans who have discovered a way of achieving superiority and keeping it by pretending to help the rest."

Slowly the Thrillators noted from his unblocked meditation that Hedstrong was getting the message. He'd quite a way to go, but he was getting there.

Collecting his thoughts, he realised Jenius had elected himself head of a spiritual planetary council, selected his inner-council, and through them created a 100-strong general council, the members of which never all met in one place at the same time. For planetary domination he relied upon what European sourced spirits could discover from trips in humans to various destinations, always supposing they ever returned.

"That is about right," Frenco confirmed. "And now Jenius is surrounding with force who will protect him from us and enforce his rule. Do you get idea?"

Hedstrong got the idea and began to appreciate where 'them' and 'us' came in.

***

Meanwhile, Phyllis was making steady progress. Her date with Bernard had gone according to plan and he was well and truly caught in her net. Sex, she concluded, was the easiest and most effective method of recruiting the assistance of her fellow beings. Years of experience had taught her how to blend candles and incense into an atmospheric influence over her chosen victim so she could gain dominance and mould him to her requirements.

Not that she had any diabolical intent. She liked Bernard and was forced to admit a sensual attraction towards him which, had he but known it, was to save him from many an unpleasant emotion. Her purpose in the surreptitious recruitment of her unwitting assistant was to enable the furtherance of her contact with the Real World. The phrase 'Real World' was not one she had grasped. In accordance with human custom she used the designation 'other side'.

To Bernard, the night of the dinner party had been one of the most glorious experiences of his life. Food, drink and incense had carried him beyond all restraint so that when he awoke the next morning, lying beside the woman of his dreams, it took him a while to comprehend that it was not all an illusion. He had to check he wasn't alone in his small, custom built flat on the City dockside, but actually had spent a physical night of actual passion and was still there, in her bedroom. The rest of the day, after he'd taken leave of his loved one, had been a blur of inconsequential routine, as were several subsequent days. At the mansion he maintained solid work, to the benefit of his charitable employers, but lived for moments of enthusiastic recreation whenever the chance came for him to meet Phyllis.

Their tours of the grounds during their rest periods were always to locations of her choice, with the orangery and walled garden targets for frequent visits. Whenever they paused, he would notice a change in his loved one. Somehow she seemed to drift into a different mood, which he mistakenly attributed to affection for him. He would put his arm around her and guide her slowly between the brick built enclosures and out into the open bedded area. When he knew they were alone, he would pause to seek her lips and she would respond to his kisses, but, especially in this part of the mansion grounds, even in his smitten state, he sensed she was different. Behind the closeness to him and the acceptance of his attentions, there was an alertness he could not understand.

Phyllis was cautious. She wasn't ready to explain her mood to him. She waited to be sure of her lover before she took him to the next stage. She was in no rush and, indeed, was compelled to admit that what she called this 'period of consolidation' had its enjoyable side. Although he managed employees and volunteers in the outside estate work, and did it well, Bernard was not averse to sharing the labouring. When he did so, he deliberately used the older, hands-on methods which helped keep him in good shape. A fraction short of male average height, he was still comfortably taller than Phyllis. She complimented him on his physique, declaring that, no matter how hard she tried, she couldn't find an ounce of surplus fat on his frame and she'd certainly tried. In the privacy of her perfumed bedroom, her explorations never failed to discover an erogenous zone which she manipulated to full effect.

For Bernard it was a blissful episode in a life which, until he'd fallen under Phyllis's spell, had at best been average and at worst dull. He had developed his appetite for physical activity during years as a professional footballer in the lower national leagues. Never quite good enough to attract premier grade he'd, nevertheless, accumulated enough cash to own his flat and avoid debt. True to his nature, he'd taken his role seriously, concentrating upon the game rather than the peripheral activities such as the alcohol and drug traps. He'd had his share of girlfriends, but none had managed to break through the inner mental barriers he automatically slid into place if a relationship began to threaten his livelihood. When he knew his footballing days were over, he'd taken it philosophically and started work as a postman. This had answered his need for continued physical exercise whilst he completed a college course in agriculture. The result was his current job which he again took seriously. He'd been thoroughly enjoying it to the exclusion of all else until Phyllis exploded into his life. She'd sailed beyond those mental barriers, ensuring that, for him, there was no return to the isolation he'd previously so successfully maintained.

When she was sure he belonged to her, Phyllis took the next step. It was a fine, sunny day and they were alone in Paradise, trees separating them from the mansion in one direction, the empty lake in another and the walled garden in the distance. It was not a public access day, so volunteer numbers were down and, apart from three select coach parties, work had been of preparation, maintenance and conservation. They were each satisfied with what they'd achieved, and Phyllis stood looking at her man, her back against the large tree where they had enjoyed their first kiss. The roots rose slightly from the ground, which meant that she gained a little in height allowing their eyes to meet.

"There's something you need to know," she began.

"What?" he replied dreamily, placing his arms around her neck and burying his head in her shoulder.

"I'm what a lot of people would call a witch."

"I know," he murmured into her hair.

"How d'you know?"

"Because you've cast a spell over me from which I can't escape. From which I don't want to escape."

"Bernie, I'm being serious," she continued. "I seem to be able to use skills others don't have. I see things they don't. It's sort of changed me."

"So?" he said, still into her hair.

"So I thought you should know and if you want our relationship it will be part of it." Bernard raised his head to stare into her eyes. "You're serious?" he said.

"I'm serious."

"And you can see things others can't," he repeated automatically. Suddenly her expression held a conviction, a knowledge that surprised him.

"Yes I can."

"What can you see?"

She had his attention. It was the moment to test his devotion. By way of an example, she explained that when they went down to the walled garden and looked between the scaffolding protecting the public from the orangery, she could see movement. Sometimes it was just shadows, and sometimes the shadows could assume shapes close to human forms. Even when she couldn't see anything, she was aware of a presence. She mentioned the occasion when she'd had to invent the two pet cats 'Stuff' and 'Nonsense' to explain away a conversation outside the shop. That made him laugh.

"Does it bother you?" she asked.

"Why should it?" He was still looking into her eyes. "I love you. You are what you are. That doesn't affect how I feel." His expression, especially in his eyes, confirmed his devotion.

"It's a good job I'm not a black witch," she told him. "Otherwise you'd suffer in all manner of ways."

He pretended to shudder at the thought and then grinned. "And I wouldn't like that," he said, "would I?"

CHAPTER 19

FRUSTRATION

"Well?" Upstart demanded, gently.

"Well what?" Hedstrong countered, playing for time.

"Darling, you know what," she urged. "We both know what the Thrillators are up to."

"That's the first time you've called me 'darling'. I think I like it."

"It's not and you only 'think'?"

The couple were alone on Eastbourne's beach, mingling in the sunshine with people sitting, walking, some bathing. Although the two spirits were not visible to human eyes, it was as if they were part of the scene, removed for a while from the purpose of their mission, relishing time spent together.

"Well, in human terms, 'darling' can mean so many different things," he told her. "From humour to threat, from love to pomposity, but the way you twitched it was... well it was nice."

"That's the way it was meant." Upstart paused a moment before adding. "I think there's nothing wrong with some human emotions, and love is one of them. The people of this planet love each other, their dogs, the freedom they kid themselves they've got, the wealth they strive for and then can't handle. Like most other items they touch, they abuse what they call love by letting their feelings drift to material things which are no more lasting than their lives, but love itself is good. I love you."

"I love you too, and it frightens me," Hedstrong told her.

Upstart wanted to know why, inspiring a long discussion upon how they were drifting into so many human ways. She suggested that fear was not a state spirits could really sustain because it either suggested a threat of pain, which could only be directed at a body, which they didn't have, or, alternatively, the unknown, which was associated with lifespans, and spirits didn't die. Hedstrong disagreed. He said it could relate to the emotions. Upstart had stimulated in him feelings he once thought formed no part of his spiritual world. Now they did, he wanted to keep them.

"Let's face it, if Antedote was still around she'd be less than enthusiastic about our relationship and would do what she could to break us up. I would be frightened of losing you." He paused, allowing his unblocked thoughts to drift between them. He was trying to cope with the concept that love, once it happened, created so many other emotions. Despite the benefit, these inevitably led to less acceptable states of mind. Hate, envy, possessiveness, deceit, aggression; the human afflictions he'd experienced in his trips beyond the Real World. That was what frightened him. "D'you see where I'm heading?" he asked.

"Tell me," urged Upstart.

"Well, over their past centuries, when two humans got together it was for a purpose: to produce offspring to keep humanity alive. Now that is often incidental and they are together simply because they gain from each other's company. They experience what they believe is physical pleasure which we can't, and which, anyway, from my expeditions into their lives, I know isn't pleasant at all unless it is mentally satisfying. The physical act is their means of a mental stimulation, or it should be. They don't always realise that and, in typical modern style, often abuse it. With us, it's sharing… a mental excitement without the need for bodily activity. It's being together."

"Aren't we being a bit physical," she twitched, "when we give each other boosts?"

That was it. That was what had triggered it all off for him. Upstart was right. Sharing with her was a very great pleasure. Added to that was his new-found ability to travel, which for him was now without the need to be confined to whatever human body he chose. He was looking at much more than he'd ever visualised.

He was looking at freedom, yet it all depended upon one feature – electrical boost.

"We still need the humans," Upstart reminded him. "They produce the power we need to be active. Well, *they* don't, but the generators they control do."

"And we get more like them every measure. That's what I really fear most." He pictured the greed, then the regulation to ensure others couldn't take from them. Bankers, solicitors, estate agents, accountants – they were all at it. Whole groups, sometimes called nations – or terrorists – were imposing rules and laws or chanting ideals to make or keep them superior to other groups around the planet, as well as endeavouring to keep each other under control. "That's what I fear. We seem to be trying to imitate them."

"So I have my answer to my initial question," Upstart twitched gently. "You are with the Thrillators. You don't like what Jenius is up to." She saw he was desperately searching to try to discover her feelings so she too left her thoughts unblocked. In typical female style they centred on the main issue: their relationship. She showed she was delighted with her lover's reaction, highlighting her feelings for him. It so electrified him he nearly materialised. There it was. She loved him as much as he loved her. She hated what Jenius was trying to do. She was also in support of what the Thrillators wanted. For a moment his fears were banished to another measure whilst they joined in a boost, leaving the street lamp they'd chosen smoking in the sunlight... for humans to repair in due course he conceded sheepishly.

***

Phyllis wasn't quite sure what was happening to her. Neither could she grasp the developing atmosphere in and around the mansion. Perhaps this was what always occurred when the National Trust took over a property. She remembered someone calling it a last resort to save the building from extinction although, with the farms, mountains, footpaths and other current possessions, she felt her participation was a very small part of a mushrooming force extending well beyond conservation. Perhaps the movement she had joined was now too vulnerable, too available for take-over by a group determined to convert it into a political voice, capable of influencing a nation.

So what? She had her own motives, which weren't entirely altruistic and her life really had begun to follow a new course. She continued her deliberations whilst she wandered through the mansion. She was on one of her breaks from the shop and she studied the crowds that trudged, group after group, through the rooms. Some listened to the details explained by helpers, others ignored the comments, waiting until the lecturer shut up so they could move on. One or two made their own way at a different pace to the rest, regardless of lecturers.

She wondered how many were trying to picture what the great edifice would have been like when fully occupied by family, friends and servants – a community, self-contained from the rest of the world, existing to its own rules and regulations. Calling on recollections of her time spent with Richard, the last Lord, she too tried to picture the complex duties and privileges of a workforce organised solely to give light and heat, water and food plus a bit of pre-central heating in an age before the outside world invaded to supply the lot. Then came the time when those greater comforts could be brought in, by pipes, cables and vehicles. Redundancy of a local way of life was inevitable, she concluded.

She began to see more and more of the spirits. First a movement, similar to what a poacher would recognise in the countryside or a soldier on patrol. Many would have ignored it, assuming a trick of light, but, for her, it was information. The poacher would freeze, look between trees instead of at them, see more movement and then spot the bird or animal. Phyllis applied similar tactics. First the spirits had been little more than an atmospheric presence. She'd been aware that they were there, but on the occasion she'd confronted Hedstrong and Compresser at the shop she'd observed more than a shadow or two. Then there'd been her confrontation with Lard.

Now, in the mansion, she detected clear visual movement. She followed it into to the kitchen and, before it disappeared through a wall towards the chapel courtyard, she caught a glimpse of a figure. A fellow volunteer greeted her, offering her some refreshment, but she declined politely. She wanted to be alone to concentrate upon what she'd seen.

Making her way out into the courtyard, she walked under the archway bridging house with chapel and down the drive towards the estate offices. She kept going past them to enter the walled garden via the intricate iron gate, and on beyond the hothouses. Rejecting the garden itself, she was drawn by more atmospheric disturbance towards the old orangery. That was when she saw them. Two soldiers standing in front of the scaffolding where workmen were continuing their task of rescuing the building. One was clad in the uniform of Cromwell's army and the other was clearly a Royalist. For a moment she thought they were human, simply dressed up for an occasion, until a workman walked through the Royalist as if he wasn't there.

Historically they should be fighting each other, she thought. She stood gazing at them, knowing she was the only human present who could see them. They became aware of her. Maybe they realised they could be seen, for they hurriedly disappeared into the cordoned off building. Phyllis couldn't follow, but when she peered though the transparent plastic coating positioned to protect against visitors and the elements, she saw more movement. Squinting in a manner she was slowly beginning to master, the movements materialised into figures. They were all soldiers, dressed in varying uniforms from differing past ages of combat.

The workmen began to take an interest in her, attracted by her intense gaze through the polythene, her head on one side and a strange expression overtaking her features.

"You OK, darling?" one of them asked, his tone and look registering approval of her neat figure and attractive features.

"I'm not your darling, thank you," she replied curtly before turning to stride away, not entirely immune to the whistles that followed her. It was good to know she could still attract male attention, and she made sure her walk kept them interested whilst she moved towards the converted building housing the estate offices.

***

Lard had witnessed the encounter between Phyllis and the workmen. He'd kept in the background as soon as he'd seen her approaching, remembering that somewhere within her body lurked Antedote. Since their encounter in Paradise he'd observed her hunting down of Bernard until she had him within her power. Was this just the usual behaviour of an extra perceptive human, he wondered, or had Antedote somehow inspired her increase in activity? Convinced that she could sense, maybe even see, the TPT force in the orangery he returned to the aviary to report to his leader.

"I wish Compresser was back," Jenius complained. "We need someone to keep an eye on her. She's probably harmless, but you never know. I could set the Thought Processors on her. Treat it as a sort of exercise, although we really should await Compresser's return with council authority to proceed. Even though it's a foregone conclusion."

"How could she be of harm, she's only human?" Lard asked.

"By interfering with my plan. I don't trust those Thrillators. The last thing we want is a distorted half human to deal with as well. I've got so far, I'm not prepared to have anything stop me now."

Lard said nothing. He wondered if Jenius noticed the extent of the block he kept on his thoughts these days. Probably not. He'd become so obsessed with developing his power base, the idea of anyone questioning him seemed beyond his comprehension. Not only was he adding to the TPT squad, he was thinking of moving his base from the aviary to what he considered might be a more impressive location. He'd discussed the idea with Lard and Kernel, and received contrasting vibes. The one, who'd had the experience of his last human trip with the Lord of the Manor, was unmoved by the idea, disillusioned at the burden of property responsibility even though it should have little impact on an occupying spirit. The other, Kernel, twitched enthusiasm for any chance of pomp without the need from him of too much effort. He was all for taking advantage of the facilities of a freehold estate humans seemed hell bent on preserving for no obvious reason. He willingly took off to research possible locations.

In Kernel's absence, Lard suggested a deferment until the return of the delegation. Despite there being little doubt of their acquiescence, he urged that it might be best to involve them in the establishment of a new central base so as not to suggest actions were being performed without their participation. His attempt failed, but Kernel unwittingly came to the rescue. He returned to report upon the benefits of sites, including the old tennis court, the servants' hall, the estate office, the leaking lake and the hothouses next to the orangery where the TPT were based. His mistake was to strongly recommend one venue above the others: the chapel.

In his absence, Jenius had already decided the chapel was to be his chosen location. Impatient though he was, his mentality would not allow someone else to claim credit for his idea. He switched to exploration of methods of enforcing the regulations they had already drafted, moaning again at the absence of the delegation and those charged with the task of experiment, especially Professer. Lard volunteered to make a trip down to Eastbourne to hurry things along. He was told that such a mission would be totally unnecessary.

"There's much still to be done in anticipation of the Council approval," Jenius twitched. "You are needed to coordinate."

Several measures passed with Lard waiting for some guidance as to what he was supposed to be coordinating. They were spent going over and over the regulations Jenius sought to introduce. 'Fine tuning' them, to use his words, although, apart from perhaps setting out an order of priority, Lard couldn't decipher any real change of tempo, melody or pitch. Eventually inactivity translated into frustration. Jenius, starved of news from the Thrillators, called his two cohorts in for what he termed an 'inner committee meeting'. Lard was becoming used to these 'action discussions' and resigned himself to another round of twitching which would leave them exactly where they were before they started.

"I believe we've given the Thrillators enough time to reach a decision," Jenius announced. "After all, it shouldn't take the inner-council this long to deliberate. Lard, I'd like you to travel down and see what's going on." It was put as if the proposal was new, without reference to any earlier rejection of the idea. Lard had no desire to question the pronouncement. A spell away from the dictatorial Jenius would be a welcome break. Knowing Compresser, he had a good idea where he might find him, especially having eavesdropped upon earlier conversations the monk and had with Thrillators before they left the mansion.

***

What Lard discovered when he arrived at the coastal town was the beginnings of a full blown revolution. He had little difficulty locating the Thrillators, still gathered in conference under the pier. All were present, together with Compresser, but Professer had been dispatched to the lighthouse upon some errand of research where he was happily testing a new idea of continental communication. It had been a unanimous twitch, including the votes of Upstart and Hedstrong who had returned from their wanderings, that to let him in on the debate would have been equivalent to a public announcement of their intent.

Lard managed his usual quiet entry and was able to remain undetected until Compresser sensed his presence. Every spirit gave off a unique pulse, so Compresser knew immediately who it was.

"What brings you here, Lard?" he asked, deliberately twitching strongly to draw the meetings' attention to the new arrival.

"Just to see how things are going," the visitor replied.

"Jenius getting agitated?" Compresser asked.

"You know how he is."

"We do not really. Please be good enough to tell." It was Frenco who sought an explanation. Leaving thoughts partially unblocked, he made it clear that the surreptitious arrival of what he considered an unwelcome official was far from appreciated.

Lard obliged, explaining that Jenius was becoming impatient for confirmation of his decision to create the TPT. Carefully he described the steps that were being taken to implement the anticipated approval, adding that they were still not beyond the point where the whole operation could be dismantled, should the Thrillators or the full council not agree.

"You think Jenius would accept rejection of the force?" Frenco twitched.

"That is not for me to say," Lard replied.

Hedstrong, who had been paying close attention to the exchange, marvelled at the diplomatic handling of the situation by the former occupant of the Lord of the Manor. With ease he was able to give this non-committal response in a manner which left his own view clear for all: Jenius would not accept rejection. Was this another technique spirits were inheriting from humans? Upstart detected his thought and quickly urged him to concentrate instead upon what seemed to be developing into a confrontation.

"I'd better go back and report, had I?" Compresser told the others.

"Report what?" Frenco wanted to know.

"It's obvious you need more time," Lard suggested. "After all, it's a big decision and some of the outer council members, remote from the speed of recent development, will be anxious to be fully consulted. I can understand your hesitation. After all, we don't want to face the delay of a full council meeting, do we? What are a few more measures' deliberation compared with that? I'm sure Compresser could explain to Jenius." After further twitching, the gathering agreed, despite their reluctance, to entrust the two officials on a report back mission.

"You can take that fool Professer back with you," Frenco muttered. "With luck he will muck everything up before we need to do anything."

The mansion officers withdrew to the Eastbourne flat to await the return of Professer from his latest mission. Encouraged by the Thrillators, Hedstrong and Upstart went with them. Being the two inner-council members resident at the headquarters, they had somehow slipped into the role of on-the-spot representatives. They were to report back to fellow Thrillators to confirm the other three had left on their return journey.

Not that they objected. It meant they could probably have time alone in the flat, a bonus that didn't go unnoticed amongst the Thrillators. Frenco, fully aware of the tie between them, still had reservations as to their loyalty and, although agreeing that to have them in contact with what he now viewed as the enemy, he was relieved that they were to remain in Eastbourne for the time being.

"Looks like we're in for a tricky period," Lard twitched to no one in particular, when all four had drifted into the flat.

"I don't suppose Jenius would back down?" Compresser queried.

"You know him," was all that Lard would concede. Turning to Upstart, he asked, "Where d'you stand in all this?"

"I'm simply here to observe," she answered, matching his diplomacy.

"And to report back. What am I to tell our leader from you?"

"Nothing," Upstart twitched, curtly. "When I'm ready, I'll report to him. I'm not prepared to have comments transmitted secondhand. That is clear, isn't it, Lard?"

Lard quickly communicated confirmation, suggesting that, with Compresser at his side, Jenius would probably be satisfied without any additions from her anyway. Then, in unusual unnecessary and seemingly undiplomatic manner, he added that this was especially so with her presence in Eastbourne being strictly a spy in the shoes of one of the Thought Processors. Upstart made her annoyance clear at what she considered a veiled threat before quickly having to block her thoughts sensing that Professer had arrived back.

The academic was oblivious of the atmosphere, launching immediately into an explanation of his progress in the communications' field. The others allowed him to ramble on a while before Lard complimented him upon his discoveries and suggested he should return to base immediately to report to Jenius. Always anxious to expound theories, Professer readily agreed and the three spirits were soon on their way.

"You don't like Lard, do you?" Hedstrong commented when they had left.

"Not really," Upstart replied. Acknowledging that that was yet another human trait, the couple shared an exhilarating surge that dimmed the lights in the whole block of flats before they returned to the Thrillators.

CHAPTER 20

GOING BACK

"I don't like it. They're up to something." If Jenius had materialised, Compresser believed he would probably have been pacing around the aviary in agitation. Not that such a confined space offered enough room. It felt congested even for spirits, especially when, for some reason, Jenius kept shifting position. In fact, Compresser decided, whenever and wherever Jenius was present it felt congested, but he kept the thought blocked.

"Maybe they've met some more opposition and are trying persuasion instead of a full council meeting," offered Lard, skating near to an untruth.

"Did they say that?" Jenius demanded.

"Not as such, but they were obviously still seeking a final decision," Lard explained carefully.

"I don't care. They've had enough time to deal with any problems by now. It's their job. Why do we have them if they get in the way?" Jenius was in no mood for reason. "We don't need them. We have the force. We can go it alone if need be."

"That would be unwise, would it not?" cautioned Compresser. The leader came to a stop in front of the monk.

"Why d'you say that? What we're doing is right. If necessary we'll have to make sure they see it our way. Won't we?" he added.

Compresser realised why he'd felt the aviary to be extra congested. One of the Thought Processors was present and Jenius's last comment was aimed in that direction. It puzzled him he'd not detected the being earlier and his thought was picked up before he had time to block.

"We've been busy," Jenius twitched. "There's still a long way to go but I can camouflage my bodyguards if I wish. All of them."

Several measures had passed since Compresser, Lard and the Professer had returned from Eastbourne. It transpired that Professer had hit on the technique whilst experimenting on the south coast and had introduced it to Jenius immediately upon his return, without bothering to tell the others.

"Good, isn't it?" he claimed, seeking to bask in the glory of what had become his discovery. "I call it 'blanket concealment'."

"Amazing," Lard agreed. "How's it done?"

"Aha!" Professer exclaimed. "I'm sworn to secrecy. It's our new weapon."

"Shouldn't we all be armed with it?" Lard urged.

"It's not perfected yet," Jenius twitched. "It takes a lot of energy and, until Professer comes up with a solution to that, it remains severely limited. In fact, I need a boost now. It was the blanket concealment attempt that really drained."

"Good, though," Professer said, cheerily. "Here, have some of mine." He gave his leader a boost and then said he was off to the shop to get himself a fresh charge.

Compresser also excused himself, explaining that he felt like a drift round the estate just to check upon the progress of human preservation, as well, of course, as keeping tabs on Professer, which was part of his mission, wasn't it?

He drifted through the rose garden in the direction of the car park hoping Professer hadn't changed his mind about the visit to the shop. He hadn't and, fortunately, Compresser found him playing with the cash computer. He'd already taken his boost and Phyllis was happy to watch him messing about, causing another assistant all sorts of trouble whilst she tried to record a sale. The assistant was beginning to think she was in charge and needed taking down a step or two.

A female customer at the head of the queue endeavoured to suppress her impatience, the line of potential buyers growing behind her. With the usual British human aversion to direct criticism the lady voiced her disapproval by complaining loudly to the one behind, who proceeded to tell everyone that the luckless assistant was 'only a volunteer' by implication apparently entitling her to sympathy and understanding.

Phyllis chose her moment to intervene, communicating to Professer to stop acting like a silly school kid, an effective admonition for a learned man for ever endeavouring to protect his overdeveloped pride.

"It's research, I'll have you know," he twitched back indignantly.

"Stuff and nonsense," Phyllis said out loud.

"Where?" one of the visitors enquired. "Last time I looked all over the place, but I couldn't find them."

Others wanted to know more and the visitor was only too pleased to explain the fable of the disappearing cats. With the Professor having stopped meddling and the cash machine doing its job Phyllis quickly left, announcing to whoever might be interested that she'd lost them somewhere, the non-existent feline friends she'd invented, that is.

"You'll have to be careful, won't you?" Compresser said, following her. "A few more outbursts like that and they'll have you certified, isn't it?"

"If you were to keep your friend in order, I wouldn't need to," Phyllis twitched at him. They'd moved away from the building to pass the temporary toilets before they were joined by Professer. Still smarting from the 'childish' criticism, he sought to explain both to Phyllis and Compresser the nature of his latest experiment.

"And how does that fit in with messing about with my cash machine?" Phyllis demanded.

Professer admitted that he wasn't sure, claiming that she'd interrupted him before he could assess the importance of what he was doing. "If you would kindly keep out of the way, perhaps I could get on with my job," he complained.

"Not if you keep interfering with my shop," she told him.

Professer was about to remind her that it wasn't her shop and that it belonged to the nation when Compresser intervened.

"You do realise you're having a conversation with a human, don't you?" he twitched.

"Am I?"

"And that she's twitching back at you without using her voice, silently?"

"I don't care what she's doing. She's getting in the… way," he finished lamely, the full impact of Compresser's words finally registering. "Fascinating. Fascinating," he repeated. "This I must investigate."

"Is he some sort of nutter?" Phyllis demanded. "And, anyway, what are you doing dressed as a monk. Is this some sort of fancy dress world?"

"It's the Real World, isn't it?" Compresser responded calmly. "How our beings are cloaked is unimportant."

"It may be unimportant to you but, standing where I am, it's comical," Phyllis twitched. "D'you play hide and seek and hunt the thimble as well like normal children?"

"I shall not remain here to be insulted by a mere human," Professer declared, and took himself off.

Compresser waited until he was out of distance before he twitched to Phyllis.

"I think you and I had better have a serious talk," he told her, forgetting to make it a question.

***

At Eastbourne, things were happening. The Thrillators had decided upon a plan of action. En block, they were to confront Jenius to give him the opportunity to explain himself. A lot of persuasion had been needed to encourage some of them into this compromising frame of mind. Frenco had wanted direct, instant action, but Hedstrong, supported by Upstart, had patiently set out the drawbacks of forceful confrontation. Their task had been far from easy, for the inner-council had occupied much of the intervening time amassing a spectacular armoury of aggressive techniques, some of which they continued to keep from the head office representatives. The meeting adjourned to allow time for final contemplation before the planning of the journey to the mansion.

Drifting across the bowling green towards the shingle banks for a last look at the coastal town, the couple took time to review the visit. What were the hidden 'weapons' the Thrillators claimed? Was one 'blanket concealment'? Upstart suggested that this was not new, and really wasn't concealment. All they did was to create maximum activity by constantly moving in a confined space thereby masking the presence of someone they wished to remain obscure. What she had heard was that they'd also devised a means of spiritual imprisonment and were close to achieving spiritual elimination. Apparently Professer had given a demonstration before he left. The Thrillators had been relieved to discover that, although he'd hit on blanket concealment, his technique was easily overridden and he was not nearly so advanced towards other discoveries as they were.

"If there was a battle," Upstart twitched, "some of us could be wiped out for ever. I can't grasp what that means. It's so gigantic, and so human. And what's to say that Professer isn't, at this mini-measure, giving some sort of demonstration to Jenius. Knowing how he rushes at things he's unlikely to have completed detailed tests."

"Surely it won't come to that. The Real World doesn't do confrontation." He thought for a moment. "Does it?"

"I fear it's going that way. Take Antedote. She was always confronting something or other. I don't think it would take much for one of us or a group, united in one aim and determined to have their way, to take to force if it was made available. Whilst no positive means has yet been found to kill us off," she twitched, "not while we're in the Real World, there are signs that when a spirit occupies a human in a particular manner, the spirit could expire when the human died. Find a means of compelling spirits out of the Real World in that manner and you have your death penalty."

"I hope there never will be," Hedstrong told her, "but I fear a way will be found. At least our fellow council members were sensible to keep Professer away from their other discoveries, whatever they may be. I suspect he was close to a breakthrough with that clock repairer before being distracted elsewhere. He's so unreliable."

"I'm not so sure he's as daft as he would have us believe."

"What makes you say that?" Hedstrong twitched.

"An unblocked moment here and a twitch there I casually managed to pick up," she replied.

"Casually pick up?"

"Of course. How else could simple little old me find out anything?"

"Darling, there's nothing simple about you," Hedstrong twitched.

"Careful," Upstart warned, "if I'm that complicated you might find yourself deprived of joint boosts as a punishment for insubordination."

"Well, if that's a possibility, it's a good job I've forgotten what those boosts are like," Hedstrong twitched. Upstart sought the nearest electrical point to remind him.

***

The inner-council remained resolved that no way were they prepared to rubber stamp the actions of their so-called leader. On their return Upstart and Hedstrong discovered they had been excluded from more deliberations. They were simply offered the opportunity to join the rest on the journey to the mansion. Believing it best to ensure that at least they all arrived back at the same time they accepted, not that they considered their presence would be of much influence on the proceedings.

In customary fashion, the Thrillators chose human public transport and made their way by bus to the local rail station. Drifting into a train they dispersed themselves between the various carriages to endure the journey. Hedstrong still felt inferior when he compared himself to the others. He assumed them to be better informed and prepared for the emotions that were crowding in. Upstart, catching the drift of his thoughts, told him he was wrong; that others were as much in the dark as he was. She claimed many were even less able to cope.

"They all fear Reality's ceasing to offer the clarity and freedom from adverse emotion for which it once stood," she said. "That's why they've separated in the train. They don't want to discuss what might be the outcome of the confrontation with Jenius. We're evolving. We're getting more complicated and the more we discover the more ambitious we'll get."

"Can't we stop?"

"We both could," she twitched, "because we've found each other, but those, like Jenius, - and probably Frenco - aren't so lucky. I'm afraid, my darling, we're about to witness the coming of a much more complex Real World."

They were nearing the capital when Upstart's musings were brought to an abrupt end by a violent shuddering. The metal wheels of the train screeched in response to emergency brakes, fusing against the track, fighting to bring everything to a halt, and failing. Some spirits, from previous human experiences, knew they were in the midst of a major accident. They kept to their posts whilst the engine hit an oncoming train, causing carriages to pile up against each other, then zigzag sideways off the track. Several burst into the back gardens of terraced houses bordering the route. One of London's inner suburbs was about to face the pressures of disaster.

Frenco was the first to twitch.

"Let us get out of here," he said. All had gathered into a group in one of the gardens. "There'll be some returning to Real World. We don't want them with us."

Using their own power, they swept through the adjoining dwelling down the street to the main road. Traffic was still moving normally, unaware of the crash. A double-decker bus was drawing away from a stop.

"Let's take that," Upstart twitched to the rest. "I think it's heading for the centre." Her thought proved correct and the Thrillators merged into the seats to complete their journey. Eventually they reached an area which was familiar to several council members, Upstart being one of them. She organised the rest off the slower mode of public transport, bogged down in traffic approaching the Oval Cricket Ground. The evening rush hour was in full flood and one or two humans were puzzled by the sudden dimming of several street lights, whilst the Thrillators recharged on their way into the tube station. Still under instruction from Upstart they drifted across from the Northern Line at Waterloo and settled into a Bakerloo train until it reached Paddington.

"You know your way about London," Hedstrong observed.

"Pity we haven't a measure or two for me to show you what some humans get up to," Upstart told him.

"I do have a bit of personal knowledge," he replied. "There may have been less vehicle activity when I was last here, but I doubt if things have changed much. There'll still be the pickpockets, murderers, tricksters. Politicians and gentry will still be swindling each other out of gains... and getting hanged for their trouble."

"You're being a bit maudlin but you're probably right, except no one gets hanged for crime now – not in this part of the planet. The so-called state looks after them. And the streets are cleaner. Disease and everything else is more subtle than it used to be. Underground and underhand I would say. That's the way things seem to be going."

The Thrillators gathered on a Paddington Station platform, their combined presence adding a chill to the already draughty extremities of the railway station. Human passengers moved away to warmer sections, whilst Frenco identified that all were present. It was agreed they take to the front carriage when the train arrived. He promised them what humans would call a conference, so they could rehearse their plan of action before they reached their destination. Having been quiet during the journey into the capital, not being a previous visitor to London, he was anxious to retrieve the leadership.

CHAPTER 21

DEPOSITION

T he first Jenius knew of the arrival of the Thrillators was the deputation leader's twitch at him in the aviary. Having travelled to the mansion with the inner-council members, Frenco had selected a small group to quietly penetrate the wooded walls. Jenius hadn't noticed their presence, which annoyed him, whilst Compresser, who was in the grounds conversing with Phyllis, saw them all. Well, he'd not actually *seen* them, but regardless of physical boundaries, was able to use his awareness to detect for quite a distance.

Phyllis had no such difficulty. She was quickly perfecting her new-found technique and, as long as there was no material barrier – such as a wall between her and them – she could pick out the Real World residents. Whilst Compresser was conscious of the Thrillators' passage Phyllis actually watched them emerge though Paradise on their way along the main footpath to the aviary. She couldn't conceal her amusement when she described them to Compresser. Clad in their various costumes from contrasting decades of humanity they looked a motley crew, giving no hint of an organised threat.

"When will you accept that the dress shown to you has no bearing in our World?" Compresser demanded.

"Oh, don't be so stuffy," Phyllis told him. "Let's get back to what we were doing."

That serious talk Compresser had sought and achieved was developing into a fledgling partnership, the two working on the mutual benefit it could offer. Phyllis's ability to converse with spirits needed refinement, especially in the thought-reading direction.

There were times when both saw what was in the mind of the other, although Compresser could effectively block. Even when he didn't, not everything got through without some supplementary twitching. Her thoughts were clear to him much of the time, whether she liked it or not, and Compresser's endeavours to educate her in the art of their concealment were deliberately not as enthusiastic as they might have been. He felt he needed some advantages, seeing that Phyllis could manipulate fellow humans to comply with her requirements in a manner totally unavailable to him.

Despite reservations on both sides, the two were getting on well, happy to agree that, at present, they preserve their unusual alliance as a secret not to be shared with anyone, human or spirit. There were the occasions in the past when Professer and Hedstrong had been witness to Phyllis's ability but it was agreed they wouldn't enlarge that knowledge at present.

"Let's hope it didn't register much with either of them," she commented. "That way we keep our advantage. Although Lard and I did communicate."

"With spirits, everything registers, but they may not think to recall it or appreciate the extent of it, don't you see?" Compresser told her. "Tell me what the Thrillators are doing, will you, please?"

"The what?" she asked.

Compresser explained and again she had difficulty containing her mirth at the thought that such a bedraggled lot could command superior positions. She reported that a small number had split to enter the aviary whilst the remaining group were beginning to gather round it. That was when Bernard joined her.

"He picks his moments, doesn't he?" Compresser twitched, in complaining tone.

"Jealousy will get you nowhere," Phyllis twitched back, remembering not to put her thoughts into human speech.

"Will you please to get rid of him?" Compresser instructed.

"Don't you tell me what to do."

Compresser apologised and rephrased his request, expressing

the hope that she would be able to dispatch Bernard on an errand so that she could give full attention to what was obviously an important moment for both of them, wasn't it?

Whilst the exchanges continued, Bernard had drawn Phyllis into the shadow of a tree at the edge of Paradise and was sliding his arms around her to pull her towards him.

"That's better," she told Compresser, noting his change of tone. She was twitching over Bernard's shoulder, a little irritated at her lover's amorous intent. "And there's no need to dispatch him. He won't get in the way." She smiled, adjusting to look into her lover's eyes, her somewhat cold expression warmed by telling him she'd missed him. Her words so illuminated his face that for a moment she shared an emotion that normal humans might call love and spirits, such as Compresser labelled unintelligible distracting reaction.

"Hold me tight," she coaxed, inciting a vigorous response. She could sense his melting into her body and felt that sharp intake of breath that confirmed his need for her. Despite herself she experienced a similar physical reaction. It surprised her and she swiftly disentangled from the embrace, promising to meet after work, cloaking her words with a guarantee of something greater than a simple embrace. He admitted he was in the middle of some task or other and should be elsewhere, gave her a swift goodbye kiss, then was on his way up to the mansion without a thought for what Phyllis was doing on her own on the edge of Paradise.

"Disgraceful," Compresser declared. "I feel sick, don't you see?"

"No, I don't," Phyllis replied. "And you don't do sick, remember?"

He claimed that he could still feel it even if he didn't 'do it', before turning his attention back to what he was beginning to call the invasion. Phyllis told him she thought the Thrillators were clustered around the dilapidated aviary but she couldn't be sure.

"There's a sort of electrical current flashing between them," she twitched.

"They'll have surrounded the place, isn't it?" Compresser

commented. "You won't see them all because they'll be in the bushes behind the aviary but I'll guarantee they've surrounded the place, you understand?"

"What for?" Phyllis demanded. "It's falling down."

"That's where Jenius is, isn't it?" Compresser told her casually, his main concentration devoted to trying to detect the identities, not of the surrounding group of Thrillators, but who was inside confronting Jenius. "Describe again the Thrillators you can see will you?" he instructed.

"There you go again," Phyllis complained. "I'm not one of your servants. And who or what is Jenius?"

Compresser sighed. He could do without such irritating human digression but, accepting he had no choice, he patiently explained that the event was of extreme importance. He needed to know whatever he could about it. He didn't mean to issue orders at her. It was just that things could be happening very swiftly and he needed brevity of communication if he, no, not he, both of them were to benefit from the encounter they were witnessing. He enlarged his explanation of what 'Thrillators' meant, and his suspicion that they had come to confront Jenius. He explained who Jenius was and slowly regained her cooperation.

" 'Inner-council', 'full council', 'need for consultation', 'executive decisions'," she repeated, "and you claim to live in the Real World? It doesn't seem much different to mine, and if what we're witnessing is a sort of United Nations gathering, where each representative pretends they're as important as the next, then I don't see how anything could happen 'swiftly'."

"Believe me, it can," Compresser told her. "This is no human gathering, is it? They mean business over there, don't you see?"

***

Inside the aviary Jenius twitched his anger at Frenco the moment he identified his presence. He could sense other Thrillators surrounding his headquarters and, apart from Lard and Professer, he was alone. He made a blocked resolution never again to be without a Thought Processor present.

"I detect aggression in your approach," he accused. "You would be well advised to acknowledge your place in this organisation."

"And exactly what is it that is my place?" Frenco twitched.

"You're no more than a member of the inner-council." The 'no more' bit was pronounced to clearly place Jenius's visitor on a lower level that he.

"And you are the different one?" retorted Frenco, rising to the bait.

"I am your leader, acknowledged and democratically chosen."

"Since when? You appointed yourself and your assumption was that the rest of us would agree."

"You have agreed. The council has given me the power, proved by accepting my position."

"Now we come to it," Frenco accused. "Power. Power, that is what you want. You are so greedy for it you want control of everything about you. You want control of Real World, and that is never what we give you."

"Let's not be too hasty," Lard cautioned. "Frenco, I think you misunderstand what Jenius is saying. By 'power' he means authority to act in the name of the council, not to control it. You must agree he needs that authority, otherwise none of the decisions we all take could be implemented."

"That is good try," Frenco twitched back at him. "But for start where does the 'we' come from? Since when you appointed council member?"

"I'm not," Lard responded swiftly, "but I identify with council decisions which, when taken, as far as I am concerned, are my decisions, and I do my best to carry out council wishes."

"And making a protective army is carrying out our decisions, is it?"

"I haven't done that," Lard stressed. "If you are referring to the

Thought Processor Force amassed in the orangery, that, as you know, is a proposal coming from Jenius and he will tell you it was created in anticipation of inner-council approval and no doubt will be disbanded if the council disagrees."

"No it won't," Jenius twitched. "It's a necessary step in the development of our community. It will give protection against aggressors. It will protect the Real World and its leader against outside influence."

"In other words it will protect you," Frenco accused. "It will protect you against us if we are in disagreement."

Lard tried again to intervene, suggesting that Frenco had got it all wrong and that might he, Lard, suggest Jenius only had the interests of the Real World in mind.

Compresser, like the circling inner-council members, was now near enough to receive the waves of twitching that were going on in the aviary. He admired Lard's agility at seeking to support Jenius whilst at the same time distancing himself from his 'leader'. The attempt to diffuse the confrontation failed, and the force of debate between the two combatants grew to an extent that they both materialised. Fortunately they had remained in the aviary, so their appearance was not visible to human eyes.

"I'm not putting up with this nonsense any more," Jenius projected. "The force is established and it stays whatever your lot say."

"Not under your control it does not," Frenco countered.

"Try stopping me."

Phyllis had kept up with Compresser. Although she was having difficulty catching the actual words, the spirits voices had risen to the equivalent of angry human volume. It was clear to her that a major dispute was growing. The couple were on the main path close to the aviary when they saw Bernard. He was alongside the wooden structure and waved to her.

"We could do without him, couldn't we?" Compresser grumbled again.

Before Phyllis could respond Jenius, still materialising, burst out with such force that the aviary shuddered. She watched the self-appointed leader sweep at the ring of Thrillators, still linked by their electrical cordon.

"Out of my way," he twitched and made to break through. There was a terrific flash followed by a thunderous roar. Compresser, unaided by the vision bestowed upon Phyllis, begged an explanation. For a moment she was too shocked to reply then, without a word, she rushed towards Bernard who was lying on the ground. By the time she reached him, he was picking himself up and shaking his head.

"That was close," he declared. "I though I was a gonner for a minute. Did you see that lightening?" Phyllis helped him regain his balance. "There was no warning, no sign of a storm, just that flash." He looked down to one side, at a scorch mark on the grass. "Good God," he said. "That was close. A few centimetres nearer I'd have been burnt up. Or did it actually pass through me?"

Phyllis lost no time in guiding him back to the mansion where she sought assistance. All thought of Trillators, Compresser and anything else was forgotten whilst she attended to her lover. Someone had already called an ambulance and they waited in the library until it arrived, both breaking the rules by sitting on the furniture. Another helper hurriedly shut the door but, by the time the vehicle turned into the forecourt with the usual flashing lights and blaring siren, a crowd of humans had accumulated in the hallway, some seeking to help and the rest just curious to watch one of their number in distress. The medics cleared a path through and entered the room to tend to the stricken man. He'd actually ceased to show signs of distress and was beginning to protest at all the fuss. He reluctantly agreed to go into the ambulance.

"That doesn't mean I'm prepared for a trip to hospital," he warned.

A few minutes after the crowd had dispersed, satisfied there was no further drama to interest them, he thanked the ambulance men for their attention. He declared that he was fully recovered and stepped down onto the gravel of the forecourt.

Phyllis, who had been anxiously waiting, immediately offered to drive him home. Their relationship was still not open knowledge to their counterparts, which meant that her approach had to be formal. With the inevitable rumours flying about, none of the other helpers volunteered with a rival invitation, content to look on and gather more food for gossip. Urged to accept Phyllis's offer and take the rest of the day off, despite his show of reluctance, the promise of time alone with his beloved influenced his decision. He nodded. He allowed Phyllis to guide him round the front of the mansion and onto the path towards the car park, volunteers returning to their posts to perform for the public.

When they passed the aviary, Phyllis looked to see if there were any spirits about. All was clear, with nothing left to evidence what had happened apart from that burnt grass... and Compresser. He'd been hovering near to her during the whole incident, but she'd ignored him, continuing to do so whilst they climbed the path alongside the rose garden. Bernard walked slowly, not objecting to her guidance on up the road to the reception area. When they reached the shop entrance Phyllis realised why the aviary had been quiet. The inner-council members were queuing through the doorway.

She bade Bernard go over to sit on one of the seats in the cafeteria area whilst she retrieved her coat and bag. Taking a deep breath she prepared to walk through the spirits, the first time she'd knowingly faced such a task. She closed her eyes and strode through the doorway, surprised that she didn't feel anything until she bumped into the head of a queue of humans waiting to be served at the counter. A minor eruption was in progress. The computer was going mad, suffering whilst one after another of the inner-council spirits took their turn for an electrical boost. A hapless assistant was desperately trying to record a sale for the visitor Phyllis had bumped into with a growing number of would-be-purchasers becoming more and more impatient behind.

"I'll take over," she announced. Looking directly at Compresser, who had followed, she added, "there must be some ghosts about. Will they kindly join the back of the queue and stop mucking up my machine."

The customers grinned, most gracefully accepting her subsequent apology allowing things to return to normal. She saw Compresser usher the Thrillators to an adjoining building housing an alternative electrical source and she didn't leave until the backlog cleared.

Having returned control to her assistant, saying she had another errand to perform, Phyllis found Bernard sitting patiently waiting for her. He made a half-hearted attempt at suggesting he was fully recovered, but happily gave way to her insistence that he was not. Phyllis was determined to get him out of the estate if only to give her time away from the spirits so she could begin to sort out in her own mind what had happened. Soon they were in her car beyond the entrance drive and not long afterwards arrived at her house.

"I thought you were taking me to my home," he commented, not at all upset that she hadn't.

"I felt it best to bring you with me, just in case there was delayed shock," she told him. "I'll take you to your home if you wish."

"No, no," he replied. "It's very good of you to offer. I promise I won't be any trouble." Phyllis said she doubted that, but if it was the case she saw no reason for him to stay and she would definitely despatch him elsewhere immediately. They were out of the car by then and she felt his arm slide round her waist to pull her to him. "What sort of trouble do you have in mind?" he asked, "as if I didn't know."

Unfortunately the promise of an interlude of sexual passion faded into the future when they entered the house. The delayed shock hit him hard and he nearly passed out on the living room floor. Lowering him onto the settee Phyllis held and consoled him whilst he regained some composure. She told him to lie still whilst she prepared a concoction.

Compresser was waiting for her in the kitchen.

"What are you doing here?" she demanded.

"What did you say?" Bernard called from the other room.

"Nothing," she told him. "Just talking to myself." Remembering to twitch she repeated her question.

"Didn't you see me in the car?" Compresser asked her. "No, I suppose you were so besotted with your lover you didn't notice me, did you?"

"You weren't inside with us," she responded, "or I would have seen you. And I'm not besotted."

"Only checking, wasn't I?" he told her. "I was under the bonnet, so as not to disturb your driving, which, incidentally is not great at the best of times, is it?"

"Don't evade the question. Why are you here?"

"Just in case you need me, isn't it?" Compresser told her.

"And why should I need you?"

"You haven't realised, have you?" the spirit asked her.

"Realised what?"

"That Jenius has left the Real World, hasn't he?"

"I'm not surprised," Phyllis retorted. "Not even a ghost would have survived that explosion."

"Oh, he's survived all right," Compresser told her. "He's in Bernard, isn't he?"

CHAPTER 22

COMPLICATION

Hedstrong and Upstart made a brief trip to the mansion for a boost before retiring to Paradise. Both were shaken by their involvement in the closed ring of Thrillators where they'd dutifully illustrated their allegiance to the council. Neither had imagined the spirit Jenius would rush at them.

They had deliberately gone the opposite way to the Thrillators and Upstart gave her lover an additional mini boost, achieving a reassuring tingle that confirmed their spiritual relationship was sound.

"I didn't think that was the plan," Hedstrong twitched.

"What? Me giving you an extra boost?" Her subdued response failed to conceal the shock she'd experienced at what had happened.

"You can pursue that plan any time," he replied, "but you know what I mean."

They both settled into a tree on the perimeter of the wooded area and allowed their thoughts to flow, uncertain what to do next. The first attempt at Real World planetary leadership was over, although Hedstrong, as soon as he'd exchanged the impression, wondered if it was accurate.

"We don't really control all of our kind, do we?" he questioned. "Let's face it, the inner-council… in fact the whole council have little or no contact with a sizeable part of the planet. Who knows how many others in the Real World think they govern it? And there must be at least some out there ignorant of us and not even knowing they have mobility outside humans. Not so many measures ago that included me."

Upstart agreed. She recalled one of her recent trips away from the Real World in Busty Bertha, a stock car driver, who welded her old cars with solid angle iron to make them virtually indestructible. With a highly tuned engine, she'd been a popular attraction, racing round small narrow oval tracks bashing into the opposition.

"They always had a world champion, whose car had a gold painted rooftop. There were as many gold topped 'world champions' as different organisers in different parts of the planet," she confirmed. "And humans have beauty competitions for women and men, with the winner declared world king or queen when only a handful of beings compete and no means of checking whether the selected ones are more attractive than anyone else who didn't take part. There are countless other examples of 'world this' and 'world that.'"

"We're doing the same if we claim we control our Real World?" Hedstrong suggested.

"It doesn't really matter because it's not our destiny to control." Suddenly Upstart was uncertain. "Is it?" she asked

Further deliberation forced them to admit they didn't know. Each could recollect their initial human entry experience plus everything that had happened afterwards, but they couldn't quite picture their arrival on the planet - how or why it had happened, or where they'd come from.

"Our origins are almost as obscure to us as the creation of the human race is to them," Upstart admitted, "yet there is something beyond recall, I know there is. I just can't reach it."

Hedstrong confirmed he'd experienced the same sensation and the belief that, if they were patient, they would eventually see through the fog of their arrival.

"We are so like humans," he twitched. "I know that now. We have emotions, desires, experience love, perhaps even hate. We're facing conflict identical to that which is killing the human race, born out of ambition, confrontation and greed for power."

"Except we can't die," Upstart contributed.

"Not yet in great numbers, but don't forget conflagration. Not that we've ever witnessed it."

Whilst they were at Eastbourne they'd joined in a thought exchange with the other inner-council members. One of their number was able to recount firsthand experience of elimination of a human, burning from within his skin. Described as an immediate combustion, the human body had been destroyed so quickly that outer garments were hardly affected. It had occurred after one of the Thrillator's colleagues had chosen to and had entered the being. There was no evidence that the spirit had survived.

"And we can't multiply," she twitched. "How ever much we love each other, we can't reproduce."

So occupied with their thoughts were they that they didn't acknowledge the presence of Compresser until he twitched his arrival.

"Don't get too technical," he observed. "Our voyage of discovery will be a long one, so we must take it step by step, shan't we?"

Neither reacted with much favour to his intervention, a mood readily apparent to Compresser through their unblocked reactions. "All right, all right," he concluded. "Now is not the time or the place, is it? Lard is suggesting we all meet in the walled garden for a conference, you understand?"

Upstart wanted to know if this was wise, so close to the Thought Processor Force, which she presumed would still be loyal to their departed leader. After a hesitation she asked Compresser if Jenius had definitely departed.

"So far as we can ascertain, you understand, yes, we think he's well and truly established in the human called Bernard. And the Thought Processors appear to have left, haven't they?" Compresser twitched. "Whether they're on a training exercise, or whether they have become aware of the…the er," he paused in mid twitch, searching for the correct word. "I think we should call it 'incident', don't you?" Taking their lack of response as agreement he continued. "Yes, the incident. They may have become aware of the incident and taken refuge elsewhere, out of detection range, if you get my meaning?"

Upstart and Hedstrong reluctantly agreed the meeting and the location, leaving Compresser to continue his rounding up of the rest of the inner-council. It took him a full measure, during which they slowly and cautiously made their way through the garden and down over the ha-ha into the adjoining meadow. Taking no chances, for fear of encountering Thought Processors, their highly activated senses acknowledged several other inner-council members travelling in the same direction. A couple joined them to pass through the wall into one of the hothouses, next to the walled garden. They stopped for a while.

"I 'av not been so close to involuntary expulsion from our world before," one of them admitted, twitching in a foreign accent. "And I 'av done some travels in my time. 'Av you seen it before?" she asked.

Upstart confessed that she had not and the two unblocked enough thoughts to allow each other to study their past human entry experiences. They found that they had much in common, except that Sexa – that was what she was named – was based in what humans called Spain and had been for many measures. The two continued to converse, drifting apart from their companions into the open walled garden. Upstart found herself exchanging information about her relationship with Hedstrong. In return Sexa offered similar details of her involvement with another inner-council member. They both agreed that the sensations sparked by their respective assignations were well worth the energy it took to guide their male spirits along the routes best suited to them.

"We sound like the humans," Sexa confessed.

"Except that female humans have lost the way," Upstart told her. "Why they ever created an illusion in their men that males were superior is beyond my comprehension. It's taking generations for them to rectify the mistake." Sexa concurred. Suddenly their thought exchange was broken by a twitch.

"So you think female spirits are in control, do you?" It was Lard who had drifted up on them in his usual subtle manner. Without allowing time for response he directed both females to the centre of the garden where their awareness confirmed that the rest of the inner-council awaited them. Upstart located Hedstrong, sparking an intimate mini surge when she joined him. Sexa drifted over to reunite with her companion.

Compresser was a little removed from the rest, hovering close to Phyllis whom he'd also invited. She was pretending to weed one of the vegetable beds whilst keeping the whole spiritual gathering in sight so she could update Compresser with visual confirmation of what his senses told him.

Lard took the lead to address the gathering, giving a brief appreciation of the progress Jenius had achieved before what he described as his 'fall from grace'. Use, more than once, of the phrase 'fall from grace' clearly signified to the gathering his disapproval of much of what Jenius had stood for. He followed this by an endorsement of the skills Frenco had commanded, describing the Thrillator's efforts as a diplomatic attempt to 'reason with a leader who was going wrong'. Expertly, he distanced himself from any blame before, almost as an afterthought, absolving the Thrillators too. He recommended that the inner-council formally elect a new leader and, having already begun to groom Frenco for it, considered that the Thrillators should give their unopposed endorsement of him as the sole candidate, which they did.

In his acceptance speech, Frenco declared that the rest of the Thrillators should remain inner-council members. Lard was offered identical official status to that held under Jenius; so was Compresser. The whole establishment, therefore, remained unchanged, except for Jenius, already becoming distant memory, and Professer. Surprisingly quiet during and after the incident, he had answered the summons to attend, but was hovering in the background where he waited in vain for appointment to a post of scientific distinction.

Visibly put out when it didn't arrive, visibly, that is, to Phyllis who saw him begin to drift above the gathering when general policy matters came up for consideration. She informed Compresser and the spiritual monk would have intervened had he not also been told by her that Lard had noticed the problem and had drawn close to the disgruntled scientist. With Phyllis describing the bodily reactions of the two of them he felt there would be no immediate disturbance of the equilibrium.

Thanks to his human female friend, he'd also been made aware of the presence of a Thought Processor, hovering in the corner of the garden nearest the orangery. Drifting away from the body of the meeting, Compresser applied his senses through the walls into the orangery. The full Thought Processor Force had returned. Organised by Kernel, who knew no better than to perform his duties in ignorance of the incident, they were on parade, waiting.

***

Since recovering from the lightening flash, Bernard had applied himself to his tasks with renewed vigour. He wasn't sure why, but felt on top of the world, even though his beloved Phyllis appeared to be avoiding him. Having just completed a visit to the estate office, he made for the garden to check the progress of the vines in the greenhouse. Entering the walled enclosure he saw her, still crouching over one of the vegetable beds, and approached.

"What are you doing?" he asked.

"Just looking for a few herbs I could pinch," she replied, straightening up to stare at him. "Were you looking for me?"

"Not especially." The comment was out before he could stop it and received the inevitable reaction from Phyllis.

"Charming," she muttered. Usually Bernard would immediately apologise and confirm he didn't mean to imply he wasn't pleased to see her. When he didn't, with a "Please yourself," she began to walk away.

"Don't forget your herbs. And you won't find them amongst the cabbages, they're over there," he called after her.

She shrugged and kept walking, making sure he noticed the sway of her hips and the suggestive movement of her body. She half expected him to follow into the hothouse area but, again, he didn't. For once uncertain, she was about to go back to confront him when a commotion in the vicinity of the orangery stopped her.

A number of Thrillators had surrounded Compresser and Professer who had been joined by two other spirits whom, from their military-type images, she took to be Thought Processors. Recalling what had happened to Jenius, she felt there was a chance of another incident, especially with several humans wandering around to inspect the current renovation work to the orangery. When she approached she could see the two Thought Processors begin to throb. She realised they were about to break out of the Thrillator circle which, she also noted, was shaping up in identical form to the one she'd witnessed around Jenius. The Thought Processors escaped before the ring was perfected, disappearing from Phyllis's view into the orangery.

"Now see what you've done, haven't you?" Compresser complained.

"We done nothing," Sexa told him in her Spanish accent. "All we done trying to do was protect ourselves." Her spiritual English slipped when, in her excitement, she forgot to adopt the usual universal technique of balanced twitching.

"Interesting," Professer commented.

"What?" she flashed at him.

"The way your twitching becomes distorted when you're aroused."

"I will make sure you are distorted," she told him, "if you fling insults at me like that."

"Now, now, let's not get heated." It was Lard, twitching from outside the circle, having drifted up in his usual surreptitious manner. "What appears to be the problem?"

Sexa was only too happy to explain, assuming the role of spokesperson for the dozen or so Thrillators who were still circling Professer and Compresser. The inner-council members, having discovered the two now restrained spirits conversing with Thought Processors, immediately suspected a conspiracy, confirmed, so far as they were concerned, when, upon their approach to the group, twitching immediately stopped and thoughts were blocked.

"They is both conversing with the enemy and it is conspiracy against us," she concluded. "For that we should be rid of them. They should follow Jenius to humanity."

The Lard technique spun into action. First he sought to establish what the alleged conspirators had been plotting, gaining a reluctant concession from Sexa and the others that they didn't know. He asked what they planned to do with their captives, having assumed them guilty of some spiritual offence. The council members confirmed they hadn't actually decided upon any specific action, apart from Sexa's outburst.

"Then would it not be judicious to allow our two colleagues the opportunity to explain themselves?" he asked.

Whilst the discussion progressed, the Thrillators gradually drifted out of circular formation, thereby allowing Compresser and Professer freedom of movement. Professer immediately took advantage of the opportunity and surged off, his angry twitches at the stupidity of the masses fading with him. Compresser stood his ground and calmly explained that they'd merely been trying to make peaceful contact with a view to discovering whether or not the Jenius force was hostile to the overthrow of their leader.

"And what did you found," Sexa demanded, "that was so important you had to block from us?"

"Nothing. You lot interrupted before we could get anywhere, didn't you?" Compresser then withdrew his thought block to prove his words, explaining that in negotiating with an uncertain force it was commonsense to impose blocking. Sexa was not convinced, claiming that there was more to the approach than Compresser was revealing. Having been the instigator of the Thrillator action she was vainly seeking to save face, an action Compresser was not hesitant to point out.

"You is traitor," Sexa flashed. "You twist things."

Another council member joined in who, by his twitches, made it apparent he was the one sharing romantic feelings with the fiery Spanish spirit. Whilst supporting her, he tried to add reason to the argument by suggesting that the two suspects be allowed a proper opportunity to explain themselves. He asked where Frenco was, establishing that he had retired to the aviary to 'consolidate his leadership' - Lard's phrase.

The lover asked his colleagues for agreement that the matter be referred to their leader. All confirmed, except his beloved. The others, embarrassed at their precipitous action, left some unblocked thoughts blaming Sexa. She read them.

"Go. Go," she twitched. "Go have your little meeting. I know they is both guilty, so I don't need it."

Phyllis had drawn closer to the group but still kept in the background just observing the confrontation. With Sexa's last outburst, most of the spirits departed, disappearing through the garden walls on their way to the aviary. Compresser left with them.

She, too, was about to depart when she noticed movement out of the walls of the orangery. Sexa's partner had stayed behind with her and was trying to persuade her to calm down. Neither of them became aware of the Thought Processors' presence until they were surrounded by the force. Phyllis watched whilst the circle grew tighter and started turning.

"I wasn't aware this area was part of your responsibility," a voice boomed out, clearly aimed at her.

"It isn't," she replied, turning to face Miss Gregory, a member of the human volunteer force who had taken upon herself the task of ensuring 'the staff', as she called them, 'pulled their weight'. "I'm on my break."

"Well, don't take too long," Miss Gregory admonished. Considering her duty performed, she strode towards the Orangery, an erect figure whom Phyllis thought would be attractive if it wasn't associated with the imperious attitude portrayed by her facial expression. Seeing she was about to walk through the middle of the Thought Processor circle Phyllis nearly tried to stop her before realising it didn't matter. Humans were constantly walking through ghosts and vice versa without ill-effect.

But this time it was different. Miss Gregory was unfortunate to enter the rotating circle of Thought Processors the moment it gathered speed to sweep over Sexa and her partner. With a blinding flash, the two council members were no more. The circle disintegrated, and disappeared through the Orangery, leaving Phyllis staring at a bewildered Miss Gregory. She rushed over to help the stricken volunteer who was sitting on the ground.

"I'm all right. I'm all right," the imperious lady declared, resisting the attempts to help her up. Struggling to her feet she again claimed she was all right. "Just a slip, that was all, a slip." She straightened her clothes, looked about her, saw Bernard approaching them and added, "And it's about time you did some work, young man," before striding off in the direction of the estate office.

"Should I be flattered at the reference to my youth," Bernard asked, "or irritated at the criticism?"

"Neither would work with her," Phyllis told him.

"She's not my type. You are." He took her in his arms and kissed her. "We shouldn't fall out. We're special."

"Are we now?" Phyllis told him. "And why is that?" she whispered into the ear she had begun to nibble.

"Because we can both see into another world and, from what we've just witnessed, there are a lot of restless spirits around."

"You can see them, too?"

"Yes, I can," he confirmed.

CHAPTER 23

CONSPIRACY

Hedstrong and Upstart had left with the main group of Thrillators to join Frenco in the aviary. The first they heard of the Sexa incident was from Compresser. He'd sensed a problem and, detaching himself from the rest, had returned to witness her departure into Miss Gregory. Hovering in the background he'd been joined by Lard. They waited with Lard to see if there was any significant effect on the human woman. Not detecting any signs of her recognising spirits, they'd both swept away to break the news to Frenco. Professer, although beyond the walled garden, had picked up the trouble signals in time to drift into the area, but they managed to avoid him. Nevertheless he followed them..

In the crowded atmosphere of the aviary, the monk was pleased to note that time and space had allowed logic to overtake the earlier impulsiveness of the Thrillators. Discussion with Frenco had reduced the complaint of treason against both Professer and Compresser to unauthorised activity.

"That does not mean we do not think approach to Thought Processors stupid," Frenco told them.

"Why stupid?" demanded Professer. "Since when is it stupid to chat to fellow spirits?"

"Since they joined army to attack us."

Lard tried his usual tactic of diplomatic intervention only to be told to shut up by Compressor. The spiritual monk stressed he'd intended no confrontation. To the contrary, his approach had been conciliatory and it had been working until he'd been interrupted.

"This is all getting out of hand, isn't it?" he twitched wearily.

"One being has got us fighting each other and, although he's paid the price, we're still at it, aren't we?" He went on to explain the negotiation he and Professer had been conducting with the two Thought Processors. "That was before you group of Thrillators barged in, wasn't it?" He stressed that, having learned of the departure of Jenius, the Processors were nervous and uncertain of their position. The two he was negotiating with had shown no hint of threat and had been on the point of agreeing to drift up to the aviary for discourse with the new leader when Sexa had led the Thrillators onto the scene.

Having received a graphic description of the fate of Jenius and noting that they were being surrounded the two Thought Processors feared a similar dispatch from the Real World and had surged off to their squad in the orangery. Compressor emphasised that no threat had been made against the Thrillators until Sexa's intervention. Her action had most likely been taken as evidence of an unwillingness on the part of the inner-council to peaceably negotiate.

"What you have now, don't you see, is a group scared of retaliation and frightened for their future. Professer and I were beginning to make amicable progress and I'm confident we would have succeeded had it not been for Sexa's attitude, wouldn't we?" He paused as if he expected an answer to his question, unlikely because everyone always ignored Compresser's questions due to their frequency. The gap allowed Lard to describe in detail to the gathering the departure of Sexa and her lover from the Real World.

"Then Sexa's pay for her behaviour," Frenco twitched with typical leadership bluntness. "And, for you two, your interference is make the situation worse. Do not try to approach anyone on your own again. You are to clear with me first. Now I have business with Lard so rest of you clear off."

Professer, who'd kept unusually quiet until that moment, was about to flash his own brand of cryptic comment into the arena when he was unceremoniously told by Compresser to shut up and follow him out. Hedstrong and Upstart, having been included in the dismissal, joined them.

"Talk about justice," Professer couldn't help twitching, as he left. "Anyone would think we were little more than robots." The four were gone before Frenco could respond, accelerating past the other inner-council members, clustered in a group on the path.

***

Frenco feared he was facing the imminent disintegration of the empire he'd just inherited. He instructed Lard to find some temporary accommodation for the visiting Thrillators and then return so he could assist in the planning of what he called 'the new order'. Lard responded immediately, conducting the inner-council members through a main window into the mansion's drawing room. Although one of the largest in the house, it was least inhabited by resident spirits. He identified Kernel, who had taken leave of his duties at the first sign of trouble and was resting in the fireplace, his recently established off-duty retreat. He seemed untroubled by the restoration work of the human volunteers who turned up most days to help the experts with the more menial chores of chandelier glass cleaning and the like.

Skipping formalities, Lard explained that Jenius had failed in his duty and was now replaced by Frenco, to whom Lard expected Kernel to show loyalty. He was to keep away from the Thought Processors until further commanded but, in the meantime, had the responsibility for accommodation of the Thrillators and their integration with the rest of the spiritual household.

Mini-measures were wasted whilst a few 'buts' a 'what's happened to Jenius?' and 'the question of allegiance' were expressed, but Lard, anxious to be back at the seat of power, soon dealt with them. Somehow he left Kernel with the impression he'd just achieved promotion to become senior officer in charge of the ruling council comforts. Any lasting doubts he may have had were dispelled by the assurance that, apart from introducing members to the house spirits, all he had to cope with was a watching brief. Lard then returned to the aviary where he began 'the moulding the new king of the empire', as he put it, but only to himself, immediately blocking the thought.

***

"This whole thing seems to be descending into chaos," Hedstong twitched when the four settled round a tree near the lake. "We have a leader carrying on where Jenius left off, an inner-council with even less power than ministers in a human parliament and an overall council believing they represent a planet with no idea what's going on beyond their own doorsteps. And now we also have a dispossessed band of spiritual outlaws floating around believing they are about to be annihilated. I think Jenius is well out of it. Everything will probably have settled down when his human host expires and he returns to the Real World."

"Aha," Professer intervened. "Aha. That's not strictly accurate."

"What bit of it isn't accurate?" Hedstrong enquired.

"The bit about Jenius's return," Professer told him. "I don't think it will happen."

"What d'you mean, it won't happen?"

"His was a forceful human entry, consciously projected by the combined action of his fellow spirits. From that we know of no method of return." The scientist was twitching in an uncharacteristic tone, dropping the usual flowery delivery expected of him. He went on to describe experiments of which he'd been a part. They'd taken place, and were probably still taking place, in another sector of the planet. They went back a number of measures, spanning generations of human lives, but all produced the same result: when fellow spirits combined to despatch one of their number into humanity, it was a death sentence. There was evidence that, as usual, the condemned spirit would have some influence on the behaviour of the human into whom he or she had been projected, but when the human died, so did they.

"That is why I was initially so excited when Kernel found himself in the clock repairer, and returned," Professer continued, "but it turned out to be a red herring. We did some further tests, and it transpired that involuntary entry without independent spiritual assistance, such as Kernel's, was different. There was no forceful action against him by fellow spirits. We're still trying to discover if there are links but, as yet, we haven't found any."

"Who's this 'we', and where are these experiments going on?" Hedstrong wanted to know.

"A long way away. Far beyond the reach of the council," Professer explained, "at least at present."

Following this revelation the four descended into silence. Hedstrong assumed the other two were having the same difficulty he was having in grasping what the Professer had just told them. For a mini-measure he even questioned if it was true, before reminding himself he was in the Real World and spirits could not lie. Mesmerised by the thought that some of his kind could actually die, he left his deliberation unblocked.

"So now you know, don't you?" Compresser twitched. "We have a serious situation on our hands, have we not?"

"You already knew this?" Hedstrong twitched. Compresser confirmed that he did. "So why are you telling me? What's caused you to share your secret?" He paused. "Oh, I see, you're thinking things are getting out of hand and you're getting out of your depth, so you want some help. And you think Upstart and I will do as helpers. Well, think again. I'm not going to participate in any experiment. I like my way of survival. I want to keep it."

"Darling," Upstart intervened, "we don't expect that. We just want you to join the team."

"You as well?" Hedstrong couldn't grasp it, and twitched as much.

"Yes, you can," his beloved told him. "You've had so much to learn in so short a stretch of measures. Compresser insisted on being sure you wouldn't divulge our secret lives before allowing me to ask you to join us."

"Don't blame her, blame me, will you?" Compresser told him. "There's so much at stake, I had to be sure, didn't I?"

"And what's made you so sure?" Hedstrong demanded.

"Observation," the monk replied. "Both of the way you have developed, the manner in which you approach Reality, calmly, cautiously, without sensation and your ability to hide feelings if the occasion demanded."

"So you set Upstart on me, to test me and to spy on me and report back."

Compresser confirmed he had; that Upstart's amorous intentions had been a ploy to investigate his existence.

"But that gave rise to a complication, didn't it?" he added. "Something we hadn't bargained for, wasn't it?" Not allowing Hedstrong's projected thought to divert him he continued, "a bond developed between you two. A genuine feeling, isn't it?"

"What he's trying to say in his roundabout way is you and she became an item," Professer intervened. "You both hit it off together. Both had it off together, did it, sexually you…"

"He gets the message," Compresser twitched, figuratively holding up a hand to stem the flow. "And you needn't revert to your haphazard professorial disguise. It's not needed here amongst us." For once Compresser wasn't ending every sentence with his usual question mark.

"Another deception," Hedstrong managed. "How many more?"

"No more, darling. This is it. You know it all and, yes, we do want you with us, and I want you as well. That's something I can't help. We're so good together, don't let this ruin us." Upstart was almost pleading and Compresser chose the moment to make an exit, taking Professer with him. He asked that they all meet up again later, outside the shop, hoping, by leaving the couple alone, they'd have an opportunity to sort things out and preserve what they'd achieved.

A typical Compresser move, Hedstrong thought out loud – here one measure and then gone almost with a flash. After the two had departed, there was silence. Hedstrong was lost for further thoughts. He drifted into the large old tree around which the four had gathered, seeking sanctuary from its reassuring physical presence. He still couldn't fully comprehend what was happening to him. He was still being carried forward by a force he couldn't identify in a world which had suddenly become strange and uncertain. How could Upstart have been so close and not told him? How could their relationship continue as it had before? He deliberately left that question unblocked, in the hope of some response.

"It can't," she answered. "It can never be the same but, don't you see, it's now more intimate than ever. There are no secrets between us. That's what I've wanted for some time and at last the others agreed."

"So you had to wait to get their permission," Hedstrong accused, almost petulantly. "It was more important to you to get their permission before telling me."

"Yes, it was," Upstart flashed back, "and if you'd just take a mini-measure you'd know why. I have a job to do and it's important. You've seen how confrontation and war can ruin humanity. It's started to happen in the Real World too, and we have a duty to stop it."

"We?"

"Yes, you and I. Both of us."

"And the others too?"

"Yes, the others too. Compresser is a good, wise spirit and he can see where all this fighting for power will lead. Professer is a brilliant scientist. You mustn't be fooled by their acts. They're deliberate, allowing them to get away with all sorts of things which are beneficial to the cause."

"And what precisely is 'the cause'?"

Upstart allowed another mini-measure to pass before answering. Then she asked if she could join him in the tree. He hesitated and she asked again. He still hesitated, but knew he couldn't hold out against her for long. When they were close, in the trunk, she requested a boost, which he reluctantly gave her.

"That wasn't a very strong one. Can't you do better than that?"

He said she didn't deserve any more than that. She asked if he forgave her, and he asked what for. She said for keeping a secret and he said that yes he supposed he did.

"But don't think you've escaped the question," he added. "What is 'the cause'?"

She was already returning the boost he'd given her and the power developed into a surge of forgiveness and enjoyment. They were together again, and all else faded into the background, including the question.

***

The four were to meet outside the shop as arranged. Hedstrong and Upstart found Compresser waiting for them. Although it was approaching midday, there were no visitors around, autumn having blended into winter and the entry gates having been closed until next year. Hedstrong wanted to know why Compresser had chosen that location.

"There's one more thing you have to know," the spiritual monk told him. "You too, Upstart. All will become clear when Professer arrives."

They didn't have to wait long. A surge of wind was followed by a flash, within which Professer momentarily materialised before settling down beside them.

"D'you have to be such an exhibitionist?" Compresser complained.

"Got to keep the image going," the scientist replied. "You never know who might be watching these days. So, let's get on with it."

"With what?" Hedstrong asked, suspicion returning.

"Right," Compresser twitched. "I'm afraid it may come as a bit of a surprise." Hedstrong gave the spiritual equivalent of a groan, before telling him to go on. Compresser asked if he remembered Antedote. "She entered humanity in a somewhat agitated, impulsive manner, didn't she?"

"You mean she's one of the ones to expire when her human dies?"

"No, of course not," Professer interrupted, "she wasn't spiritually forced out of Reality. She went of her own volition, only not quite as willingly as one might usually go."

"That's an understatement," Upstart contributed, experiencing an emotion a human might describe as jealousy.

"But it was agitated... impulsive," Professer continued, "and any departure in the human direction which is less than premeditated tends to have interesting results. There appears to be some sort of electronic response by which the human brain identifies the intrusion and converts it into an awareness foreign to human normality. We are yet to establish how and why but are fortunate to have identified at least two guinea pigs within these grounds. The problem, however, is that, being in what might become alien territory, the situation is far from ideal for research of the nature required to advance our knowledge."

"You call this better than his scatterbrained image?" Hedstrong twitched. "What's he trying to say?"

"In a nutshell, when a spirit unwittingly or forcefully enters a human, it gives the human the ability to see us and communicate with us, is that clear enough?" Compresser told him.

"So it's Antedote that's given that human witch the power of spiritual sight and communication?" Upstart asked. The Professer confirmed it had. "Charming," she declared.

"Not only that," Compresser added. "Her lover Bernard now

has the same power, after the Thrillators projected Jenius into him."

"What's so fascinating, really fascinating," Professer contributed, "is that we have one of both."

"One of both what?" Hedstrong asked.

The Professer explained that, upon the human demise of Phyllis the witch, Antedote would probably be back amongst them, whereas the forceful ejection from reality of Jenius by fellow spirits meant that when Bernard was deceased, their former leader would likely die with him.

"Probably?" Hedstrong queried. "You mean you don't know whether Antedote will be back or not."

"Precisely." After further explanation, in which Professer described earlier experiments in another part of the planet to establish that, although the humans involved could see the spirits, they did not know why. They themselves were unaware that they were inhabited, just as the spirits were deprived of their consciousness until they returned to the Real World. In the case of Jenius, he would never have the opportunity of the return and recall of what was his last human experience… probably.

Hedstrong caught Upstart's thought and realised some of this was new to her as well. A few measures ago he would have begun to doubt his sanity upon being faced with these latest revelations, but so much had happened to him, indeed still was happening, that he just accepted what he was being told and asked what was the next step?

"We meet the two subjects and converse with them," Professer twitched at him, as if it was an obvious course.

"We need their help, don't we? They can see what we can only sense and their sight sometimes carries further than our perceptions, unless there's a barrier, like a wall, in the way, d'you understand?" Compresser said reverting to his question mark habit.

"D'you have to use that way of twitching?" Hedstrong complained.

"Sorry, but yes. Like Professer said, it keeps me in the mood and, what's more, I rather like it, d'you see?" He went on to remind them that two forces were beginning to match up to each other – the inner-council fearing attack from the Thought Processors and the Thought Processors convinced that they had to fight for their survival.

"So how do we go about 'meeting' these two humans?" Hedstrong wanted to know.

"They're in the shop, aren't they?" Compresser replied, sticking to his questioning approach. "All we have to do is go through the wall and I'll introduce you, isn't it?"

CHAPTER 24
COMING TO TERMS

Since his latest return to the Real World, Hedstrong's control of time seemed to be leaving him, one measure somehow appearing to merge into another. Before that there'd been no need to do more than exist, observe, choose his next being and travel wherever his human host had carried him. He'd lately begun to acknowledge how much he'd liked that… the simple, clearcut existence without responsibility. Now everything was complex, confusing and somehow he'd been drawn into a situation where the Real World was beginning to crumble into humanity. Time was becoming important.

"It's not that bad, darling," Upstart urged. "At least we've found each other."

"Until some Thought Processor group surrounds us, and then we're gone. For ever."

"Then, we won't let it happen," Upstart twitched.

They'd just left one of the strangest meetings imaginable, not that spirits were too hot on imagination. For the loving couple, uncertainty was creeping into their beings. They weren't indestructible. They'd become nearly as vulnerable as humans, all because one of their number had tried to take control: to dictate to the rest of them.

Entering the shop with Compresser and Professer, they'd been formally introduced to Phyllis and Bernard. For some reason she didn't understand, Phyllis had experienced a surge of animosity the moment she observed the two spiritual lovers. Noticing the reaction, Compresser had attempted to explain how, before Antedote's entry into Phyllis's body, she'd been rejected in the Real

World by Hedstrong who had demonstrated his preference for Upstart. Phyllis needed to fight to maintain politeness in Upstart's direction.

The meeting was even more complex because of the frequent pauses to allow Bernard to begin to understand what was happening to him. Hedstrong, who made little attempt to respond to Phyllis's gestures of goodwill, nevertheless identified with the predicament facing her lover. He considered it not so different to his own precipitous projection into a strange, confusing existence. The only factor preventing him forming a deeper bond with Bernard was the knowledge that Jenius was lurking somewhere within the human's flesh. Still, by the time the exchanges terminated, a liaison of sorts had formed between what were clearly three differing teams - the two humans, who could see the spirits; Upstart and Hedstrong who could see the humans but could only sense the presence of fellow spirits; and Compresser and Professer, equally blind to the sight of their compatriots but with a knowledge of the Real World far exceeding even Upstart's experiences.

"Where d'you think we go from here?" Hedstrong twitched when the two were alone.

"I think we wait and see. Nobody has asked us to do anything. Professer's gone off, no doubt to lecture his learned colleagues on the complications of the third world."

"What third world?" Hedstrong interrupted.

"The one that seems to be a halfway existence between human and spirit. You know, where forceful or unpremeditated entry into humans gives them the ability to see us. Like Phyllis. Only she's in a category of her own I suppose." If Upstart had possessed physical presence she would have shrugged before adding, "I don't know. Let's leave the speculation to someone like Professer and twitch onto something more enjoyable. I'll race you to Paradise."

She was off with a surge which dislodged the hat of one of the volunteer gardeners. Hedstrong's sweep carried it beyond the poor woman's grasp when she bent down to retrieve it, but he missed the unladylike language that followed.

***

For a while after the incident with the Thought Processors, Miss Gregory failed to notice anything untoward, except that she felt different. That terrible woman Phyllis Leblank kept watching her, which was irritating to say the least. And the superior lady's eyes did seem to be playing up a bit. Sometimes, when she looked in certain directions, shadows crossed her vision. At first she blamed her stomach and thought of changing her diet, but her intake of food was as regulated as the rest of her life. Then she worried that she was losing her sight. She booked an appointment with her optician.

Things appeared worse when she was within the grounds of the mansion, to an extent that, in a weak moment, a rare weak moment, she allowed her composure to slip. She was in the walled garden about to reprimand that nice young man Bernard when she could have sworn she saw some misty figure flit across her vision. Then there was another, much clearer, and suddenly all seemed to get too much for her. She staggered, stumbling onto her knees near a well tended patch of sprouts. Emotion, an experience generally foreign to her, erupted into an anguished cry, and the last thing she remembered was plunging her head in the soil between two rows of succulent green plants before she lost consciousness.

Recovering quickly, she was soon complaining she was all right whilst a concerned Bernard tried to assist. Regardless of her protests, he remained with her, slowly helping her to her feet. She was about to get really angry when a feeling foreign to her strict disciplined existence began to develop. She'd experienced it before, when she was much younger and a man had attempted to pay her attention. The discovery that his overtures had been designed to win a bet had put paid to any further amorous interludes but, despite herself, it was here again.

"Really, I'm all right," she managed, her voice lacking the usual enforced authority. "It's nice of you to be concerned, but I'm all right." With an effort she raised herself onto one knee before standing, leaning on Bernard for support.

"You are clearly not," he replied. "Come with me," and he slowly led her out of the garden, guiding her into one of the lean-to enclosed sections. Its sloping roof, attached to the high wall, was without illumination, leaving small, none too clean, windows allowing the light to deliver a reluctant attack upon the gloom. It took Miss Gregory a moment to become accustomed to the contrast.

"Thank you," she managed whilst Bernard sat her on an old wooden chair, having hurriedly attempted a one handed sweep of dust and debris off it.

"Sorry I can't offer you the comforts of the big house," he said, kneeling beside her, "but this will give you a chance to recover. Shall I get help?"

"No," she assured him. "Just a little while to get my breath back and I'll be sure to be all right."

Bernard ventured to seek an explanation for her fall, cautious not to prod too enthusiastically and mildly surprised at the gentleness of the responses from this usually dragon of a lady. Declaring that it was kind of him to attend to her, and keeping her arm around his shoulders whilst he continued to kneel beside her, she admitted to some concern at what appeared to be a deterioration in her sight. Asked for a more detailed description of the affliction, she told him of the shadows that seemed to flit across her vision.

Bernard wanted to know if she'd tried to have a good look at them. Receiving a negative reply he suggested that she should. Miss Gregory's usual self would have told him not to be so stupid, but for some reason she dismissed that reaction almost before it had materialised. This young man, who really wasn't quite as young as his appearance allowed, was, after all, trying to help, and it was rather nice to be sitting there using his body for support, even if the chair was hard and still probably quite dirty. So, in her gentler mode, she asked him why on earth she should do that?

"Because I think you will find that your eyes are perfectly all right," he told her. He knew of the previous incident with the Thought Processors, having discussed it at the meeting with the others in the shop. All had expressed the hope that the forceful entry of Sexa into Miss Gregory's frame, with or without her companion, would not have allowed her the type of vision he and Phyllis were experiencing. "I believe you've been singled out, and have been awarded the gift of sight of what they call the Real World."

"The what?" Miss Gregory demanded. Some of the old superiority was returning, although she still clutched Bernard around the shoulders. "Are you sure you're not influenced by someone else's rather way-out practices?" she asked.

"No," Bernard replied calmly. "I'm not."

"But I suppose she introduced you to these notions." Miss Gregory was, of course, aware of his liaison with the Leblank woman whom she considered to be of dubious character, totally unsuitable for inclusion in the workforce. Although not exactly part of her job description, she believed her responsibilities to include knowledge of the backgrounds of the staff employed by the Trust. After all, they may be slaves to any amount of hidden agendas in their anxiety to be part of the lost age of so-called luxury. That woman Phyllis Leblank topped her suspicious list of questionable characters and she had added Bernard as a close second the moment she had unearthed their unhealthy relationship. Yet now she was minded to modify her view of him in recognition of his demonstration of concern for a woman in distress. In fact, she felt, with her guidance, she may be able to remove him from the list altogether, and she gave his shoulder a squeeze. "You really believe in such things, don't you?" she ventured, resolving to try to humour him.

"I'm afraid there's no question of belief," Bernard told her gently. "I can see them, and I think you can too."

"Don't be stupid." Miss Gregory's superiority was back, showing her characteristic impatience when faced with opposition to her fixed beliefs. Then, to her surprise, she sought to soften the blow by adding, "unless you can give me proof." She held him even closer to her before adding, after a deep breath, "Bernard… may I call you Bernard? I don't wish to sound sceptical, but all this is very strange." It was clear he needed to be saved from the clutches of that witch of a woman who had obviously sunk her lecherous fangs into his innocent life. She stood, shakily at first, but, getting a grip on herself, allowed him to guide her out into the daylight. "You may call me Susan," she told him, linking an arm into his.

"Be prepared for a shock," he warned whilst they followed the path to the orangery. The ancient building was still surrounded with scaffolding but there was not a workman in sight. When he gestured that she thread her way through plastic and the metal pipes, she objected at first, waving at the warning notice and stressing that it was a hard hat area. "A brief look inside won't hurt," he encouraged, and that strange feeling of excitement she'd experienced a few minutes earlier returned. "Close your eyes," he instructed. To her surprise she did as she was told, allowing him to guide her into the ancient room that was once an old-fashioned greenhouse, before, she recalled from her research, a play room for the children of the house. "Now open them," Bernard instructed.

At first she thought she was in the midst of a fancy dress party. The gathering was grouped towards one end of the building, seemingly in deep debate, although she couldn't hear their voices. Several were wearing uniforms she recognised dating from the Second World War, whilst others represented fighting forces of a much earlier age - one even clad in a suit of armour. Suddenly they were joined by two superior looking personages, whom she could have sworn drifted in through an outside wall. Neither spoke, but she understood what the newcomers were saying. They were telling the others to beware, explaining that they were being infiltrated. Slowly the group stopped what they were doing to turn in unison to stare at the two humans.

Susan Gregory fainted again.

***

Hedstrong and Upstart spent a very long measure in Paradise, sometimes drifting between the old trees, many bare of their leaves whilst others refused to bow to winter, maintaining their green cloaks despite the winds that sped across the valley. The couple would stop, maybe rustling the grass under the boughs, a little less cropped than in the areas more frequented by the public, or disappear into a sturdy trunk for a quick shock. They had no desire to return to the Reality of their world and would probably have remained indefinitely within the presence of each other had they not begun to run short of power.

Reluctantly they made their way back to the shop, each to seek a boost. Hedstrong tried the cash till, hoping to have some fun by sparking off a response.

"It's switched off," Phyllis told him. "The shop's closed. They're moving it down to a new location next to a restaurant."

"That's a pity," Hedstrong twitched casually. Neither he nor Upstart had expected Phyllis to be there, and hadn't noticed her until she spoke. "I was hoping for a bit of entertainment."

"I'm sure we could think of something," Phyllis told him.

"Such as?" Upstart demanded. She'd finished taking a boost from a wall plug and flashed over to join her lover.

"No need to perform like that," Phyllis said. "I'm not about to entice your lover boy away, even if I do have your rival embedded in my flesh. She can have a go when she returns to your world."

Upstart was prevented from reply by a banging on the door. Phyllis moved to unlock it, and was nearly knocked over by Bernard bursting into her presence.

"I think we have a problem," he announced.

"All right, all right," Phyllis told him. "Calm down. Whatever it is, I'm sure we can deal with it." After a few more platitudes, Bernard was encouraged to collect his thoughts, which Hedstrong and Upstart struggled in vain to read. Achieving a measure of control, he described his interlude with Susan Gregory.

"Since when have you called her Susan?" Phyllis demanded.

Bernard was in no mood to react, his anxiety to recount the whole experience for a moment outweighing his devotion. Waving aside the question, he told of the encounter with the Thought Processing Force. Being ignorant of their purpose or title he simply described their ghostly appearances, especially the two black Processors who came into the orangery through a wall to warn the others of the human presence. It had taken Bernard some time to revive the stricken lady and apparently, when he'd succeeded, the Real World people had all disappeared. He'd escorted her to the estate office to rest and to receive the administrations of other members of the staff.

"And how did you revive her," Phyllis demanded. "By the kiss of life?"

Upstart had heard enough. With a twitch at Hedstrong, she was off through the wall.

"Hang on a minute, I haven't had my boost," he complained.

"We'll call in at the chapel on the way. There's enough points there to keep you going."

"You could give me a boost," Hedstrong suggested whilst they sped up the drive.

"Yes I could, but I need all I've got. We've work to do, and quickly."

When they reached the chapel, she waited impatiently whilst her lover connected with the house electric supply. She kept urging him to hurry and in the end had him so flustered he materialised, frightening a volunteer cleaner who had sneaked through the corridor out of the mansion for a cigarette.

"Now see what you've done," he complained, quickly resuming his normal state to sweep after her up the steps and along the drive towards the estate office.

"Don't fuss. This is important." Upstart would say no more until they were in the vicinity of the buildings adopted for administration. Only then did her pace slow. She made Hedstrong circle with her, concentrating to detect any other spiritual presence. "We seem to be alone," she concluded.

"Are you going to tell me what's going on?" Hedstrong asked. He was wondering if this was just a reaction to Phyllis's overtures in the shop. Whether there was a pang of jealousy influencing their swift departure.

"No, it's not," she twitched, reading his unblocked thought. "Don't you see? We have another human with sight of us and she passed out in the presence of the Thought Processors. What if they realised? What if they use her as a weapon? That would neutralise the advantage we have."

"You make it seem like we are at war," Hedstrong replied.

"Aren't we?"

He had no time to respond, for Upstart was off again heading straight for the estate office. She was relieved when she established that they were still the only ones present from the Real World. Miss Gregory was sitting in a chair, more comfortable than the last, and by her protestations that she was 'all right' showed every sign of return to full, active consciousness. She was about to get really angry at the fuss that was being made by the members of permanent staff when she looked up and saw the two spirits floating in front of her.

"Maybe I should take the rest of the day off," she said abruptly. "If you would be good enough to convey me home, I should be obliged." The worker to whom she had spoken looked surprised and for a moment uncertain.

"That's if it's not too much trouble," Miss Gregory snapped. "It's only down the road and I'm not sure I should walk at present."

"No, no, that's all right. I'll get the vehicle," he stammered. "Yes, just wait there and I'll be back."

When the Land Rover drew up outside the office door, Upstart and Hedstrong were uncomfortably installed under the bonnet. It was the only location they could find which guaranteed a barrier between them and the occupants so that they could remain undetected during the journey. Miss Gregory was in the passenger seat and the two spirits were fully occupied trying to avoid inadvertently shorting the electrics. The last thing they wanted was to ruin the vehicle's mechanical progress and delay the moment when they could get Susan Gregory to themselves.

CHAPTER 25

TIME FOR ACTION

The moment Phyllis realised Hedstrong and Upstart had left the shop she pushed Bernard out of the door, locked it and ushered him up the hill towards the mansion. Ignoring his protestations, she maintained a power-walking step until she reached the pedestrian way down past the rose garden. Only then did she slow, instructing her lover to keep his eyes open.

"What are we looking for?" he managed between breaths.

"Compresser."

"Why?"

"Oh, for goodness sake, Bernard, why d'you think? Someone else can see the spirits like us. You said yourself that was a problem."

Bernard acknowledged indeed he had, but failed to see why his news had scattered everyone from both worlds in all directions. He wanted to know what Phyllis thought she could do about it, especially with those other two spirits having taken off like tornadoes. He suggested they would be well ahead by now.

Phyllis didn't bother to reply. She'd just spotted the Monk drifting along the main path below. Shouting to him caused several human volunteers to respond, each wondering what she or he had done wrong. With several 'not yous!' she surged past them eventually to catch up with Compresser.

"Phyllis," Bernard gasped, seeking to keep pace with her, "you do know you're making a fool of yourself? If you stop here and, as far as they're concerned, start talking to yourself they'll think you're round the bend."

"Follow me, will you?" Compresser twitched, leading the way

from the path into the formal garden, out of view and earshot of any others. "Now," he started, "I think you humans would say, 'Where's the fire?'"

"Don't try to be clever," Phyllis retorted. "We have trouble."

Compresser wished he had the full capacity to read human minds. Experiments existed, especially with those where there was known entry of one or two spirits from the Real World, but he'd not grasped the formula sufficiently to always succeed. Obviously something was wrong, so now was not the time to take the risk. He needed all the details, accurately, or at least as near to the truth as humans could manage.

Phyllis obliged. She announced that Miss Susan Gregory had acquired the ability to see into the spirit world and knew it. Those were the two facts he extracted from the account she gave him, her anger neatly suppressed by her clipped, level tone. He also sensed a hint of a suspected liaison between the other woman and her Bernard. Phyllis wanted immediate action, suggesting that the whole world could be in imminent danger if Miss Gregory was not stopped before she realised what power was within her grasp.

Avoiding mentioning they were probably somewhat removed from the centre of planetary activity, Compresser, nevertheless, took the development seriously. He should have foreseen the result of Sexa's departure and done something about it. He certainly didn't want matters to grow ahead of experiments elsewhere.

"Come on, then," Phyllis urged, making off in the direction of the walled garden.

"Wait a minute… just stop a minute, will you?" Compresser said sweeping in her footsteps. "We need to consider…"

"Stuff considering," Phyllis shouted. "We need action," and strode on. The three of them were out of the formal garden and halfway across the path leading to the walled area before Bernard, who was several paces behind his love, suddenly halted.

"Phyllis, stop!" he shouted. The command, delivered at maximum volume, was such a surprise that she did so abruptly;

Compresser passed through her before he, too, could brake. Then the storm broke.

"Who d'you think you're telling to stop! I've just had about enough of you today. First you go off with that woman, no doubt falling for every trick she chooses to perform, then you casually mention she might ruin all we're trying to achieve here, and now you think you can tell me, *me*, what to do." If she expected the reprimand to bring her man into line, she was mistaken. He stood his ground, glaring at her. "I don't know what's got into you these days," she hissed. "Ever since that lightening struck you, you've shown an aggressive streak. I'm not sure I like it. In fact, I'm not at all sure I like you."

"I'm not sure you ever have," Bernard replied. There was a calm in his voice which infuriated Phyllis even more. Her anger was almost too intense to allow speech, but somehow she managed.

"After all I've done for you, now you betray me," she shouted.

"No, I'm not. I'm trying to help you. Stop you making a big mistake. You're in no mood to confront Susan. In this state you'll do more harm than good. Look at the exhibition you're making of yourself. People are beginning to stare."

"We can't have that, can we?" Phyllis spat at him. "We can't have anyone thinking our lovely, obliging, creeping Bernard was anything other than a nice human being." Compresser tried to intervene seeing, like Bernard, that others were taking notice. "And you can butt out too," she shouted, "with all your theories about who and how your lot are supposed to take us over."

Compresser materialised between the two humans, with his back to Bernard.

"They are not theories," he twitched, "and we do not 'take over'. We occupy. Don't exaggerate what we do or your own importance."

It was the first time Phyllis had looked closely at a ghost in the flesh so to speak. The expression pulsing out of his eyes, plus the countenance of his face, were beyond anything she had ever experienced. She wanted to reach out to touch him, but she couldn't. She wanted to be angry with him, to chastise him, to embrace him, love him, yet she was paralysed in both speech and body.

"Now," Compresser continued, lapsing to his usual questioning style, "let us make our way calmly along this path until we are away from public view, all right? Then I shall be able to resume my normal state and we'll begin to plan a sensible course of action, isn't it?"

Fortunately no one on the estate had been close enough to hear more than voices raised in anger or to be sure that suddenly a monk seemed to have appeared out of thin air. Interest in the altercation soon declined to a casual noting of the extraordinary, the more sceptical concluding that it was probably some experimental rehearsal derived to pep up the image of what was just another boring old pile of aristocratic masonry. They went about their activities, leaving the strange threesome to wander down the path, through the gate and onto the tree-lined driveway.

**

Miss Susan Gregory's house was a modern contrast to the ancient world in which she spent her working hours. The dwelling was neat, detached, two-storey and hiding with others in a small select estate on the perimeter of the village. The land might once have been considered suitable for local authority housing of the working classes. However, four bedrooms, albeit smaller than older council designs, plus minute gardens conforming to modern desires, and space for the motor cars which had brought affluence out into the country, confirmed the units to be speculative owner-occupied residences. The Land Rover threaded between the overflow of cars parked along the cul-de-sac.

"You can turn at the bottom," she instructed, not wishing to have the vehicle reverse off the estate road onto her pristine double-garage approach. "Thank you for your courtesy," was the only acknowledgement she allowed, before leaving the vehicle the moment it drew to a halt.

"Stuck up bitch," the driver muttered, watching her stride towards her front door. His language deteriorated even further when the Land Rover's engine petered out.

"Oops," Upstart twitched, pleased to be away from the confines of the bonnet. "Was that me or you shorting his electrics?"

"Me, I think," Hedstrong told her. They both waited whilst the whirring of the starter motor laboriously attacked the stubborn engine, eventually bringing it back to life with a burst of thick blue smoke. By then Miss Gregory was safely in the house leaning against her closed front door. The two spirits came in through the wall to hover in front of her. She didn't see them. She stood with her eyes closed taking deep breaths to combat an unfamiliar feeling of inadequacy.

When she eventually straightened her back to resume progress she walked through the ghosts before her sight adjusted to the greyer light of the hall.

"She didn't see us," Upstart twitched.

"Perhaps we're worrying unnecessarily," Hedstrong suggested. "Let's find out." He followed the proud lady into the kitchen to watch her pour a glass of water from her purification jug, moving to sit at her dinner table looking at it. Hedstrong drifted over to face her, and waited. When she looked up she groaned.

"Tell me you're not real," she managed. "Tell me I'm just hallucinating and all this will go away."

Hedstrong shook his head. Matching his thoughts with his twitching, he tried to reassure her that she was not mistaken and that he did exist, but not in her world. It seemed he was getting through, because she answered his projections, demanding to know how he could prove he was not an image conjured up by a twisting of her mind. He said that he couldn't, only she could, and asked her what he looked like.

"Don't you know?" she demanded.

"I'm afraid not. In the Real World, we don't see each other. We just know we're there," he twitched. "Try describing my appearance. It may convince you and I'd certainly be interested to know. But if it's not a good one, try to leave out the bad bits, 'cause my beloved is present."

"This is stupid," muttered Miss Gregory. "You're talking a load of nonsense. Go away and leave me alone."

"Sorry, no can do. We have to communicate. My world is under threat and we need your help."

"We?" Miss Gregory demanded. "Who's 'we'?"

Upstart, who had been hovering in the hall, drifted in to appear beside her lover. The human lady tried to keep control of her emotions.

"D'you know how stupid this is, your appearance, your suggestion that you can't see yourself? And what on earth do you mean by a 'real world'. This is the real world and I'm in it." She paused. "At least I think I'm in it. Unless I've died and this is some sort of purgatory." She stood up. "Whatever it is, just leave me alone."

With that she strode out of the kitchen to collapse in one of her armchairs in the lounge, abandoning the two spirits to look at each other, except, of course, that they could do no more than sense their continued presence.

"D'you honestly not know what you look like?" Upstart asked.

"How could I?"

"Never mind, I think you're rather cute, in a masculine invisible sort of way. In fact you've got a sexy presence that a girl finds hard to resist."

"And are you trying to resist?" Hedstrong asked. Upstart conceded that she was not and the two lost track of time whilst they merged in a sizzling, spiritual embrace.

***

Miss Gregory, in an uncharacteristic neglect of caution, had forgotten to secure her front door. She ignored the ringing of her bell and the knocking, simply sitting staring straight ahead, unwilling to believe that anything was real any more. Phyllis tried the handle and, with the door open, rushed down the passage to the kitchen followed by Bernard. Both came to an abrupt halt at the image confronting them.

"What in God's name's that," Bernard blurted out.

Slowly the mini tornado stopped spinning to separate into Upstart and Hedstrong.

"Something you and I try for but have never achieved," Phyllis told him. "Pure, complete, unrestricted sex."

"Sorry," Upstart twitched, figuratively trying to re-arrange herself. "We didn't register your arrival."

"Don't apologise," Phyllis told her. "I only wish I could share such an electrifying experience." It was a compliment, expressed in admiration with a depth of feeling that conquered any jealous revolution that may have stirred from Antedote's spirit within her. Further communication in that direction was arrested by the arrival of Compresser. Agreeing it was best for Miss Gregory to be greeted first by two humans, he'd stayed in Bernard's car, hurriedly collected from the staff car park for the journey after they'd confirmed where she'd gone. Patience exhausted, he'd passed briefly though the lounge and observed the traumatic state of Miss Gregory.

"At least she's away from the Thought Processors, isn't she?" he commented.

"But for how long?" Phyllis asked. "We've got to take control of her." Unfortunately her words were spoken out loud.

"Who's there?" cried Miss Gregory.

With a twitched muttering that echoed something like an oath, Compresser told the rest to stay where they were and went to see the lady. In an attempt to reassure her, he materialised and approached from the hall. Fortunately the door to the lounge stood open, which assisted in an almost natural humanistic entry, his elevation a centimetre above the floor and static feet concealed beneath the flowing gown. Miss Gregory stared at him.

"Are you human?" she asked in a tired voice. He smiled and shook his head. "Then can you explain what you are?"

Compresser found this difficult, not just because of the need to educate yet another in spiritual communication but also because he'd never quite been able to answer that question to his own satisfaction. Somewhere, so many measures ago, he could recall... but no matter, she wouldn't comprehend anyway. Adopting a combination of twitch and thought projection, matching intention to his benevolent expression, he began the training of a suspicious, questioning pupil.

In human time, it took over an hour of conversing before Miss Gregory showed signs of relaxation. Despite her difficulties in coming to terms with notions beyond her world, she was no fool. Compresser concentrated on the mysteries of the universe, eventually gaining her concession that there were many features still beyond human knowledge. Somehow he managed to convince her that he was one of them.

"All right," she surrendered. "But why on earth am I suddenly involved in all this?"

Another 30 human minutes passed whilst Compresser sought to describe the conflicts that were beginning to rack his world. Painting his small group as 'the goodies' and the Thought Processors... not quite 'the baddies'... more the ill-informed, he described the efforts of first Jenius and now Frenco to take on the role of leader. When he got to corruption of power into an appetite for control, the picture he created was so likened to human attitudes that he was winning. He felt the moment had come to introduce the others.

"May I ask my colleagues to join us?"

"They're here?" It was a simple, unemotional question, for Miss Gregory was past the point of incredulity. "Then, bring them in."

During the whole of this time, Upstart and Hedstrong had been listening to and translating into human thought processes the scene taking place in the living room. Bernard was unable to penetrate proceedings through walls and Phyllis, despite her supernaturally claimed attributes, fared little better. The two spirits nearly lost the battle to keep the humans in the kitchen on several occasions, so the invitation from Compresser came as a welcome relief.

Hedstrong was asked to join him first, Compresser urging that he come through the wall, preparing Miss Gregory first by describing exactly how and from whence his spiritual colleague would appear. He was impressed by the way she received the apparition.

"Despite what you tell me, I still find it difficult to convince myself that I am not in some sort of dream world," she said. Compresser communicated he understood and instructed Upstart to bring his two 'human colleagues' out of the kitchen, entering the lounge in the traditional manner. He explained that as they were human, like her, any attempt to walk through walls would result in serious injury. Their arrival in the lounge stimulated mixed feelings. Bernard, Miss Gregory was able to welcome, but not that witch of a woman! She was a different matter.

"I might have known you would be involved," the lady declared, surprising the gathering by actually twitching the response instead of speaking. Changing to human language, she added, "at least this should convince me I'm not in a dream. I cannot imagine how even my subconscious would entertain your presence."

"Susan," Phyllis started, which was a mistake.

"Who said you could call me Susan?" Miss Gregory demanded. "I certainly didn't."

"All right, all right, Miss Gregory, then. Whatever you feel about me and whatever I think of you, it is important that we work together."

Susan Gregory was at pains to stress that she had absolutely no feelings for Phyllis Leblank whatsoever but, with attempted soothing words from Bernard, who infuriated his beloved by calling her 'rival' by her Christian name and getting away with it, she calmed down.

Agreement was eventually reached to discuss the current predicament rationally, after which Compresser excused himself for a mini-measure to take a boost from the standard lamp, dematerialising at the same time.

"I can't imagine why you materialised in the first place. I can see you almost as well in your so-called 'real state'," was Susan Gregory's final thrust before she subsided into meaningful debate as one of an increasing unlikely band of warriors.

CHAPTER 26

CRISIS MEETING

T he problems of leadership hit Frenco from the start. He received a full report of the incident involving Sexa's dispatch into the body of Miss Gregory, possibly with her lover. He agreed Lard should be the one to negotiate with the Thought Processor Force whilst he remained in the background. The commission was to Lard's liking. He was known to the TPT from his contacts with them during the reign of Jenius, so was accepted in the Orangery, if with some reservation. He took his time, allowing the Processors to voice grievances. He asked for suggestions as to how they saw their future. Only then did he begin to negotiate. It took a lengthy measure with many pauses before he left to report back.

Frenco's stay in the background neither prevented him from insisting upon hearing every detail, nor his criticism of any step he considered ill-conceived or fruitless. He finally ran out of patience.

"This I do not find acceptable," he thundered. "I drift around this little crumbling structure, fit for no more than birds. Not even for them, and the rest of inner-council lord it in manor and you allow yourself to be manipulated into inactivity."

"A little harsh," Lard responded.

"Not harsh enough. Either I get protection of Thought Processor Force or we get rid of them. There is work to be done. How else can I take control of things?"

Lard refrained from questioning what 'things' needed to be taken control of, seeking once again to calm a leader who appeared to be developing the usual characteristics he imagined his position demanded.

"They're just a bit jittery at present," he urged.

"And that is all that is holding them back? You know what a frightened being can do," the leader twitched. "If they think they are threatened, they will fight."

"I'm not sure you can assess their reaction in human terms," Lard tried. "After all, we are all spirits. Perhaps we should afford them the recognition of the superior intelligence vested in all of us by our Real World. Although I have to admit to one human tactic: the art of keeping them talking. It often removes a lot of the aggression."

"That is rubbish," Frenco countered. "They have realised their existence is in threat. What would you do in their position? Would you trust Thrillators you hardly know? Of course you would not. You would protect your space and if there was suspicion of attack you would want to strike first blow."

Lard suggested that the Processor Force might not think like that. He felt that, after a period under Jenius, when they had practised discipline and obedience to what they'd been told was a higher being, they were simply at a loss to comprehend the present situation. Frenco ruled that that made it all the more important for someone to take control of them...him. However hard Lard tried, he was unable to convince the disgruntled new leader that no one, apart from him, had aspirations to take control and that his position was not under threat... not immediately anyway.

"Immediately!" twitched Frenco. "That is point. It may not be 'immediately' but it is there, and if we do not stop it now it will be ten times harder to deal with later. No, they have had chances. They have to be dealt with."

Lard ventured to ask how he felt this could be achieved, and was unceremoniously instructed to arrange a meeting of the inner-council. Frenco declared the aviary unsuitable for such a crucial gathering, which would have had spirits floating in and out of the structure as if it didn't exist. Lard was to proceed to the mansion to organise an acceptable location so that Frenco could gain authority for action.

"Having spent your last human existence in the place, at least you should be able to achieve that without more delay," was Frenco's final jibe.

A lesser spirit would have taken such criticism badly, but to Lard it was of no consequence. Maintaining a dignity and regality he considered befitting of his position, he drifted from the aviary, but didn't embark upon his latest commission straight away. He sensed the imminence of Compresser and, with a twitched greeting, joined him in the formal garden. The benevolent monk was well aware of the problems, taking seriously the assessment he was given of Frenco's state of being. The two debated possible solutions to the growing threat of confrontation, but failed to come up with a course of action they felt would avoid violence.

"You know this sort of thing's happening elsewhere on the planet, don't you?" Compresser said. "If we were just facing a minor hiccup in one small corner of our Reality there would be no lasting effect, but we're not, are we? Wherever one of us tries to assert pressure and gain control over others, there's elimination and we lose more, isn't it?"

"We've caught the human trait," Lard agreed. "Down through their centuries they've used force to control. I sometimes wish they hadn't created alternative, readily available power sources, then spirits wouldn't have found their freedom. Exercising it seems to have made us greedy for more. I suppose we're now faced with the emotions which keep humans in conflict... envy, jealousy and the fear someone else will achieve more than the rest."

"Maybe that's what we're on this planet to experience, perhaps even learn to cope with, d'you think?" Compresser wondered.

Each agreed that, if they survived the current atmosphere of conflict, they would seek to implement the one human feature capable of rendering aggression ineffective. They would endeavour to achieve a state of organised chaos which would cripple attempts at domination by any individual. They would preach democracy.

***

Compresser had persuaded what he christened his 'middle force' to remain at Miss Gregory's house whilst he surveyed the situation at the stately home. Following his discussion with Lard, he sped back to them, pausing only to gain a top-up electrical boost at a street light, illuminated to denote the end of another human day. When he arrived at the dwelling he was relieved to discover that the occupants had maintained an uneasy peace, principally through the two spirits slipping up to a bedroom where they partook of a romantic surge whilst the three humans concocted and consumed an evening meal. All were recharged physically or electronically by the time Compresser made his presence known.

"There will be only one outcome to the current situation up at the manor, you know? There will be war, isn't it? Sooner or later there will be war, don't you see? I'm familiar with similar incidents in other sectors of the planet, aren't I? Where you have an ambitious leader like Frenco, anxious to take control of all around to build an empire, faced by a force maybe still loyal to the deposed leader, what will he do? He will seek to eliminate it, to substitute his own force, loyal to him, won't he? And how do I believe he will try? By mobilising the inner-council, won't he? He's become so impatient he's convinced himself there's no time to start building an army from scratch, so he'll try to use what's already available to him, isn't it? War is inevitable, you know?"

Hedstrong suggested that the Thrillators would be no match against the Thought Processors. He felt every effort should be made to solve the problem by negotiation. Whilst Upstart sympathised with his pacifist approach, she felt that any attempt in that direction would only inflame matters. If anyone could have succeeded, Lard would have done so and, according to Compresser, he hadn't.

Miss Gregory, now reconciled to the situation in which she found herself, was anxious to reassert authority over what she considered 'this motley bunch of ghosts'. She was fast mastering their technique of conversation and advocated the direct approach, believing that both sides should be told not to be so stupid and have their heads bashed together. Phyllis responded, quite unnecessarily in Miss Gregory's eyes, by pointing out that spirits didn't have heads capable of being bashed.

"We're better trying to influence from afar," she said.

"That's typical of you," Miss Gregory pronounced. "What do you suggest? Cast a spell on them?"

"We use the power of thought," Phyllis replied, sensing she was onto a winning argument. "At least you can't fault that. Religions have been doing it for centuries, even yours."

Miss Gregory attempted a dismissal of such 'typical black magic mumbo jumbo', but, with so many unnatural goings-on around her, was eventually forced to accept failure. Bernard attracted attention and earned condemnation from both females for suggesting they do nothing and see what happens.

It was well into the human night before a plan was agreed. Compresser had deliberately allowed the debate to ramble on, knowing, from his earlier reconnaissance, that little or no action was likely until at least another new human day dawned. Lard had told him he was not about to rush arrangements for the meeting Frenco required, and had planned a last attempt at persuading the TPT to show allegiance to the new ruler. Phyllis said they should get some rest beforehand, and won an invite to occupy one of the Gregory bedrooms until morning. To her annoyance she had to allow Bernard to be channelled into another. His was next to Miss Gregory's chamber, and she refused to be consoled by Bernard's whispered insistence that they should not embarrass Susan by openly flouting their relationship.

The spirits were amused by the demonstration and the difficulties all three humans faced in having to take time to sleep. After the performance, Hedstrong and Upstart assumed position in the rafters to enjoy their particular measure of union whilst Compresser drifted off elsewhere. They all agreed to meet in the lounge of the Gregory establishment at nine the next morning – human time – each of the spirits selecting some sort of signal that would afford a suitable indication of the hour in question. That's when they would finalise how to implement the strategy they'd accepted, which was 'to observe'. In essence, Miss Gregory concluded, it was to do nothing, as Bernard had suggested.

***

Lard embarked upon a new measure before he finally made his way to the mansion. A further attempt to convert the TPT into an army for Frenco had failed. They'd insisted they wanted to keep their independence whilst they observed how Frenco and the Thrillators behaved. They were not convinced that the elimination of Jenius, their leader, was not the start of a plan to do away with them all. Although Frenco and his council couldn't lie, they could change their minds.

Kernel was found and told to help plan a Thrillator meeting. He was to proceed to the dining room after a couple of mini-measures. Lard selected this location because it was central. He wanted time for reflection before setting wheels in motion. Spayed and Baybe were ready to act as door guards to the room and, never having got so far as joining the TPT, they could also be commissioned to act as lookouts. The first task, which he undertook immediately, was to persuade mansion residents to vacate whilst the Thrillators were in session.

Lard was relieved that the spring opening of the estate to the public was still a few further measures away. Spirits were not unduly troubled by visitors wandering about, but it would reduce distraction if they could have their conference without an endless procession of humans trying to imagine themselves presiding over nobility at the head of the large table. Nobility, Lard thought, allowing himself a moment of reflection on his last trip into their world. The public had no idea of the problems of entertaining in a big house: the crumbling masonry, the eternal draughts, stuck with the now admired drapes, floor coverings and surviving antique furniture which was not falling apart, and some that was, because there were insufficient funds to buy replacements.

Despite the limitations of his last human host compared with the wealth of his predecessors, Lard still had a soft spot for the place. At least, he thought, for a worldly generation or two, preservation for the nation avoided young pupils or senior citizens having to suffer the adaptation of an unsuitable building as a school or nursing home. His meanderings, uncharacteristic for a spirit, were interrupted by the arrival of Kernel, who enquired whether he should now summon the Thrillators.

"Good idea," Lard twitched. "You get them and I'll tell Frenco. And I've asked all the house residents to vacate. See if you can locate them and have them gather elsewhere, in one place." He had become fond of Kernel, happy to accept the low level of application to tasks he was commissioned to undertake. He was easy to command and could be relied upon never to be unpredictable, a benefit not to be cast aside in these times of Real World stress. He knew the Thrillators would be assembled and waiting as required.

"About time, too," the disgruntled leader told him when Lard returned to the aviary. "What kept you?"

For once Lard dropped his guard, failing to counter with a pacifying response.

"It's not as if there's any need to rush," he twitched.

"Do not be stupid. Of course there is need. Do you think that those Thought Processors are going to stay waiting for us to decide how to deal with them?"

Lard didn't consider the question needed response and simply explained the arrangements he'd made for the meeting.

"And how long is it going to take that stupid Kernel to round everyone up?" Frenco demanded.

"They should be ready now," Lard told him.

"Then they can wait. How do you plan that meeting should be arranged? What should content be? Do I ask for views and let them talk before I tell them what we do? Do you produce Agenda for discussion?" Again Lard's response was less than courteous.

"I assume you'll just tell them what to do and explain how you plan to deal with the Thought Processors. You don't need an Agenda for that," he twitched. "Incidentally, what are you going to do?"

"If I have to decide for everyone, what is use of Council? I am not dictator. Members have right to express views and come up with suggestions. We will 'av an Agenda."

"Of course," Lard accepted. He knew Frenco had no idea what he was going to do. "Then, if you're ready, perhaps we should go."

"We? What do you mean 'we'? You are not Thrillator. This is to be closed session… only elected members. If you have not made that clear to Kernel you had better do so quick. I want guards posted at doors, and all other stupid spiritual occupants of house kept well away." Lard didn't think it worth confirming he'd already arranged this.

With that final outburst, Frenco aimed out of the aviary, gathering momentum during his swift, direct journey to the dining room. So swift was his progress that upon entry through the walls in between, he suffered a brief materialisation. Whilst trying to stop he overshot and had to gather his being together in the gravelled forecourt before he returned through a large window. He allowed the assembled inner-council members to sense his arrival and greet him as if his entry had been all part of a plan, including the overshooting.

Following on behind, in more leisurely fashion, Lard identified

Kernel, separating him from the rest. He asked if his arrangements were being implemented.

"Already done," Kernel told him. He was communicating by transference rather than twitching and Lard was surprised to discover that the spirit was maintaining a block on his thoughts as well as using a process which probably didn't reach the others in the room. "Baybe and Spayed are on the doors, for what it's worth, and the rest of the permanent residents are assembled in the chapel."

"Lard," Frenco twitched from the other end of the room with unnecessary strength, "are we all present?"

Taking advantage of another thought transmitted from Kernel, Lard said all except two: Hedstrong and Upstart, who couldn't be located.

"They not really one of us anyway, so is better they not be here. We shall begin. Kindly exclude yourself."

"As you wish," Lard twitched back. "Kernel and I are leaving. Come on," he said to his spiritual colleague and the two swept up through the wall, making it clear to the gathering that they were departing.

Satisfied that all was secure, Frenco began the proceedings with a lengthy report upon the happenings about the estate, managing to imply that all was within his view and under his control. By the time he was on to describing the purpose of the meeting, Lard and Kernel were hovering below the alter of the church, pleased to have deserted the so-called seat of power. The other Real World permanent residents were there. The two exceptions were Spayed and Baybe, who remained circling the dining room as bodyguards to the Thrillators, doing their best to connect with the waves of discussion.

***

Lard congratulated the mansion residents upon their patience and restraint during the recent past, especially as they'd suffered the presence of sometimes less than courteous beings in their midst. Although most of them hadn't really noticed much difference, even fewer realising they'd suffered until it was put to them, they happily joined with him in sharing memories of the measures when they'd enjoyed the freedom of the house with only the odd frustration of having to tolerate the occasional outbursts of Antedote. They agreed, a return to those times would be welcome, although accepted Lard's pronouncement that this was unlikely. Nevertheless, he said he would do his best to preserve the comforts that made their existence in the Real World enjoyable. They thanked him.

***

Compresser had not been idle. He'd assembled what he called his small force for action. With each of the spirits taking care to plug in for an electrical boost on the way, he led them back to the estate. It wasn't far up the road from Miss Gregory's establishment and their approach was through the gates by the lower lodge. The humans amongst them were striding along the driveway when Phyllis twitched everyone to stop.

"There's movement ahead," she said.

"She's right. What a strange crew they all are," Susan Gregory commented. "How anybody could take them for an organised army of resistance is entirely beyond me. Although they do look a little menacing."

"Too right, they do," Bernard agreed. "I think we should keep well away."

Compresser wanted a full description as the force was still not near enough for him to detect any spiritual presence. Like Upstart and Hedstrong, he was solely dependent upon the commentary the others were giving. Miss Gregory was the one to describe progress. The Thought Processors had obviously moved out from the Orangery via the walled garden onto the drive. They were now progressing towards the mansion. Compresser wanted to know how many and the humans agreed there were no more than eighteen.

"Hang on, there's one behind the rest," Susan Gregory reported. "He's holding back, leaving them to carry on ahead. I'd say a cut above the others. Somewhat academic in stature."

"Professer," Phyllis said smugly.

"What?" It was more a challenge than a question, Susan Gregory not quite sure whether the witch was being insulting. "What d'you mean 'Professer'?"

It was Hedstrong who gave the explanation, twitching in a manner sufficiently conciliatory to avert the threat of another confrontation between the two women. Compresser asked for more detail and was told that 'Professer', a word Miss Grogory had difficulty repeating without looking down upon it, was now heading their way. She was told not to worry, he was a friend, or at least had acted so last time they'd met.

"Aha," the learned man pronounced, completing his approach. "I thought you humans wouldn't be allowed out on your own." He beamed in on the presence of the three spirits, and greeted Compresser with obvious affection, but his attitude was not well received by Miss Gregory who took badly to the suggestion that she was being in some way controlled, and said so.

"Don't be so stuffy," Professer told her. "Just keep your eyes on that happy band of mercenaries and tell us where they're going."

"I shall not," Susan Gregory declared. "I am not prepared to stand here and be insulted, especially not by a mere spirit."

"In that case," Professer invited, "you'd better shove off. Try the estate office. It could do with your input. The minions aren't doing much and they may actually let their hair down and really enjoy themselves. I'm sure that would be against the rules."

"I'm not staying here to be insulted," Miss Gregory repeated.

Hedstrong was about to intervene when Compresser stopped him.

"Let her go, won't you? She'll be nowhere near the Processors, will she? She can't do any lasting damage and she can keep the staff busy and out of the way, can't she?"

Bernard wondered if he should go with her.

"No, you don't," Phyllis told him. "You're needed here."

The rest paused to watch Susan Gregory gather herself to her full height. One look at Bernard confirmed he wasn't about to join her. She glared at him, ignoring his apologetic look, and, whilst Phyllis took his arm to stake her claim, the lady strode off through the ornamental gate. Professer's carefully calculated remark had hit the target, ensuring she was on what she considered to be her most direct route to tackle whatever mess the estate office had managed in her absence.

"Shall we continue our surveillance?" Compresser urged.

The slightly smaller group followed his lead, tracking the Thought Processors along the pedestrian path, through the meadow, into the formal garden and on up towards the mansion.

CHAPTER 27
NEW ORDER

T he inner-council meeting was getting nowhere. Members, having had opportunity to mix with the house residents, were becoming accustomed to a less pressurised, peaceful way of life. They had adjusted to the comfort of their surroundings, and were not inclined to easily give up their new-found luxury. The cold and draughts, the smell of dust and the odour of decay had no effect upon their beings, so residence in the manor was much to their liking. They couldn't believe their leader was talking of war, especially against fellow spirits. What purpose would it achieve? Why was it necessary? There was ample space for everyone to drift in their own sweet way, so why spoil things?

Frenco lost patience and was about to show his frustration when there was a commotion at the side door. Baybe's twitchings were becoming more forceful, and waves of similar reactions from Spayed at the main dining room access penetrated into the meeting. Others of the Real World were attempting access, and weren't impressed by the messages of restraint they were receiving.

Frenco called a halt to discussion. He twitched Spayed for a report, but any response was negatived by the entry of two of the three senior Thought Processors. They made their presence known whilst the third bypassed Baybe through a wall to join the gathering.

"This is private, closed meeting," Frenco twitched cautiously.

"We are aware of that," one of the Processors told him. "But it was considered appropriate for us to enter into discussion whilst you were gathered together."

"And who is this 'we' that 'considered'?" Frenco demanded.

"The Force set up by Jenius."

"Jenius no longer leads so there is no Force. I now lead."

"If Jenius no longer leads and there is no Force, then there is no Leader and no council."

"You are inaccurate. I am elected by inner-council, who have planet recognition."

"We do not agree, either that your 'council' represents the planet, or that your inner-council has authority to select a leader. We consider your actions to be a dictatorial attempt to seize power."

"This is not true. I am leader, properly appointed and stand in the shoes of Jenius. That means that those responsible to him are now responsible to me. You and your force are responsible to me," Frenco claimed.

"That does not accord with the chain of command laid down by your predecessor." The other two Processors twitched their confirmation.

"This is nonsense. Jenius had no power..."

"He had every power and he exercised it fully," the same Processor countered. "We deemed it appropriate to appear in your midst, amicably, to explain the transference of power."

"I am power," Frenco asserted.

"You are not." The Thought Processor went on to explain the clear orders expounded by Jenius several measures before the arrival of the inner-council. He had feared an attempt at his overthrow and dictated that, if it were to happen, his power of leadership was to immediately transmit to the three senior Thought Processors. They would take control and would have the authority to implement necessary action to stabilise the situation.

Frenco tried to argue there was no situation requiring stabilising. He again suggested that Jenius had no power to transfer leadership. He said that leaders had to be democratically elected by the Real World and that his appointment had been by the elected representatives of all the planet's spirits. The leading Thought Processor declared that his argument failed because absolute power had been vested in Jenius and had been exercised by him. In the exercise of that absolute power he had chosen his successors.

"It is with that power that we three approach you. We are prepared to enter into negotiation with a view to harnessing the obvious qualifications of you and your fellows so that Thought Processors and Thrillators can work together for the greater benefit of the Real World."

Frenco hesitated, but neglected to block thought of the audacity of these mercenaries to even consider they could dictate to him. He had manoeuvred hard and long to achieve his goal, and no jumped-up soldier was going to take it away from him.

"I am sorry you take it that way," the Processor twitched. "We came in peace to negotiate."

"Then you had better go whilst there still is peace and tell your force I am leader and they must answer to me." Frenco awaited reaction, but none came. He tested to establish the whereabouts of the three Processors and even twitched other Thrillators for assistance in locating their exact presence. No one could. The confrontation was over. The Processors were no longer present.

***

Compressor's small part-human/part-spiritual group had moved diagonally through the formal garden and were positioned on the path leading to Paradise. The aviary was between them and the main house, which allowed distance but kept in view a motley collection of military personnel. Phyllis had seen their three leaders detach from the rest to drift into the mansion through the drawing room. She described how the remainder had spaced out, some, she thought, disappearing to complete a circle of the building.

"There's insufficient to create a strong enough force-field that big," Professer twitched. "But if they close in."

"What if they close in?" Bernard twitched.

"Obvious," Professer told him. "Don't be stupid. You know what happens."

Bernard didn't really know, but felt it best not to admit to his ignorance. The group waited, and he occupied himself by pretending to show interest in the grass verges. It was strange to see his fellow workers attacking their human duties, unaware of the turmoil going on in what he was told was the Real World. To maintain the pretence of doing something, he pointed out non-existent border features to Phyllis, who was too busy watching what was happening to notice. She reported that several of the force looked over at them and Compresser doubted if Bernard's subterfuge had them fooled. None moved out of the circle and she described the return of the three leaders to join the line around the house.

"Can you hear their twitch?" Professer asked Compresser.

"No, but if they remain in position I think I can guess, can't you?" the monk replied. "We may be in for quite a wait, might we not?"

"Shall I go in and see what I can discover?" Phyllis offered.

"Bit risky," Professer told her. "Always a chance of conflagration if you get tied up in the midst of battle."

"Surely there won't be a battle?" Bernard twitched.

"If you're so sure, you go in," Professer replied. In an unblocked thought he added, "he's daft enough to."

Hedstrong was about to object to the learned man's attitude when he saw Miss Gregory. She was marching along the path separating the front of the mansion from the formal garden, stepping round Thought Processor sentries until she encountered an obvious leader. Phyllis explained to Hedstrong, Upstart, Compresser and Professer the reason for the lady's somewhat circuitous route, the sentries being invisible and beyond their sphere of detection.

Miss Gregory appeared to make communication with the leader. It was a swift exchange before she continued in her purposeful manner, now heading directly towards them.

"And what have you been up to?" Professer asked.

"I'm not sure I like your tone," the lady replied, her dignity and confidence fully restored. "At least I haven't been drifting around doing nothing like the rest of you."

"And we thought we'd got rid of her," twitched Professer.

"What have you been up to?" Phyllis demanded, echoing Professer's enquiry with equal bluntness. Usually, faced with such a confrontational attitude, the lady would have invited the purveyor to mind her own business, but the nature of the Gregory news was of such impact that she felt obliged to convey it to the rest.

Apparently there had been little to attract her attention in the estate office. Contrary to prediction, all appeared to have progressed smoothly without her, it being made politely clear that her continued presence, although acceptable, once a National Trust person, always a National Trust person, was not what might be described essential. Having failed to impress the staff of her importance, she'd taken her leave, proceeding along the drive up to the main house entrance.

Other Trust servants had the front door unlocked in anticipation of the arrival of an expected coach party of children, on a special visit, so she'd been able to enter unimpeded. Not only had she reached the dining room in time to witness the spiritual confrontation between Frenco and Thought Processors, she'd remained afterwards to learn the reaction of the Thrillators.

"A little man of French appearance and accent with ideas above his station seemed to consider himself the leader and the others appeared foolish enough to believe him. Having obviously lost in the exchange with what, for some reason, you call the Thought Processors, he was visibly angered. He proceeded to preach confrontation, warned of potential annihilation and whipped his group into a frenzy of fear and aggression." Miss Gregory paused for effect. "I left them planning a united surge out of the mansion to avoid what the little Frenchman called 'the enemy.'"

"And you told this to the Processor you talked to on the outside," Professer concluded for her.

"If you mean that soldier who was polite enough to acknowledge me, yes, he did show some interest, and was of far greater stature than the Frenchman," she replied.

"I pray we be saved from the stupidity of humans," Professer twitched. "You know what will happen now, don't you?" The question was addressed to the gathering as a whole. There was no time for response.

First the noise of a lively group of children came from the direction of the rose garden up the hill, some distance from the house. Upstart floated off to investigate and swept back to report that a column of girls and boys were descending.

"They're coming down the path along the side of the garden. I think they're heading for the mansion," she said.

Realising the danger if they got too close to battling Thrillators and Thought Processors, Phyllis told Bernard to go and stop them. He asked her how and she told him not to bother, taking on the task herself. She managed to divert the children back to the rose garden where they waited, expectantly, one or two amusing themselves by kicking newly tended borders.

The Thrillators chose that moment to burst out of the mansion. They linked in a pulsing circle to drive the surprised Thought Processors back into the grounds. Behind the circle came the other Processors sweeping through masonry from the rear of the house. For a mini-measure there was speed of movement, then all was still. Phyllis had rejoined her group to witness the scene, describing it to the four spirits. The inner-council members remained linked to each other, but were surrounded by a circle of Thought Processors, now also linked. The whole gathering had drifted further away from the house. They headed towards Paradise and the old lake below the watching group.

"Do tell me they're not equal," Professser twitched. "Pray they don't equal each other in number."

"They do, I think, is you," Compresser told him, having strained his senses to count. "Wait. No, there's one more inner-council. I don't think they're equal, are they? Phyllis, am I right?"

The inner circle of Thrillators were bunched together, each maintaining contact with the other. The outer ring of Thought Processors were better spaced. It appeared to Phyllis that they were attempting negotiation whilst still surrounding their captives. To her fellow spirits, all that was visible was a movement of grass. Phyllis, unable to verify the numbers from her viewpoint, told the others to 'hang on' whilst she moved closer.

"Don't," twitched Professer, but his warning went unheeded. As Phyllis approached, there was a sudden surge by the Thought Processors. Their circle began to spin, creating a mini tornado which multiplied in speed and force. A human second before they clashed with the inner-council, Phyllis became enmeshed in their midst. A clap of thunder, followed by a flash of lightening frightened the waiting children. Their teachers moved to avert their view as disaster unfolded on the grass below.

"You were right," Professer twitched to Compresser. "The numbers were odd, until that stupid female human was taken in. That equalled it out."

"What in God's name's happened?" cried Miss Gregory.

"Conflagration," Professer told her. "Those idiotic spirits have annihilated each other. Your stupid human joined in and that made the numbers on each side equal. Equal force against equal force eliminates even with a part-human/part-spirit to make the equal number. I've always said so and now we have proof. Inevitable. It will feature in my next thesis. What's more, what she stupidly did caused the spirits to seek her out as a human entry escape. No part-human like her, probably not even a whole human, could accommodate such a large number of simultaneous entries. Therefore, we have combustion. Yes, that's it." He sounded pleased. "I've got it. Good job those children were far enough away otherwise it wouldn't have worked. Yes, I've cracked it. Total immediate elimination."

"What d'you mean, elimination?" Hedstrong demanded.

"Gone. For ever. Ceased to exist either in the Real World or the human one."

Bernard was already running off the path down towards Phyllis, except there no longer was any Phyllis. Her clothes appeared almost undamaged, heaped against what little remained of a smouldering human body, seemingly consumed by a tremendous heat. A scorched ring of grass showed where the circle of spirits had been. The teachers, and those children that had refused to turn away, had witnessed a female Trust worker, the one that had officiously herded them into the rose garden, striding down towards the lake to be suddenly hit by a tornado, a bolt of lightning and burnt to a cinder.

Susan Gregory rushed to comfort a distraught, confused Bernard. She warned him against revealing any knowledge of the Real World to fellow Trust personnel. Some had witnessed the latest incident. Several were hurrying to assist and others to help frightened children.

"They would simply consider us mentally disfigured by what, to them, was a death by a flash of lightening," she told him. "An act of God."

With this newborn compassion stirring within her bosom, no doubt influenced by the spiritual entry of Sexa, she placed her arms around him and allowed him to bury his sobs in her accommodating chest. Observing the scene from close quarters, Compresser was satisfied that the surviving flesh and blood part of his small force could be left to the mercies of human tragedy. He invited Professer, Hedstrong and Upstart to follow him to the chapel. In the event of conflict he'd agreed with Lard that it would be a good place to regroup.

The other spiritual house residents were still assembled amidst the pews, ornaments and rafters. Spayed and Baybe had joined them after the Thrillators' surge out of the dining room. Some house spirits wanted to investigate, but had been arrested by warnings from Kernel. Lard had added his recommendation of restraint, advising that time be allowed for the measure to unfold gradually.

The residential spirits accepted the authority of the Real World occupier of the last Lord of the Manor. It was he who greeted Compresser and the others when they arrived. The rest of the measure was taken up with exchange of information, followed by the hatching of a plan devised to secure a return to normality. Lard was officially appointed head of a group which included Upstart, Kernel, Hedstrong and several others. 'Leadership' did not feature, a growing spiritual version of 'democracy' managing to enter so much into the equation that, afterwards, Compressser confessed his satisfaction that nothing sensational would happen for some further measure, isn't it? The Professer agreed.

"Until some idiot seeks to introduce too much control and stifles everything by rule and regulation," he added. The two had left the chapel gathering to drift across the grass, past the scorched earth where disaster had struck.

"Lard's crafty enough to avoid that," Compresser suggested, "don't you think?"

"Self-importance gets them all in the end, but hopefully that's a long way off and will give us time for experiment."

"You've certainly got some specimens to study now, haven't you?" Compresser twitched. "Two half-human/half-spirit examples. What more could you ask?"

"Not a lot," Professer agreed. "D'you realise, we're about to become a centre of study and excellence?"

"Careful, you're beginning to use the sort of drivel a human would employ when he can't think of anything constructive to do, aren't you?" Compresser warned.

"There's one factor which will need careful research," Professer said, ignoring the comment. "I'm not sure the conflagration of Phyllis the witch eliminated Antedote. She could be out there somewhere with a few scores to settle."

"Let's leave the Lord of the Mansion and his trusty friends to worry about that, shall we?" Compresser told him.

They'd reached Paradise, passing close to an oak occupied by Hedstrong and Upstart, who had also taken the first opportunity to leave the chapel. They'd felt they deserved some romantic time on their own, but paused in mid-spiritual embrace when they caught echoes of Professer's and Compresser's conversation.

"Surely that can't be true," Upstart commented after the two learned spirits had left their range.

"Does it matter if it is?" Hedstrong twitched back. "No one can take away what we've discovered. Not so many measures ago, I was alone. Now I have feelings and you. Nothing will change that."

There was a rustle in the surrounding trees from which, for a mini-measure, Upstart thought she caught a familiar drift. Hedstrong seemed not to have noticed. Could Antedote really have returned? She kept her sudden sensation blocked, not noticing Hedstrong was blocking too. They devoted their energy to giving each other a loving, reassuring boost.